NO WAY HOME

NO WAY HOME

JODY FELDMAN

sourcebooks
fire

**ASSEMBLE
MEDIA**
assemblemedia.com

Copyright © 2022 by Assemble Media
Cover and internal design © 2022 by Sourcebooks
Cover design by Ploy Siripant
Cover images © beemore/Getty Images, Inside Creative House/Getty Images,
zdenkam/Getty Images, Anton Shakhmin/Shutterstock,
19srb81/Shutterstock, Freepik.com
Internal design by Danielle McNaughton/Sourcebooks

Published by Sourcebooks Fire, an imprint of Sourcebooks
P.O. Box 4410, Naperville, Illinois 60567-4410
(630) 961-3900
sourcebooks.com

Cataloging-in-Publication Data is on file with the Library of Congress.

Printed and bound in the United States of America.
LSC 10 9 8 7 6 5 4 3 2 1

To Debbie Poslosky.

We would have been friends in high school.

CHAPTER ONE

I DON'T KNOW HOW I GOT HERE.

Not *here* here, in the back of my parents' car, heading down the Beltway toward the airport. I mean I don't know how I got to be the one from my school who's going to Rome.

"Today," I whisper to myself. "I can't believe it's already—"

My dad swears under his breath. Traffic has come to a complete standstill. My mom sighs and searches her nav app for a nonexistent alternative route, all panicky about being late. I have plenty of time—my plane doesn't leave for three-plus hours—but we're meeting Sofia, the student from Italy who I'm switching places with. She'll do English immersion here, living with my family, while I live with her parents, the Rossis.

Sofia's plane landed five minutes ago. We're still fifteen minutes away.

"Don't worry," I say. "She needs to go through customs first."

Not that I'm an expert on international travel, but I've done my homework. At least about that. "We'll be there."

"And if we aren't…" My mom turns around, a dark strand of hair trying to cover the worry crease between her eyebrows. "How would you feel, Tess, if the Rossis aren't there to meet you?"

She has a point—I'd probably crumple in the middle of the Rome airport, heart pounding, tears gushing until I finally got the sense to call my host family or my extended family who lives in Italy still.

They're why I applied to Exchange Roma in the first place. Aside from my dad, my great-aunt and cousins are my only direct link to my grandfather, who I call *Nonno*. I used to beg Nonno to take me to Italy so I could see and taste and feel the village where he was born and after wander the streets of Rome where he grew up. "But you've been," he'd say. I'd remind him I was four years old at the time, I could barely remember anything, and besides, I wanted to see Italy with him. "Someday," he'd say. "Someday." But he passed away before that could happen.

I poured all that into my application essay. And though I don't really speak Italian and though there were seventeen other applicants to the program from my school, *I* was the one who got accepted. The essay must have had something to do with it.

My mom sighs again and shifts her anxiety from the traffic to me. "You have everything, right, Tess? Phone, laptop, chargers, passport?"

I've been basically attached to my passport since this entire fantasy came true. I wave it at her for the third time today. And traffic magically clears.

My dad starts driving like a wild man. He makes it to the airport twenty-three minutes after Sofia's plane landed, pulls to a screech near the airport entrance, shoos my mom and me out of the car, then goes to park. I humor my mom and sprint with her toward the gates.

Fifteen minutes later, Sofia finally comes striding out from the security area like she's a supermodel on a runway, debuting impeccably chic, totally wrinkle-free black clothes that cannot have traveled thousands of miles. Her mass of long, dark hair frames her heart-shaped face and flows behind her in near slow motion.

I knew she was gorgeous—we've FaceTimed her and her parents weekly since we were paired up—but seeing her in person... Is there a step above breathtaking? Even her long, manicured fingernails are perfect. If every girl in Italy is like Sofia, I'll be utterly ignorable.

She races up and gives us each the double-cheek kiss. "Ciao! Ciao! Ciao! *Famiglia* Alessandro! Finally! We meet, how you say? Head-to-head. No, no. Face-to-face!"

"Face-to-face! Yes!" I say, trying to sound much more interesting than I am. If only I had a few days to absorb this aura she's beaming out.

My dad, a good three inches shorter than Sofia, grabs her carry-on, gets that sparkle in his eyes, and tries to show off his Italian. "*Benvenuto a* Washington, DC. *Speriamo che lo...*"

She waves him off. "We keep the talk with the English. More easy for you. Me, more practice." Then she turns to me. "Your *Italiano*? Is okay now?"

When we first FaceTimed, it was a total fail on my part. "I'm getting there," I lie.

The truth is, my Italian is terrible. My dad had me check *intermediate proficiency* on the Exchange Roma application and told me that I really would get there. But so many people applied, and my chances were so slim, that becoming fluent enough would have only raised my hopes then crushed my dreams when the program chose someone else. Then when I *did* get accepted, I scrambled and tried to learn by streaming Italian movies and TV with English subtitles. People pick up languages like that all the time.

It didn't really work, and my three years of high school French—Italian and French are supposedly similar—didn't help much either. Now, I keep wondering how long before they discover I'm a fraud.

"*Si.* The language, she's hard." Sofia tilts her head, sympathy filling her eyes. "But is no *problema*. My parents. They make you fast learn. Do all the things. You will see. They make sure you have many, uh, honest times." She shakes her head and laughs. "No. Mean, you will...you will no forget your time."

"We expect your time to be unforgettable too," my mom says.

Even with that awkwardness, we manage to talk about food and weather and whether Sofia might see the Washington Monument and the White House. Or even the president. And we tell her about life here and how my friends want to meet her and everything.

By the time we take her bags to the car, swap them out for mine, and get me checked in for my flight, I still have nearly an hour before I need to go through security. We head to a juice bar inside the airport.

"Berry blast smoothie," I tell the woman behind the counter.

"You too?" Sofia says. "Me too!"

The woman nods. "Sisters do that."

We laugh.

"Cousins, then? You've *got* to be related."

We look at each other. There is some resemblance. "I guess it's the Italian in me," I say.

Sofia grins. "Same! Italian in me! Selfie!" She blasts a few of us laughing then hands me her phone so I can see. I look acceptable. She still looks like a supermodel.

We pass the phone around the small table, and once my dad gives it back to Sofia, he clears his throat like he does when he's about to tell one of his stories. Ugh.

"You know, Sofia," he says, "we have family in Rome. My own father grew up there."

"Yes? I want to hear!"

He launches into the full version of *My Italian Family Story: The Immigration Years.* It takes him five minutes to tell her how Nonno constantly argued with his father, even more so after Nonno's mother got sick. One day, Nonno had enough. And with his mother's blessing—*go forth and please do right by our family*—he left for the United States.

"He brought only his clothes, a few mementos, and forty-six dollars. He was only fifteen years old," my dad says. "Can you imagine?"

Even I shake my head. My dad never told me that Nonno was only fifteen when he immigrated, neither speaking the language nor knowing where he'd live and what he'd do. It's weird enough that someone is taking over my life here—my room, my parents, my friends. Then there's the awkwardness of living with total strangers and the dread that the exchange program will discover just how little Italian I can speak. But Nonno's story changes things.

At seventeen, I have money, a credit card, and a return ticket home, plus a phone I can use to translate anything or call anyone, anywhere in the world. Nonno's courage has me feeling fearless.

It may be a little early, but I jump up and lead the way to security. First, I give Sofia a hug, then my mom, and my dad last. He hugs the tightest of all, his cheek lightly scratching my temple. He lets go, mostly, and slips a small package inside my backpack.

"What's that?"

"The perfect thing for this trip. Wait until you're in the air, though." He gives me an even bigger hug and looks like he might cry.

I can't leave him like this. I resort to the one Italian saying, pretty much a family motto, I've known since birth—something he's always said when I'm sad or frustrated or scared. Just before I get swallowed up by the people in line, I start it. "*Chi cerce…*" *Whoever searches…*

"*Trova!*" both my parents call back. *Finds.*

Simultaneously, Sofia chimes in, "*Non trova.*"

Doesn't find?

Her eyes reduce to slits. She smirks.

And my blood runs cold.

CHAPTER TWO

I GRIP THE HANDLE OF MY WHEELIE BAG TIGHTER, WHITE AT my knuckles, light in my head. I look back through the crowds of people, but Sofia and my parents have left.

Breathe, Tess. In four, hold two, out six, hold two. Repeat, repeat, repeat. I take one more cleansing breath and shake it off. Sofia's look meant nothing. Either I misinterpreted it or I mistook her smile for a smirk. It's just all this nervous excitement.

I get to the gate an hour before we board the plane with little to do but tap my foot, check my phone, and watch people stare at theirs. A family sits in the seats opposite me, and I play a long round of peekaboo with their little girl, who can't be more than two. Their parents thank me, but I should thank them for the distraction.

Sad that the two-year-old won't remember a thing about this trip. I barely remember my only visit to Rome, and I was double her age. I haven't flown overseas since, and I've never flown alone.

My best friend Carly has done both. When she came to say

goodbye this afternoon, I had her double-check my bags to make sure I didn't forget anything.

"You might want to carry on a full change of clothes in case your big suitcase takes a detour to Barcelona." She inspected its contents and pulled out a ratty stuffed bear. "Beanie Cubbie? He's not coming with." She sat him back on my windowsill. Then she held up three pairs of black jeans and three blue shirts. "Just no."

"The shirts are not identical," I said. "Besides, I want to fit in. Not look like some flashy American."

"You'd rather be boring?" She tossed out one shirt and one pair of jeans and added a romper and a sundress. "You'll thank me," she said. "Three reasons. It can get hot in Rome. Italy might be the fashion center of the universe. And it can't hurt to look cute on occasion. Listen to me. *Conosco i miei polli.*"

"What the hell? I know my chickens?" Ever since I got accepted to Exchange Roma, Carly's been learning Italian idioms with me, but that was a new one.

She shook her head. "I know what I'm talking about."

"Of course you do."

"No. That's what it means." We both laughed.

Now, I send her one last same-time-zone text, a gif of chickens.

She FaceTimes me back, but all I can see is the ceiling until her face whips into view, tight curls piled in a messy knot on top of her head, green eyes open wide. "Need more fashion advice?"

"Of course," I say. "What does one wear to a *festa*?"

"Unless it's a party for doctors, not these." She grabs up a new pair of scrubs.

I gasp. "You got it!?" She'd applied for a prestigious internship with a pediatrician, but when she hadn't heard back in forever, she was sure it went to someone else. "When were you gonna tell me?"

"Now? Just got the email. But I haven't said yes yet."

"Seriously? It's all you've ever wanted, Dr. Carly CureKids."

"What if I suck at it? Or can't handle it?"

"Carly. She chose you. You handle the sick kids. I'll take care of Rome."

We keep talking until they announce it's time to board.

Carly holds up a finger. "Before you go, one more saying, my favorite, but *do not* use it. It's so old-timey, people will look at you funny. Here goes: *Non calare le brache!*"

I give *her* a funny look. "Don't pull down my pants?"

"It means don't chicken out. Go there and kill it!"

"You too, Carly. Call Dr. Abrams and accept!"

"Only if you promise to stop worrying about Sofia's smirk. It was nothing."

I promise. Then I walk down the jetway, channeling the confidence Sofia showed coming out of security. But one step inside the plane, and my heart speeds up instead.

The flight attendant directs me to my immediate right. I find row twenty-three, stash my wheelie in the overhead compartment, and awkwardly scuttle past the man sitting in the aisle seat to get to mine at the window. He greets me in some language I don't recognize then lowers his eye mask and falls asleep. Now, I'll have to climb over him to use the bathroom.

I can't worry about that now. I lean back and close my eyes, replacing every bad thought with visions of me, arms outstretched, twirling in the center of Rome.

I sit with that and with the passing landscape below us until we've been in the air for fifteen minutes. Then I pull out the package my dad gave me. The small box is tied with a ribbon the colors of the Italian flag—green, white, and red. I slip it off, open the lid, and move the card aside. Underneath is a silver locket engraved with lines and curves that remind me of the space where a tree trunk might meet its branches. Even more, where flower petals meet the stem.

I read the card.

Dear Tess,

Don't groan. This is not a total repeat. I'm skipping the part where Nonno came to the U.S. with only his clothes, etc. But here's what you don't know. Your great-grandmother handed him this just before he left for America, to remind him from whence he came. When you were born, Nonno passed it along to me, ribbon and all, to give to you on your 18th birthday. Knowing how you wanted to travel back to the old country with him, 17 is close enough. Nonno would agree.

All our love,
Nonno & Nonna
Mom & Dad

Inside the locket are pictures of Nonno and my grandmother, Nonna. I hold back tears. My grandparents were both killed in a boating accident three years ago. I miss them so much. But it's like they're always looking down on me. Maybe that's the answer, in a greater-universe sense, to the question of how I got here—on this plane, into this program.

I close the locket, give it a kiss, and slip the chain around my neck. Suddenly, I feel a sense of peace, as if the locket were my new superpower.

I roll the ribbon, place it inside the box, tuck it into my carry-on, and pull out my new journal, a gift from Carly.

Inside the front cover, in big balloon letters, she wrote "Tess's Roman Holiday." Underneath, she glued in a picture of orange flowers. Snapdragons are her favorites. The next several pages are filled with messages from all our friends—some private jokes, some advice, some hoping I have fun. I draw individual picture frames around the messages to make them even more special. Then I decorate the margins with flowers and stars and fireworks. And I may have just turned this journal into a sketchbook.

I haven't told anyone, not even Carly, but I want to get better in art. Or just more confident. Not that I have any talent, but sketching gives me a sense of calm. No one has expectations of me, and I have zero expectations of myself.

On the first empty page, I sketch the locket—the chain, its shape, and the lines and curves of the flower-not-a-flower. Not bad. On the next page, I sketch the man next to me in seat 23B. Without staring at him, I start with the curve of his jaw, the hint of his bushy mustache and eyebrows, then separately, the fold of his hands on his belly.

The man shifts. I cover the page even though there's zero chance he'd recognize himself. To call the sketch amateur would be an insult to amateurs. I'm better off sticking to lockets and flowers-not-flowers.

I sketch a full flower and turn it into a field of tulips, leaving space for a haiku.

Even in fields of
Fully fluttering feelings
Flowers find their feet.

I'm not a poet, but I love haiku. Counting the syllables, finding the right words, drawing mind pictures—together, they rival the calmness of sketching.

But I'm jolted from the calm as the pilot's voice crackles over the plane's speaker, announcing something-something-something and that the weather in Rome is beautiful.

Just as he starts to repeat it in English, a woman comes bustling down the aisle, spewing a string of words so fast, I can't be sure it's Italian. She's flagging a flight attendant, her saggy cheeks flapping in time to her underarm flab, the obnoxious scent of perfume wafting behind her.

If my friends were here, we'd laugh hysterically. And I can't even exchange glances with the man next to me, who's been lightly snoring for too long now.

I should sleep too. It'll be morning when we land. So, I find that calm again, close my journal, lean my seat back, and plug in some music. Three songs play. Five songs. Fourteen. Still no sleep. Well, maybe I doze for a minute. Maybe.

I stretch my legs, open my eyes, and…hold in a gasp. Mr. Mustache, who'd been sleeping next to me, is gone, and in his place is Perfume Woman. There's no hiding that odor, a combination of baby powder, rose petals, and wet dog. She gives a crooked smile.

I smile back, but my heart is racing. Something about this feels completely off. Is it the smile? The perfume? Did I pass out for hours? I press on my temples. My breathing comes rapid-fire. *Breathe, Tess.* In four, hold two, but my out-six whistles like a windstorm.

My seatmate is now looking directly at me. She rattles off something in Italian, but the only part I understand is her asking if I'm all right.

I nod, and she pats my arm.

I nearly recoil, but I manage to look back at her, hoping she'll stop staring at me. "*Grazie.*" I point to myself. "*Bene oro.*" That should mean I'm fine now.

And I am. I'm going on an adventure. In a foreign country. Filled with so much beauty.

I might not have friends there, I will need to fake my proficiency, and I may feel awkward and uncomfortable and ignorant sometimes. But I have it pretty good.

Though I could do without one more minute of the woman and her perfume.

CHAPTER THREE

Seriously? Does this woman need to stay on my tail? No matter how fast I walk off the plane and into the Rome airport, her perfume drifts from behind. Either that, or it's permanently implanted inside my nose. I stay in the middle of the crowd, hoping to lose her.

Eventually, the space divides into two areas: one for arriving passengers with European passports, and the other for the rest of us. As I veer toward mine, the smell fades. Thank God I'll never have to see her weird smile again. And thankfully, the immigration guard at the end of the long line speaks English. *Why are you here? How long are you planning to stay?* I answer, then he looks me in the eye and gives me my first passport stamp.

Outside of security, Sofia's parents are holding a sign with balloons. *Ciao, Tess!* Even without the sign, I'd recognize them instantly. There's no question that Anjelica, from her long fingernails to her smoky eyes—maybe she'll teach me—and her long, dark hair is Sofia's mom. But unless Anjelica uses a straightener, Sofia gets her curls from Francesco. His lighter brown hair with its natural highlights falls every which way in medium-length waves. Add in his scruff of facial hair, and he'd almost look like a bad boy, except the glint in his eyes shows a true soft side.

I trot up to them, and they, to me. Their hugs are so warm, and their smiles so big that I feel at home already. We start walking, all three of us talking over one another in a mash-up of Italian, English, and sign language.

I get my voice to break through. "I can't believe I'm finally here! Meeting you in person!" Ugh. I meant to say that in Italian, but it just burst out in English. I start to repeat it like I'd practiced, but they're already saying pretty much the same thing back to me.

They insist on carrying all my bags, and we walk through the airport, their longer legs outpacing me so much I need to run every few steps to catch up. We grab a taxi at the stand. Anjelica and I climb into the back seat, while Francesco sits in the front. He turns around and gestures to himself and Anjelica. "*Niente auto.*" He simultaneously shakes his head and motions like he's steering.

Okay, so they don't have a car. Or they don't know how to drive.

"*Questa volta abbiamo preso il taxi. Solitamente usiamo la moto,*" Anjelica says. "We have *moto. Capito?*"

I do understand. Some of it. Maybe. Usually, they drive motorbikes? I roll my fists like I'm revving a motorcycle. "Vroom-vroom! *Si?*"

"*Si!*" And Francesco pantomimes how it would be if the three of

15

us and all my luggage were riding a motorbike through the traffic. "*Tre pagliacci.*"

"Three…" I start translating aloud. "*Pagliacci?*"

Anjelica flops her feet up and down and makes goofy, animated faces.

"Clowns!" I say. "We'd be three clowns. *Tre pagliacci.*"

And all three of us do our best clown impressions until I'm laughing so hard, I can barely see. I finally take a breath, and a beat of quiet, to look out the window at all the traffic, mostly small cars and Vespas whose drivers don't seem to notice that they're weaving past ancient buildings, far older than any back in DC. "Wow!" I say. "Wow. Wow."

"Welcome. To. Roma," Francesco manages. And for the first time, he turns and faces front, holding up all five fingers on his left hand. Then like a countdown, he lowers his fingers one by one. We turn the corner, and he points out the window.

I gasp. Out of nowhere, right in front of us, is the Colosseum— four stories of arches and stonework, a giant stone layer cake. This place with all its competitions and all the death, this ancient half-ruin, sits in the middle of the city like any normal building.

"It's so amazing!" I stare and stare. "There should be signs and lights and trumpets to celebrate that it's still standing after two thousand years."

Francesco and Anjelica look at one another, clearly confused.

I barely know the Italian word for *bathroom*. How do I explain? I grab my phone and have my translation app say that for me.

"*Si, si!*" says Anjelica. "We take granite."

I smile and put the phone down. Apparently, they see it so much, they take it for granted.

The taxi weaves past countless piazzas—town squares—some major and some barely noticeable. All these neighborhoods, all these twisty, narrowing streets—it's dizzying. I'd be utterly terrified to find my way around this city or anywhere, really, if it weren't for nav apps.

Francesco has the taxi stop at the entrance to a "street" that's only wide enough for half a car. *"Benvenuti nella Capitale!"*

I understand that: Welcome to central Rome!

Anjelica tugs me and my smaller bags down the narrow street like the cobblestones are smooth as glass, even in her heels. I barely take a step without tripping. Francesco catches up from behind with my big suitcase. We dodge motorcycles and pedestrians past ground-level stores, cafés, and a gelato shop, getting occasional whiffs of a Rome I've only imagined until now.

Above the businesses are five- and six-story, old-stone buildings in shades of brown, tan, gray, rust. And one that's ocher, but a dirty yellow with stains streaking down as if the mortar between the stone blocks has been weeping for decades. It almost makes me shiver. *Please. Any building except this one.* But Anjelica points straight at it. *"La nostra casa."* Our house.

I get an instant shiver. Why can't it be the rose-colored one with the gelato shop underneath? But I need to stop judging the book by its cover. And Sofia said I'd love it.

Sofia was right. Up four flights of stairs, the bright apartment has clearly been renovated. The living room has picture windows, white leather sofas and chairs, a human-sized floor lamp, and, on the wall, large Renaissance-type prints in sleek, contemporary frames. Straight ahead is a short hallway, and to the right is a small dining area, a dazzling kitchen, and a spiral staircase.

Francesco picks up my suitcases like they're empty and heads up the winding stairs, but Anjelica leads me the other way, down a short hall. She points out the bathroom, then we stop at a small, bright bedroom. Sofia's room. But now, there's no furniture, one of the walls is torn up, and leaky stains snake across the ceiling. In the middle are paint drums, buckets, ladders, and other construction materials.

"Sorry." Anjelica shakes her head. "*Problema qui.* You no sleep *qui.*"

She leads me back to the spiral staircase and its wooden steps that are attached to wrought-iron handrails. The unrenovated space up here has no bathroom. Its only window, eye-level, is the size of a shoebox. And the room itself is… Well, to say it's cozy would be generous.

Anjelica gestures that I should unpack later. "*Un pisolino.*" She pantomimes with her cheek resting on folded hands, eyes closed. Yes, I do need a nap.

"*Grazie,*" I say as she leaves, then I try to adjust my expectations. In fact, this dark tower room is sort of fairy-tale romantic. I take a picture of the window then a selfie of me with the stairs spiraling down behind. I post them. My Roman hideaway!

Then I FaceTime my parents like they asked. When they pick up, I show them a 360 view of the room.

"This is it! My home away from home. The spiral staircase, my bed, and a wardrobe, which I think Francesco said he built himself."

"Careful going down those stairs at night," my dad warns.

Really, Dad? "Anyway, we have a night table, alarm clock, lamp, shelves, little mirror, picture of flowers. Enamel crucifix for you, Dad. Sorry, Mom. No Star of David. That's about it." I tell them about the construction downstairs. "If I understood right, they packed up almost everything this past Wednesday when the roof started leaking."

My mom's worry crease deepens. "Sort of bare."

"But I have this vase," I respond, trying to keep positive. "Anjelica bought the flowers for me at the market. And a monkey figurine, because everyone needs a monkey figurine."

My dad gives a laugh, but not my mom. "Will you be okay up there?"

"Not just okay. It's my own private retreat!" I put extra enthusiasm into my voice and hope that sounds convincing. I test out the small bed and yawn. "So comfortable. Sooo comfortable."

"That's what's most important," my mom says. "Need a nap?"

"Definitely. Love you!" I disconnect, close my eyes, and…

Anjelica is hovering over me.

I shoot up.

She laughs.

According to the alarm clock, it's one o'clock, and by the light eking in from the tiny window, it's afternoon. That means it's 7:00 a.m. back home. I slept for a couple hours, but my head feels like it's been stuffed with cotton.

Anjelica taps her phone, and the translator speaks. "Clean up and change clothes if you want. We will take a walk to show you the neighborhood. We will go to the market, get some lunch at a café. Gelato too. Keeping busy is the best way to recover from jet lag. Yes?"

"*Si. Grazie.*"

Half an hour later, we stop at a small restaurant on Via della Scrofa, a few narrow streets away. We don't talk much while we're waiting for our food. Well, Francesco and Anjelica do, but mostly to each other. I look out the window at the people going by, then point to a plaque on a house across the street. "Amerigo Vespucci lived there?"

"*Si,*" Francesco says, smiling at me like I'd asked a ridiculous question.

I run out to take a picture. In that one spot, I could take a thousand of them. And I take nearly that many of my pizza, the best—*la migliore*—I've ever eaten.

Francesco points to my pizza. "*La migliore?*" He shakes his head. "*No. Domani! Pizzeria da Michele a Napoli!*" He kisses his fingers.

He wants to go to Naples tomorrow just for pizza? We don't need to. I mean, I just got here a few hours ago. But they seem so excited to share that with me, I can't let them down.

I wipe my mouth, push back, and I stand next to them to capture the moment. "A picture of you? Of us? *Una foto?*"

Anjelica covers her face. "No. *Evitiamo i selfie, vengo male nelle foto.* Me. Photo. *Brutta.*"

There's no way Anjelica could take an ugly picture. She looks so much like Sofia, and Sofia looked amazing in our selfie.

Before I can protest, Francesco gestures to a kitschy decoration of a fat chef with a ruddy face over a steaming pot. "Photo him. More pretty."

I laugh, but they seem serious...*too* serious, and so different from the people just seconds ago.

My good mood starts to fade. So little has gone like I'd imagined. The weird woman on the plane, the bedroom, a sudden trip to Naples, and now this. Maybe it's exhaustion or homesickness, but I suddenly feel like I'm going to cry.

CHAPTER FOUR

I EXCUSE MYSELF TO SPLASH WATER ON MY FACE BUT FIRST LEAN into the small bathroom mirror. There's a blob of pizza sauce on my cheek. If I didn't feel it, I must be exhausted.

I come back to the table shaking my head. "You didn't see? Um. *Hai visto?*" I point to my cheek. "Giant zit of sauce. *Gigante salsa...* Zit." I pantomime popping it and break into a wide grin. The mood resumes.

Back outside, we take the streets uphill to *Il Pincio* and its breathtaking overlook of central Rome. Below us is a world of crowded busyness, a patchwork of rooftops in reds and tans and browns, and countless church steeples, massive and small. The view is *so* worth the hike, but I love the gardens up here even more. Fresh and green, calm and quiet. Along its paths are marble busts of famous Italians. Dante, Leonardo da Vinci, Marco Polo, hundreds more. Sadly, some of them are littered with graffiti. But somehow, I fall in love with Boccaccio and his Sharpie'd eyebrows, mustache, and soul patch. I stand next to the poor guy, take a picture, goofy expression on my face, and post it immediately.

"Is this whole area *Il Pincio*?" I ask Francesco. Anjelica has wandered a few steps away.

"Questo è Villa Borghese." He sweeps his arm around and points to a large building. "*E lì giù c'è il museo.*"

"Museum?"

"Museum." Francesco nods and points to Anjelica. "*Sua*, uh, *cognata*?" And when I clearly don't understand, he launches into a bunch of words and motions.

"Oh," I finally say. "Anjelica's sister-in-law works there?"

"Sister-in-law. *Si.*"

Anjelica comes back and gives him a playful swat. *"Nessuna famiglia oggi. Solo Tess."*

Sweet. No family today. Just me.

I ask/pantomime if we're going into the museum.

"*Non vendremo oggi*," Francesco says. "You. *Scuolo. Credo.*"

He seems to think that the school will take us to the museum. If not, we'll go back another time. So instead of going in, we take a rowboat onto a very small lake, which is total perfection after all that walking, except for the moment that Francesco nearly capsizes the thing.

The Rossis sense that I've reached my limit, so we make one last stop at a market. I help Francesco pick out fruits and bread and mostly vegetables. He's making minestrone for dinner and asks me to be his sous-chef.

He started soaking the beans this morning, but he has me chop

23

tomatoes, carrots, zucchini, garlic, and celery. He contains his hair with a headband before he handles the other ingredients, especially the onions so I don't cry. With everything in the pot, we sit down to a game of Scrabble.

Anjelica takes on a sly smile. *"Solo parole italiane."*

Only Italian words? "No fair!" I find a way to communicate that in Italian.

"Si. Non è giusto." But it will be fairer, she says, if I use my app.

By the time I stumble through and lose terribly, the soup is ready. And with the crusty bread and hunks of cheese, it tastes so incredible.

It has me smiling even when I wake in the morning. And when I'm halfway down my spiral stairs on the way to the bathroom, Anjelica, still in pajamas, comes to greet me.

"I hope I didn't wake—" I stop and try to say it in Italian.

She tells me I didn't wake her, though I think she's being kind and that the sixth and ninth steps apparently squeak. I'll remember that so I don't wake anyone again.

Immediately, though, the Rossis have me get dressed and eat a quick breakfast. Then we hustle to the Metro station near the Spanish Steps. It's not so different than the Metro in DC that I've ridden hundreds of times. We take a quick ride to Termini, the main station in Rome, get off, and head to another area with dozens of platforms. Very different than the Metro in DC.

I'd be totally lost if I were by myself, but I keep up with Anjelica and Francesco, and we board our train, which leaves just minutes after we find our seats.

The high-speed service whirs us through industrial rail yards and past graffiti-lined walls, announcements coming in both Italian and English. It doesn't take long before the concrete changes to green countryside, mountains in the distance. Then the landscape becomes flat as far as the eye can see.

I never knew that a long train ride could be this calming and relaxing. What seemed so overwhelming yesterday is utterly *perfetto* today.

I turn away from the window to say all that to Anjelica and Francesco, but they're huddled together, speaking low. Instead, I let myself be mesmerized by the passing scenery. Then in a snap, just over an hour since we boarded, we come to an area very different than the Rome I've seen so far. To my right are modern skyscrapers like in any city. I'm hoping there's more charm to Naples than this.

The Rossis arranged for a driver, chauffeur's cap and everything, to pick us up. Soon, we leave the generic cityscape behind and move into the Italian quaintness I'm already loving. Even the driver's chattiness is charming, though I wish he'd keep his eyes on the road instead of glancing back at Anjelica and me. But he manages to weave past pedestrian- and motorcycle-only streets without swerving even once. He must know his chickens.

The driver lets us out on a cobblestone street—nearly an alley—that is crammed with four- and five-story apartment buildings in reds and pinks and yellows. Laundry lines strung from building to building, with their clothes and sheets flapping in the breeze, act almost like a canopy Plants, flowers, and Italian flags decorate some of the narrow balconies. And I catch an occasional aroma of onions and tomatoes cooking in these families' kitchens.

Many of the buildings have small shops on the ground floor. Anjelica leads us past a number of them until she ducks inside one filled with knickknacks and antiques.

While they examine every goblet on the shelves, I glance into the jewelry cases. My dad likes interesting watches and my mom, unusual earrings. It would be so great to bring gifts home to them, except I don't have that type of cash, and they'll see everything that goes on my credit card.

In the third shop, I do find the perfect watch for my dad, one with a 24-hour dial instead of the standard 12-hour. I take a picture in case, at the end, I still have enough money to go halfsies with him. I'm sure he'd love that. I might even be able to navigate here by myself.

We meet our driver at the end of the fourth street we've wound down, and he hands Francesco a slip of paper with a number. "*Circa quindici minuti.*"

Fifteen minutes for what? It turns out that the wait for Pizzeria da Michele is more than two hours long, but not for us. The driver went there and brought back a line number.

We go right in and sit at a small table against a wall of green and white tiles. I face the curved, blue-tiled wall with its arched ovens. The flames are blazing, a blast of heat occasionally brushing my cheeks. A man with a long-handled paddle pulls a pizza from one of the fires.

The menu is on the wall and… This wouldn't fly in the United States. Only two choices: pizza with cheese, and pizza without. No toppings.

When in Rome…or Naples. Pizza margherita, it is.

Through the translation app, the Rossis explain that they take pizza-making so seriously in Naples that the city regulates who gets to own pizzerias and exactly how the pizzas are made.

When ours come, I follow the Rossis' lead and cut my pizza into quarters, fold the outside corners of one piece into the middle, and take a bite of heaven. It's that good. Pure. Simple.

I nod to Francesco. "You're right. *Il migliore.*"

He says something in Italian that's probably the equivalent of *I told you so,* but he doesn't rub it in. When we're done, he has the driver take us to a whole different area where a blue sea spans before us. We get out and stroll along an arm of the Mediterranean, eating gelato amid the cruise ships, private yachts, grand hotels, and expensive restaurants.

I could stay here for hours looking out onto the waters, but we need to head back to Rome and to the reason I'm here. Suddenly, my stomach is twisting in an all-too-familiar jumble of excitement and dread.

The Exchange Roma welcome party is tonight.

CHAPTER FIVE

I HAVE JUST ENOUGH TIME TO GO BACK TO THE APARTMENT, clean up, and change clothes. Also, to get in a FaceTime pep talk from Carly.

I give her a tour of the place and a quick intro to Anjelica and Francesco. Just before they turn away, Carly takes a screenshot of them.

"Why'd you do that?" I tell her about Anjelica's ridiculous camera phobia.

"Sofia will love it. I'm meeting her tonight."

"Wish I were there. Or really, that you both were here." I go up to my room and ask Carly to talk down my anxiety. "Eighty-three new people. I can do this, right?"

"You'll kill it," she says. "Except, what are you wearing?"

I show her my black-jeans, blue-shirt uniform.

"Just no. Wear the romper."

"But I want them to meet the real me."

She gathers her hair in her hands and sighs. "The real you actually picked that out. Be daring. Look cute. Good impression and all. That's number one. Number two, stop being ridiculous. Have you checked your Insta? Do you see how many likes you got just this morning? And remember it's not even eleven here. On a Saturday. We love you here, they'll love you there. Stop obsessing. Promise."

"If you promise you'll say yes to your internship. Monday morning. No excuses."

"And no excuses, you. Go there, meet everyone, report back."

That's all I need. I change clothes and head downstairs.

Anjelica gives me a twirl. "Ooh! *Molto bella!*"

"*Perfetto,*" Francesco adds. He hands me a key to the apartment. "*Ma non necessario.*" Not necessary because they'll always be here for me, or they'll keep the door open.

I give them each a hug. And even though it's early, I'm ready to go.

Francesco and Anjelica walk me to the program's school tonight so that I can get there by myself on Monday. We head south, one block off the Tiber River, and pass by a long, wide strip of green space. Well, greenish space. The grass is both green and muddied out.

"*Cos'è quello?*" I expect a shrug or a wave of their hands.

But Francesco smiles. "*Circo Massimino.*" Circus Maximus.

I stop. Stare. The Romans once held chariot races in that very spot. I imagine the thunder of hoofbeats, the waving of flags, the roar of the crowd.

I catch back up to the Rossis, and just a bit farther, we move from ancient times to apartments and businesses. Then, at the next corner, Anjelica and Francesco, who don't want to be embarrassing parents, point out the rest of the way and send me off with kisses.

The main school building is set back from the street, a treed lawn to the front and sides. Probably in back too. This place has grounds. Then again, it's a private school, where the students mostly come from rich or important families. My friends and I found some of the other Exchange Roma people online, and their families seem rich and important too. Mine is neither, which also has me freaking. I don't want to play one-upmanship with anyone.

I'm nearly twenty minutes early, so I walk off to the side, sit under a tree, and pull my journal and pencils out of my backpack. Carly tried to convince me not to take them, but here I am, sketching the branches and leaves above. Sort of. It looks more abstract than real. I add lines to signify a bird. Then a squirrel.

Behind the building, partially visible, is the edge of the party tent. I'm about to sketch it when two people, already chatting like they've known each other forever, enter the grounds and head back there. The girl has spiky, blond hair with red tips. The guy is tall and thin like a string bean.

Before I can sketch Red and Bean, another guy wanders onto the grounds, moving like he both has a sense of purpose and not a care in the world. The ultimate confidence. I'm jealous.

I try not to stare, but as he nears, I manage to catch his wave of light brown hair, his ruddy cheeks, and especially his eyebrows that dip close to his blue-green eyes before they raise to a perfect curve.

Our eyes connect. One of his brows arches up, and he shoots me a lopsided grin but just for a second until some other girl calls out to him.

Even still, my cheeks are hot and I'm kicking myself for not smiling back or waving or something. I go back to my journal and sketch the perfect quirkiness of that arched eyebrow, the oval of an eye beneath, the outline of its pupil, the—

A shadow comes over my page. I freeze. *Please, not him.*

It's him.

I slam my sketchbook closed, which makes my pencils tumble toward his feet. I lunge for them, hitting my head on his knee.

He topples backward into the grass and sits back up with a laugh. "I am so sorry." Then he scoots a few inches closer. "Truly sorry."

"No, it's my fault. I should be the one apologizing."

"Shall we start over?" The Eyebrow's English accent shines through. "I'm Devin Kessinger-Scott. And I believe you've captured my eyebrow."

"I what?" My cheeks don't lie as well as my mouth does. "No. My friend says if you can sketch an eyebrow, you can sketch an eye then a nose then a mouth then…"

"Right." At least he doesn't ask me to explain. He just points to himself then back to me.

Is that some British thing?

"Right, then," he says. "I must've been too vague. One more try. I'm Devin Kessinger-Scott, British, London, England. And you are…?"

"Oh, sorry. Tess Alessandro, American, Washington, DC."

"Tess Alessandro, artist and liar."

"Guilty," I say. "Not of being an artist, but for my one small lie. I'm a terrible liar."

Devin picks a few blades of grass. "Yes, you are. You looked to the left before you talked about the eyebrow."

"I what?"

"It's a common tell. Something about the right side of your brain being the creative area, so people look left when they're fabricating lies, you liar." He throws the grass at me. "My tell is this." He raises his left eyebrow.

I smile. "Socking that away for future reference."

He raises it again.

I try. Fail. "How do you do that?"

"It's my only talent," Devin says. "Otherwise, I am talentless, talent-free, talent-negative."

"Oh, I doubt that!" The voice lilts from behind me.

Two other people walk around and join us on the grass.

The girl is striking. She has perfectly streaked, shimmery hair that falls in choreographed waves framing her flawless skin. The guy she's with, her height, has a smattering of freckles and a wide smile that crinkles his eyes. She gives his sleeve a tug. "Should we be speaking Italian?"

"*Dah, si, oui, ja...*" He keeps going with yesses in all the languages.

Before I can give him a full smile, the girl looks at me. "You're Italian, right? You look Italian. Do you speak—"

"English," I say. "I'm American. Tess, from DC."

"I'm Bright. As in bright lights. I was on Broadway when I was seven. Revival of *South Pacific*. Eight-month run, four shows a week." Let the bragging begin. "I met Nicolas"—she nods to the guy with her—"at the Newark airport. He was scheduled for the direct flight, but—"

"Hey, Bright," he says. "You know I can actually speak."

"I get carried away sometimes." She gestures for him to go on.

Nicolas moves his mouth, but nothing comes out.

We all laugh. Then he explains how a thunderstorm headed directly toward Chicago O'Hare had him catch an earlier flight to Newark to avoid it. They met there.

"Not only that," Bright says, "but they assigned us to the same teacher here. And we both got upgraded to business class. Unless you were already in business class, Nicolas?" She doesn't wait for him to answer. "His father works for the NFL. Tell them."

Nicolas scratches his shoulder. "He's not a player, but yeah. He travels to games on Sundays."

"NFL?" says Devin.

"National Football League," Bright says. "American football. Not your football." She leans into Devin and laughs.

I am so out of their league. Literally.

"So, what's your deal, Devin?" Bright asks. "Where do you come from? Who do you know?"

"I know her." Devin nods at a girl who's walking toward the tent. "Larissa. She's already been a sous-chef at a four-star restaurant in New York."

Seriously? Another prodigy? "I was also a sous-chef." Somehow, I keep the sarcasm out of my voice.

"You were?" Devin asks.

I nod. "For my host dad last night. We made minestrone." I laugh. "And I hate to brag, but I have this other talent. I can pat my head and rub my stomach while I hop on one leg."

They make me show them.

"But don't be too impressed," I say. "That's the extent of my coordination. Me, mountain biking, wall climbing? Total fail."

And the conversation morphs. Bright can do a perfect dolphin impression. Devin can fit his whole fist into his mouth. Nicolas can turn his eyelids inside out. He does.

Bright screeches. "Stop it! You're scaring me."

"Good." He puts his eyelids back. "I need company, because this whole exchange thing has me scared as shit. Who are these strangers I'm living with? How can I possibly speak Italian for eight hours every day? And now I'm inside an alternate universe with a dolphin, a hand eater, and a stomach rubber." We all laugh.

A voice comes over a speaker from back by the tent. "*Benvenuti!*"

The four of us race over there.

A man slightly younger than my dad, balding with black-rimmed glasses, stands at the front of the tent. He gives us a smile and a salute, which makes everyone else, already seated, turn and watch us scramble for empty chairs at a back table. The man continues speaking, distinctly, but it's all Italian. I catch a few phrases, but whatever's making some people laugh flies over my head. I understand enough to put together that he's Signor Matteo, director of Exchange Roma.

He goes on to explain the program. I know this only because I

34

read about it again and again and again. During the first two weeks, we'll be taking field trips almost every day. To start, they'll center on different topics—history, theater, government, art, religion, industry, whatever else—to help us decide our personal areas of concentration. During our last week, we'll be giving two full presentations, one individual and one group. In Italian.

Before that reality fully freaks me out again, Signor Matteo calls up the professional chef and four culinary students who will prepare our lunches daily.

Bright tugs a strand of hair at her temple. "I bet you a back rub, Devin. That girl you met, she'll be in their kitchen before the end of the week."

"*Si,*" says the girl next to her, the one Devin talked to before he caught me drawing his eyebrow. Larissa. "*Assolutamente e parler italiano.*" And she'll be speaking Italian. Apparently, in the advanced proficiency class.

I'd be turning three thousand shades of red, but Devin doesn't blush. "Hello again. I mean, *ciao di nuovo.*"

Bright remains cool too. She introduces herself and us like we're old friends. Then says how she can't wait to visit Larissa's restaurant in New York.

I nearly pinch myself. I sketched an eyebrow, I performed a stupid party trick—both beyond embarrassing—but fifteen minutes later, I'm settling into this incredible new group of friends. How?

It doesn't matter because, suddenly, everything—*everything*—is going to be okay.

CHAPTER SIX

By morning, with the sun sneaking through the little window, in the surprising comfort of this tower room, I can't stop grinning about last night. Bright, who we dubbed the Ambassador, made sure to introduce us to every person there. By the time the evening ended, she'd identified everyone in our particular class—intermediate proficiency—and put all the contact info into her phone. She's already planning a party.

I lie here until clicks and aromas lure me downstairs. Francesco, who can draw much better than I can, is sketching the row of glasses on the shelf, but each of his is a little different—some crude, some ultra-elegant—as if he were going into goblet design. Or has some strange fascination with them, the way he and Anjelica picked up every single one at that shop in Naples.

I point at his drawing and give a thumbs-up. And he says something, maybe how their family loves glasses? I have no clue how to respond, so I just smile and tell him—or try to in Italian—that I'm teaching myself how to sketch but I'm only brave enough to use pencil.

"*Spero che tu sia migliore di me.*" He's wishing me something. No clue—he talks so fast—but I smile anyway. Then he closes his book and slips it under a framed picture of Anjelica, Sofia, and himself just as Anjelica brings us hot chocolate and rolls with jam. *Deliziosa.* Almost before I put the last bite into my mouth, the two of them have me out the door to wherever we're headed.

"*Dove oggi?*" I ask, impressed with myself for asking where without mentally translating my question.

Francesco simply gives a sly smile. "*Ti piacerà.*"

Of course, I'll like it. I've liked everything else.

Our taxi navigates narrow streets then larger ones to the Colosseum, which opens just as we get there. Anjelica and Francesco already have tickets, so we head straight in.

They lead me around, giving me time to read the pages in our bilingual guidebook that correspond to where we're standing. We start at the top of the structure then navigate down and around stone bleacher seats, enough for eighty thousand people. NFL stadium size. But everything looks bigger, thicker, and much more imposing. We get closer to the surface where, in ancient times, they'd sometimes flood the floor to hold boat races. Inside an arena. Insane.

There's an area tucked underneath the bleachers called the hypogeum, where animals and gladiators would wait. Like a green-room before death matches.

"We go. *Si?*" Anjelica says.

Francesco contorts his face and bares his teeth. "*La! Leoni. Tigri. Orsi.*"

"Ah! Lions and tigers and bears."

We clamber down steps to the shadowy area, an underground system of tunnels and windowless rooms. Francesco and Anjelica hang back while I wander deeper into a small space—a cage for animals that were imported for battle or for the gladiators who were kept under control after Spartacus's rebellion. This space may be smaller than my tower room, but even if it isn't, at least I have a window and stairs to escape. Here, some hoisting mechanism would drop the victims to a brutal ending. Just imagining that has my heart pounding.

Soon, the Rossis call me out of there. We need to leave for whatever they have planned next. It takes twenty-five minutes in a taxi and a walk across the Tiber River before I recognize the church in the distance.

"The Vatican?" I ask.

"*Si,*" Anjelica says.

The approach to St. Peter's Square is lined with vendors hawking everything from food to toys to selfie sticks. Nonno and Nonna would hate the gaudiness and, especially, the sellers who are trying to profit off one of the holiest places on Earth.

We pass through the gates where a mass of people is gathered, all facing St. Peter's Basilica, a church with multiple domes and columns and arched windows. Anjelica turns me to one particular window with red curtains and something like a tapestry, red and gold, hanging from a balcony. Not ten minutes later, the pope himself comes out there to speak. I've never heard such a hush come over such a huge crowd.

His address seems to be more of a Sunday sermon than a prayer.

More than ever, I wish I'd studied Italian. And I wish I could have come with my dad and, especially, Nonno and Nonna.

At the end, after he blesses us all, we beat the mass exodus and grab another taxi, which takes us close to home. Francesco gestures that the apartment is toward the left, but once we get out, we veer right to stop for lunch in Piazza Navona, the largest square I've seen so far. The open area, supposedly constructed in the shape of a stadium, was once the site of some sort of competition (that's all I understand) and is circled with yet another church, a museum that was once a palace, buildings—maybe apartments?—and restaurants, all with outdoor seating. People are flocking to a large restaurant in the corner, but Anjelica waves a hand at it. "Bah! *Troppi turisti!*" Too many tourists. She makes a beeline to a smaller one farther down.

We sit where I can look out over the three fountains and the row of artists in the middle, some stationed next to their makeshift galleries, some painting new pictures on the spot.

After we order, I get a closer look. The first artist has paintings of people walking along the Tiber. They're good. The next artist is practically leering at me, not even pretending to paint but just surrounding himself with pictures as if that makes his staring invisible. I rush by the creep. The third artist, though, is finishing a picture of a woman in a red dress, holding a yellow umbrella under a blue sky and walking by the closest fountain, *Fontana del Nettuno.*

This is how I want to remember Rome—the sights, the smells, the sounds, everything here in this place of beauty and inspiration and aspiration. My mom would tell me I'm waxing poetic like my dad sometimes does, but I don't care.

The painting will be ninety-five Euros, the artist tells me, nearly a third of my spending money. If this were week six, and I'd saved enough, I would buy it on the spot. Maybe I'll come back. I'll definitely come back.

Anjelica shows up—our food is here—and she takes a picture of me with the artist and the painting. I post it immediately.

We stay at lunch for nearly three hours, which seems like three minutes. Then we continue walking, but my energy soon lags.

Francesco loops his arm through mine. *"Ho un'idea!"*

Anjelica, as if reading his mind, lights up. "Buns! We get... No, mean, we go buns!"

"Buns?" I pat my stomach. "Too much pasta. Uh. *Troppo pasta.*"

By her expression, it's the language barrier again. Instead, she loops her arm on the other side, and as a conjoined trio, we make a sudden turn.

I ask if we're going to a bakery, but they laugh. "No good English," Francesco says. Anjelica mimes sleeping then jerking awake, eyes bugging out. If I'm reading her right, wherever we're headed will wake me up.

Where we're going, though, is another church. They want me to pray for energy?

Anjelica pulls out two big scarves and covers her shoulders with one and mine with the other. No going sleeveless in churches here.

They enter first and cross themselves. I almost feel like I should, but being raised in a mixed-religion house, my dad never had me do that, so I just follow behind.

The sanctuary has black-and-white marble floors, about a dozen rows of dark wooden pews down the middle, and ornate arches on the sides. The Rossis aren't kneeling to pray, though. They steer me toward another space. Then Anjelica pulls the scarf over my eyes. "Okay?"

"Why? I mean, *per che cosa?*"

She takes the scarf down. "A sup, sup…supplies?" She opens her mouth into an O, and her eyes follow.

"Oh, surprise. You want to surprise me."

"*Si, si.* More *speciale. Fidati di me.*"

Sure, I'll trust her. I help her cover my eyes. They each take a hand, and soon we're going down a staircase amid a crowd of people. We get to the bottom, walk a little farther, a little farther, then she lifts my scarf. It takes my eyes a bit to adjust to this room with decorative doorways and arches and bridges made mostly of—

I gasp.

Francesco and Anjelica laugh.

These aren't buns. They're *bones*. Skulls. Hundreds and hundreds, maybe thousands of skulls line the walls. The coat of arms above a fireplace-like alcove is, literally, crossed arm bones. The clock and the decorative trim along the ceilings and walls, bones. Even the statues standing there are skeletons. Not the kind from biology class. Real, from people, skeletons. And if I understand right, that's skin still clinging to them. Five rooms of human bones in all: the Crypt of Skulls, Crypt of Pelvises, Crypt of Leg Bones and Thigh Bones, Crypt of the Three Skeletons, and one more I didn't catch. I hope I can forget the whole thing before this gives me an eternity of nightmares.

It takes a long walk back outside in the hot Roman sun before I finally lift the scarf from my shoulders. I give one huge shudder. "*La cripta dei cappuccini. Molto oro.*" I have no clue if I said the crypt was scary or it had a lot of gold.

Either way, they laugh.

"*Ti ha svegliato, sì?*" Anjelica pantomimes someone waking up.

"Yes. *Sì.*" It definitely woke me up. And freaked me out. I could use a Disney princess movie to counteract it all.

But we get another gelato, apparently the energy snack of champions, and walk while we eat, turning down one street, and another. At the next corner, Anjelica stops and gets out the scarf. Church again? But no. She uses it to blindfold me and leads me forward, it sounds, toward a large crowd of people. A rushing noise too. We stop. Francesco takes my other elbow and has me step onto a ledge, maybe a foot or two high. Anjelica gently bends my neck forward, lets some light in from the bottom of the scarf, and, once my eyes adjust from the dark, fully lifts it.

"Oh! Wow!"

I knew the Trevi Fountain was large, but this thing is massive. I look up a few fast facts. It's eighty-six feet high and 161 feet wide and was completed in 1762, which makes it older than the Declaration of Independence. I put my phone away and get hypnotized by the sight. It's like a myth come to life with tritons, horses, chariots, and the Greek god Oceanus.

We're at a height from the fountain itself, so we make our way down through the crowd, to the water's edge. And just stand there, Francesco and Anjelica letting me be.

It's hard to look away, but after some time, I turn my back and toss a coin with my right hand over my left shoulder into the water. With that, according to legend, you're destined to return to Rome. I'm already figuring out how to do that. I'll be way more skilled with the language next time, though I'm not sure it matters. I'm getting by one word at a time.

I take one long, last look for now, and we move on.

I wanted to stop by the Pantheon earlier, but it was too crowded. Now, though, closer to dusk, it's pleasantly busy. I pass through the eight columns and the squared entrance into the breathtaking rotunda. I almost hate to walk on the checkerboard floor, large squares and circles of marble in red, gold, blue-gray, and white. The walls are lined with more marble: columns, panels, alcoves, tombs, statues. And it's unbelievably pristine.

I fix my sight on the real reason I'm here. The oculus, a large open space in the dome's ceiling and the only source of light. It's also thought to be an opening to the heavens. I center myself directly below it, the last of the sun's rays falling into the centuries-old structure. I close my eyes, tilt up my chin, and will the angels, the powers, or the God of any religion to beam down positive waves for my first official day of Exchange Roma and its full Italian immersion.

If the oculus's connection to the heavens works, I don't feel it.

And the energy from the gelato has officially left me. I turn to the front of the Pantheon, but there's no sign of Anjelica. Francesco, though, is talking to an equally tall, older man off to the side. I head that way, and a strange grin spreads over the man's face. He looks me up and down: slowly, deliberately.

Like with roadkill, I look away, then look back...

Because that man. The artist, the creepy one, from Piazza Navona. It's him.

CHAPTER SEVEN

I SHAKE IT OFF. IF HE'S THE SAME MAN, FRANCESCO WOULD HAVE talked to him at lunch. It must be his leer. Our driver in Naples had it too.

I double back to the oculus. Press on my temples. Look up. *Please make me stop imagining bad stuff. Let me just have fun.* I close my eyes, take a deep breath, and the man is gone. Prayer semi-answered.

I tell Francesco I went back to say one more prayer.

"*Ottimo*," he says. "*Una preghiera.* Prayer. You need."

"*Si*," I say, in case that's a question. I pray it's not a statement. "Anjelica?"

Francesco types into his translation app. *She will meet us later.* He walks ahead, even faster this time.

I didn't know I'd need to work out to prep for today. "Where are we going? *Dove?*"

"*Scalina Spagna.*"

About ten minutes of run-walking later, we're at the base of the Spanish Steps. Anjelica waves, shopping bag in hand. *"Ciao! Per te. Per domani!"*

"For me? *Grazie.*"

But she doesn't hand it over. *"Per domani,"* she repeats. No smile.

I squeeze back a shiver, still left over from the bones and the man, I guess. Fine. I'll find out what's in the bag tomorrow.

Francesco whips past us and up the Spanish Steps, Anjelica on his heels.

Who are these people? They've been sightseeing for hours, must be at least a couple decades older than me, and still have ten times my energy. I have to get in better shape.

About halfway up the 138-step staircase that leads to the Spanish Embassy, Francesco turns, climbing backward. *"Il primo che sale le scale ordina la cena per tutti!"* He faces forward again and picks up his speed, Anjelica right behind.

No clue what he said, but it doesn't matter at all. So far, they've given me a practically perfect day. Except for the creepy man. And the bones. But even the skulls were disturbingly cool.

We go into a restaurant at the top and get seated at an outdoor table with a spectacular view of Old Rome. I swipe on the camera to capture everything, but Anjelica covers it with her hand and points to her eyes. "Love with *occhi.*" Then she taps just above her temple. *"Ricordi qui. Si?"* She shakes her head. "No fun."

"No fun?"

Anjelica nods.

"Oh! No phone."

"No phone. *Si*. Yes."

"Right. I should make memories of my own. *Ricordi qui.*" I tap my head. "So also, I shouldn't…" I mimic keyboarding. "*Si?*"

True. I did put my phone away at the Trevi Fountain and the Pantheon, and I soaked it all up. Not just the sights, but the sounds and the smells and the feels. But now this means no translation app all dinner long.

I don't need it at first. Francesco waves away the menus when the waiter comes. His self-proclaimed prize for winning the race is ordering our dinner. The five dishes for us to share come out at random times: *supplì,* fried rice balls filled with meat, tomato sauce, and mozzarella; *cacio e pepe,* my favorite pasta, just cheese, and pepper; Caprese salad; *orate,* a fish with artichokes; and for dessert, *maritozzo,* an opened-up sweet roll, overstuffed with fresh whipped cream, raisins, and pine nuts. All the while, we sip Frascati, a sparkling wine, which has my head spinning on the walk back.

It's been *una notte fantastica*, an amazing night, something I want to revisit forever, but once we get back to the apartment, I can barely find the energy to get ready for bed. One quick FaceTime, though. My parents are expecting it.

They answer, huddled over the phone. "Tess!" they say simultaneously, like they rehearsed. "We miss you!"

"I miss you too. Rome is amazing!" I recap the day, everything except the wine. They might freak, even though I only had one glass, maybe two. Francesco kept topping it off.

"*Domani scuola?*" says my dad.

"Someone's been studying Italian. Yes, school tomorrow." I rattle on about the beautiful grounds and the fun I had with the people again, just so they don't hear my one last bit of nervousness. Italian immersion in just nine hours.

"Where's Sofia? I want to wish her luck at her school tomorrow." Actually, I'm hoping to get one last boost from her aura.

"We'll tell her," my mom says, no worry crease at all. "She's hanging out around the Lincoln Memorial with her group. She's been lots of fun. So glad you're having fun too."

"I am. Tonight, especially, has been a *notte fantastica*."

"Doesn't sound like you mean it," says my dad. "We know you're stressing."

"Of course I am." I need to sound more convincing. "But it's just the language now. Everything else is amazing. And it is almost midnight here, you know."

"Get some sleep, sweetie. We miss you," my mom says. "Love you."

"Love you too."

Now, with a bit of second wind, I try to sketch the picture in Piazza Navona. Just no. I move my journal to the night table, turn off the lamp, and in three breaths, I...

I sit up straight, clawing my way out of some nightmare like someone awful has been in my room, staring at me.

"Hello?" I'm alone, but the lamp is back on. I turn it off and bury my face in the pillow. But I'm thirsty and have to use the bathroom and understand my body well enough to know that if I don't drink and pee, I'll lie here thinking how I'm not really thirsty and can hold out from peeing until morning.

I take the spiral staircase down, slowly. My head feels so fuzzy.

Voices. Loud voices. Anjelica. Francesco. Too loud for this time of night. Too fast to understand. Too Italian. I don't want to bother them, but—

Creak! That ninth step.

The talking stops. So do I. Then it starts back up.

I stand there like a lurker. If I'd just come downstairs like a normal person...

I turn. I'll start over. Make it back to bed, wait five minutes, then—

A hand grips my elbow. Spins me around. Anjelica.

Francesco slides past, standing between me and the tower room.

Now, sandwiched between them, I can only march downstairs.

"What...what's..."

"You're finally up," Francesco says. "You should join us. We're having a little party."

"Yes." Anjelica hisses so close that her breath brushes my ear. "It took you long enough. I thought the lamp would wake you up. Or Francesco standing there, staring. But no."

My breath leaves my body.

They're speaking perfect English.

CHAPTER EIGHT

"English? You?" I press a finger into my temple. "I thought...you didn't, you don't—"

"You have no clue what we do or don't." Anjelica shoves me into the kitchen and elbows me toward the table. "Sit." Her eyes, cold and hard, don't match her too-big smile.

This is no party. She presses me onto a chair, and Francesco swivels a laptop around.

Sofia's close-up fills the screen, something long and silver flashing at her cheek. She widens the view and slides the object, the flat side of a knife, along her jaw. She turns the camera and pans across a door. Dresser. Window. Headboard. The tease of a pillow. My mom's face. My dad. Completely still.

It's just after eleven there. They rarely go to bed before midnight. "Mom? Dad?"

No answer. "Are they—?" I can't bring myself to say the word.

"Sleeping." Sofia moves into the hallway. "Deeply sleeping. Peaceful. For now."

For now? "What kind of sick joke is this?"

"A really good one," she says.

"Good for us maybe, but not so good for poor Tess." Anjelica laughs.

"You tell her, Mama," Sofia says. "Tell her the punchline."

"The punchline or the gut punch?" Anjelica strokes my arm. "What happens next depends on you. So far you've been a disappointment." The stroking turns into a tight squeeze, nails denting my skin. "Sleeping through our first nudges. Having us wait. Almost making Francesco go upstairs again. Then you sneak down, eavesdropping, like a common narc. Bottom line? You do everything we say, or they will die." Anjelica gets fully in my face, stale coffee breath assaulting my nostrils. "It's as simple as that. Your parents will die."

With that, Sofia flashes the knife against her cheek again. And the screen goes black.

I can't catch my breath. Can't even scream. Only crude, guttural sounds come from the back of my throat until Anjelica holds up a hand, and I swallow back the noises.

"By six-fifteen a.m.," she says, "you will do the following. You will leave here and find your way to Viale Europa twenty-two. It's an address. Repeat it now."

"Wha…what?"

"Repeat it!"

"Viale Europa twenty-two."

"Again. Vee-al-ee. Air-oh-pah."

"Vee-al-ee. Air-oh-pah."

Anjelica nods. "The old woman who lives there takes her little, white dog for a brief walk at seven-fifteen each morning. You will slip into her house, unnoticed, steal the silver canister from her coffee table, and return here. Remember this: Sofia is quick. Sofia is skilled. It will take twenty seconds to murder both your parents. If that. They are weak and soft. Like you. You talk to anyone on your way, or try to get help, and we will know. Your parents die."

I try to swallow. Can't.

"You'll need most of an hour to get there," Francesco says, "but you will be back in time for school. Your first day of school in Rome! Aren't you excited?"

Somehow, I manage to nod.

"Good. That's a good girl."

CHAPTER NINE

I'M IN A NIGHTMARE, SLOGGING UP THE SPIRAL STAIRS, ONE BY one by one, slow motion. Except I'm awake. I wait for the sobs to come, but rage and fear and confusion have dammed up my tears.

More than anything, I need to warn my parents.

But… I can't. Sofia's right there with a knife, practically daring me to be stupid. I need to warn someone. Aunt Debbie and Uncle Dale would laugh that Italy's twisted my imagination. The Bethesda police? They'd either call it a prank or call me a drama queen. Even if they did take me seriously, they'd investigate, find happy people, then call me a drama queen. After that, what's to stop Sofia from killing my dad and dragging my mom away in chains until I did what they told me to in the first place?

I have relatives here. But my great-aunt, Zia Elena, doesn't speak English. And my dad said that his cousin Arsenio and family would be out of town my first few days.

I'm alone.

Wait. I am alone. How hard would it be for someone like me to disappear? No one would catch on for at least a day, except… Sofia is there, ready to kill. In seconds. Then what would stop the Rossis from killing me?

I press on my temples. Is it my parents, specifically? Me? Is this some kind of slavery ring? Is that creepy old man waiting to kidnap me?

I can't let my mind go sideways. Not now. I have to believe that if I steal some canister, this will all be over. And if that man comes anywhere near me, I'll scream and kick and fight any way I can. If only I'd taken Krav Maga with Carly.

No time now. I need to leave by 6:15. Or before, really. It's too easy to get lost here. According to the clock on the night table, it's 5:42, but I don't trust it. Not anymore. I reach for my phone.

It isn't there. Not surprising. In my exhaustion last night, I probably slipped it into my backpack after I talked to my parents.

But it's not there either.

I dump out the entire contents of my purse and my backpack. No phone. No computer. No credit card. No money. No passport. No identification. No way to leave Italy.

I have no way home.

The shaking starts in my shoulders, then launches into my neck and head. Inhale, four. Hold, two. Exhale… I don't have enough air to make it to six. But the threat of death, the threat of being an orphan, propels me to get dressed. I can't afford to break down right now. Just do what they say. But how?

I can't find the address without a nav app or without taxi money if it's too far to walk. And if I ask anyone for help, I'll have no parents.

I pull my hair into a ponytail then collect the right clothes— black jeans and blue, button-down shirt, sleeves cuffed to the elbows. Black Converse shoes. I'd blend in anywhere.

I leave the semi-safety of the tower room, maneuver down the stairs, to the bathroom, and—

I stumble back. Hands on knees. Head down.

There's blood on the mirror. Blood-red writing.

I fight for air. Finally realize. This is not my parents' blood. It's just lipstick.

DO NOT WRITE. MEMORIZE ONLY.

WALK—SPAGNA STATION. TAKE THE MEA ANAGNINA

SWITCH AT TERMINI—MEB LAURENTINA— 9 STOPS TO EUR PALASPORT

WALK—LEFT ON VIALE AMERICA, RIGHT ON VIALE PASTEUR, LEFT TO VIALE EUROPA 22

I read it multiple times, even mumble it out loud.

Anjelica barges in and points at the mirror. "You saw that?"

I nod.

"Tell me you saw that."

"I saw it."

"Memorized?"

"Memorized."

She takes a rag and wipes the words away. Then she puts the shopping bag from last night onto the counter. "A present. Use it." She leaves.

On top is a train pass paper clipped to a Metro map with the Spanish Steps station circled. I'll board the train there then switch at Termini. Same as Saturday. *And you're comfortable with local trains, Tess.*

Underneath is a crossbody courier bag like everyone has here. Probably big enough for the canister. It's empty and feels like it'll float away. I throw in some tissues, my case of pens and pencils, and my journal just so it hangs semi-normal.

At 5:58, according to the watch my dad practically forced me to wear—*but I'll always have my phone*—I take a breath of morning air and stop myself from running to the police. Instead, I retrace our route from dinner last night and easily find my way to the station. I board the train, hyper-aware of every single person there. No leering man, at least not yet. I ride the Orange Line to Termini. Navigate that station. Board the Blue Line to Laurentina.

Still no man. But anyone could be tailing me. That guy reading the paper. The one on his phone. The woman staring out the window. I want to stay here, ride the train until every one of them leaves. But I can't sit here paralyzed. The clock is ticking.

A few others get off the train with me at Eur Palasport. I walk upstairs to the street, pause to get my bearings or, really, to make sure no one is following me. They all pass by.

With my back to the building, I turn left to go down Viale America. Right at Viale Pasteur. Left again on Viale Europa. 6:46. Better early than late.

Number twenty-two, like many of the buildings, has storefronts at street level and apartments above. A locked gate, metal-bar construction about eight feet high, blocks the entrance into a courtyard and the access to the private residences. Even if I had the muscles to climb over, it would draw attention. I need another option.

Across the street is a similar building with shops below, apartments above, and a gated courtyard. I settle on a planter in front of a clothing store where, even through the trees and parked cars, I can stake out my target.

The building has four floors of balconies, meaning four floors of apartments. Why couldn't the Rossis write the apartment number on the mirror? Another of their sick games? Anjelica said I'll know. But how? Do they want me to fail? Do they want to kill my parents?

"Stop!" I whisper to myself. They may think I'm "weak and soft," but I'm also smart and observant.

Only seconds later, someone opens the gate next to me and turns toward a large, white church far down the street. It takes fourteen seconds for the gate to close. If these gates are identical, and they appear to be, I could make it across the street before it locks back up, *if* someone opens it and *if* I don't have to wait for cars to pass. More are passing every minute.

I go back across the street and lean against a tree, semi-facing the gate. I shake my hair out of its ponytail to hide my face enough that no witness, if it ever comes to that, can identify me. Then I pull out my journal and pretend I'm an art student, drawing the church's imposing walkway. Or trying. I can't draw a straight line to save my life. Hopefully, I won't have to.

Still, I keep my pencil hovered over the page, adding grass strokes, but mostly watching for anyone watching me.

Several strokes of grass later, an older woman, without a dog, nears the gate from inside the apartment complex.

Go time! I stroll several steps closer, move my journal into the bag, and pretend to rummage for my keys. When I glance up, ready to feign surprise that—lucky day—someone is coming out just as I'm going in, the woman holds the gate open, almost smiling at me.

I smile back and decide not to say *grazie* so she or anyone won't hear my voice. I nod, though.

The woman nods back and bumps into me hard enough to whip my courier bag to my back.

"Oops. Sorry," she says. "Have fun." And she scurries out, the metal bars clinking shut behind her.

CHAPTER TEN

She said what? Have fun? In English?

How the hell could she know I speak English? Unless she's part of this.

Her perfume wafts behind and my stomach twists.

It's her—the woman from the plane.

I look left. Right. Turn behind, like a paranoid squirrel. Who else is here, watching me?

Anyone might be staring out these courtyard windows. Thieves. Killers. Good Samaritans who will call the police if they see me breaking and entering...in eleven minutes.

The courtyard is a small, grassy area with a few trees and two benches. The walkway to the building's entrance slopes upward so much that it takes only five steps to reach the main door. Unlocked. Hooray for small things. I go inside.

With four apartments per floor, I have a one-in-sixteen chance to get this right the first time. The door on the far right has a welcome mat with a picture of a little white dog. Anjelica said I'd know, and I probably do now. But unless the woman keeps her door unlocked, I'm no closer to breaking in than I was a minute ago.

I go back to the courtyard. The dog-mat apartment is even farther uphill, its balcony more like a patio, just a step above the grass. Two of its windows are open. There's a way in! Except… Putting aside felony theft in a foreign country, I've never climbed in or out of any window. Weak and soft? In this case, the Rossis are right. How can I possibly find the arm strength to hoist myself in? Maybe I won't have to. Maybe they don't lock things here.

I stay in the shadows, watching the patio door. 7:12. A white-haired woman moves toward the slider. A little dog follows.

I keep my eyes up, head down, hair in my face. I become that art student again. I reach into the bag for my journal, but my fingers find a folded piece of paper that wasn't there before. I unfold it and—

Don't scream. Don't scream. Don't scream.

There's my mom. My dad. Sofia. A selfie of them at our kitchen table, making goofy faces, a block of knives clearly pushed forward on the counter, one missing from its slot. The picture has to be from dinner yesterday. It's only 1:13 back home, so they're still sleeping. And not dead, not yet.

I breathe. Again. Again. Again. Until…

On schedule, the woman and her dog come out through the patio door. They turn toward the street and go out the gate, not even glancing my way.

I shove the picture into the bag and wait to make sure the woman is really gone. Also, to stop from shaking. I finally stand, brush myself off. Make my way onto the patio, past two chairs, a small table, and two dog bowls. Grasp the handle on the patio door. Locked. Next, I move back into the building itself. Her apartment door is locked too.

I'll have to go through the window. But I've never managed a single pull-up in gym class. And the table and chairs are chained together like this area has a theft problem. Ironic.

I toss the courier bag in, grasp onto the chest-high windowsill, and jump, the toes of my Chucks scrabbling against the wall for some leverage. And I drop to the ground.

I need to reach farther inside, grab onto the walls of the sink that's directly underneath. One, two, three… I jump, stretch one arm in, and push up with my toes. I manage to inch my other arm in, a little more, a little more. And somehow—strong toes, sheer will?—I make it to my waist, half in, half out, poised over the kitchen sink.

I pause to listen, prepared to leap back if I hear someone coming, but everything stays silent except for the ticking of a retro cat clock on the wall. I swivel the faucet to one side and walk my arms across the white porcelain, my legs scraping the windowsill.

Somehow, I make it over the sink and swing my legs to the kitchen floor.

It's ugly, but I'm in.

So are my fingerprints.

Just last year, I watched a documentary about a college student who was wrongfully accused of murdering her roommate, then the hell she went through for years in a godforsaken Italian prison. Even if no one in the world has a record of my prints, I still don't want them with the Italian authorities. The Rossis could be capable of anything.

I grab a kitchen towel from the counter and wipe down everything I've touched so far.

Beyond the kitchen is the living room. In the center of the coffee table sits the silver canister. It's about ten inches tall with a diameter half that. Its surface is peppered with random cutouts, each about half the size of a baby fingernail. I grab it with the towel, shove it into the bag. And with that, a thrill, nearly electric, shoots down my spine.

No time to celebrate. It's 7:26. Time to get the hell out of here.

Too late. The door to the apartment creaks open and the old woman's voice drifts in.

"Ah, bambina! Sei stato così veloce stamattina! Tempo per la tua colazione. Nom, nom."

I retreat into the bedroom, heart pounding. I close my eyes and try to picture the rest of the apartment. Try to process a plan. Or just find the right moment and bolt. Otherwise, I'll have years to process. In jail.

Breaking and entering. Stealing a silver canister. And a kitchen towel.

Nom, nom.

Sounds like the woman is about to feed her dog, and the dog bowls are on the patio. She has to go out there. She has to. Please. Please.

The thrill, just seconds ago, has totally vanished. My legs wobble. I can't fully catch my breath. Or am I holding it?

A scraping sound, like a spoon in a can, drifts from the open bedroom window. She's on the patio.

I race out of the bedroom and use the towel to open the front door. And to wipe off the prints on the outside where I tried to get in. I pull the door shut. Too loudly.

Did she hear? By the volume of the woman's conversation with her dog, her hearing isn't all there. Soon enough, though, she'll know she had a thief.

A door closes on the floor above. High heels clop down the hall.

I stop myself from running to the courtyard, out the gate, and back to the train. Can't draw attention.

One step at a time.

I reach the door to the courtyard and put the towel on the knob, but I can't get a grip. *Use your hand. Wipe the knob.* Into the court-yard. *Pull open the gate, then wipe it down.* Except more people are on the street now. And the strangeness of a girl wiping metal bars with a towel would be suspicious. Memorable.

The high heels are still plinking behind me.

I jam the towel into the bag and kneel in the shadow of a tree, hair in my face, retying a shoe that doesn't need it. If Signora Second Floor opens the gate, her fingerprints will be the last ones on there.

The gate opens. I have fourteen seconds to slip through without touching anything. Thirteen, twelve, eleven... *Move!* Nine, eight, seven... *Slower.* Five, four... *Out!* Two, one... *Steel yourself for a scream.* What's Italian for *thief?*

Whatever it is, no scream. And none down Viale Europa, down Viale Pasteur, down Viale America. None in the train station. No sounds of feet chasing me. No leering men. No Italian sirens.

Still, it's not until the MEB starts moving that I remember to breathe.

I sit at the very back of the very last train car, where no one can surprise me from behind. I've been blindsided enough for a lifetime.

But I did it. My cheeks start creeping into a smile. Then they stop.

I am officially a criminal.

Why me? Maybe I'm just the lucky, random exchange student assigned to the Rossis. It's not like they would have specifically asked for me. Unless they did. But again, why?

I press on my temples. It's too much, too much...too much adrenaline and too little sleep. And too theoretical. One thing isn't theoretical, though. The canister.

The two other people in this train car are sitting near the doors, staring at their phones. More will be boarding. I have just minutes to figure out what I stole. And maybe why.

I peel back the flap of the courier bag, maneuver the canister to sit upright, then pop off the ornate lid.

The only thing inside is yarn.

They threatened my parents' lives over tangled strands of pastel yarn? No. It has to be the canister itself.

I tap it inside and out. It's sturdy, but thin all around. No hidden compartments. No writing on it either. It's just an innocent knickknack, probably available at three thousand places online. So why did they make me steal it? A power thing?

I have no answers, and I won't have the canister for long. In case I need to remember it… No phone. I can't take a picture. I try a quick sketch instead, too quick. The size and proportions are all wrong.

Seven people are in the car, all near the doors. I keep everything low on my lap, the seatback in front of me acting as a shield.

I lay the canister on a second piece of paper and mark off the dimensions, top to bottom, side to side. Much more accurate. Now for the details. My preschool teacher would be proud. I wrap the paper around the canister and start a rubbing, the random rectangles appearing exactly where they're supposed to.

The train stops again. I'm only a quarter of the way through, but four passengers head closer. Too close. I hide everything in the bag.

My first drawing will go in the nearest trashcan. But I fold the rubbing then put it inside my shoe. It's the best hiding place I have for now. From the police and from the Rossis.

The Rossis. I have to escape from them. Escape from Rome.

But how? I have no passport. No phone. No credit cards. No money.

All I have are two smiling prison guards.

And a psychopathic teenager, poised to kill my parents.

CHAPTER ELEVEN

I walk from the Spanish Steps Metro stop to the apartment, my mind racing through all the questions I have for the Rossis. If that's even their real name. I won't ask a single one. Too dangerous. But I can win this battle. I'll walk into the apartment like it's been another morning of sightseeing.

When I get back, Francesco and Anjelica—Anjelica, not such an angel—are lounging around the table, drinking coffee. I don't need my key; they left the door cracked open. Anjelica pops right up but, surprisingly, doesn't snatch away the courier bag. Instead, she gives me that double-cheek kiss. "*Buongiorno! Qualcuno si è alzato presto questa mattina.*"

So, we're back to pretend. Fine. I manage a smile. "This is for, I mean, *questo è per te.*" I put the bag on the table.

Anjelica reaches for it, but I pull it back faster. "*Minuto.*" I take out my journal, my pens, and pencils. They can keep the tissues, the towel, and the Metro map.

Anjelica pulls the threatening picture from my bag. She laughs then burns it in the sink.

Francesco makes me hand over my journal and thumbs through it: the friend messages, sketches of my locket, flower field, and the haiku. He stops at the man on the plane. "Anjelica! Look! He had a fake mustache!"

My blood runs cold. They knew the man sitting next to me. Him *and* the Perfume Woman. Who else?

Francesco turns the pages past more haiku, a growing list of sights we've seen, sketches of the tree, the eyebrow, the painting in Piazza Navona. He stops at the sketch of the church. Waggles a finger and rips it out. Blank, blank, blank the rest of the way. Except...

Near the back, there's one page of contact info for my family here in Rome. I have to hope the Rossis don't question it, or use them to get to me too. I can't grab the book back, and I can't sit here, panicking, as he goes page by page. There are 420 of them.

"Bathroom?" I say. "*Il bagno?*"

He nods.

I don't have to pee, so I trickle sink water into the toilet, flush, and wash my hands—really scrub them. When I come back out, my journal is sitting next to my breakfast. No mention of my relatives. Either he gave up or ripped it out without interrogating me.

"*Mangia!*" says Anjelica.

Eat? I can barely produce saliva. But they're watching, so I take a nibble and another and, in the middle of my third, Anjelica finally sets the canister on the table. Then she waves the kitchen towel over her head like a rally flag. "*Un bonus!*" She laughs like it's the best joke ever.

Anjelica gets Sofia on the computer and shows her the canister and the rally towel. *"Guarda questo."* Watch what?

She wraps the towel around Francesco's head like a bandanna. Then she ties it around her wrist like a bracelet. Laughing, laughing, laughing. Then she stops. And she loops the towel around my neck from behind. Tugs.

I am not dying today. I wedge my fingers underneath.

And she lets go. Laughing again. "Just kidding, Tess. I wasn't going to hurt you. However..." She motions me back to the computer.

Sofia's in my family's kitchen, sharpening the knife.

No! I did everything. But I stay silent, a bit of roll drying on my tongue.

Sofia shrugs, puts the knife back into the block, then walks into my parents' bedroom.

My dad is softly snoring. My mom shifts slightly. It's like nothing ever happened.

Sofia goes into my room, crawls under my covers, and says goodnight. The call ends.

"Adesso va tutto bene," said Francesco.

Everything's good? Maybe for him.

Anjelica leaves the room and comes back with the courier bag, now filled with the contents of my backpack and a few Euros.

"I'll speak in English, so you understand completely." She holds up my phone. "Isn't technology grand? Now, we can see everything you see, watch everything you type, listen in on every conversation. Send love notes? We don't care. Watch porn? Go for it. Talk about this morning? Say anything about us?" She shakes her head. "Slit throats can be such a messy business. Maybe poison? Electrocution? So many ways to die."

She slides my phone to me, and her face softens. "As for social media, thank you for not posting every five minutes. It would be a full-time job for us."

"What do you mean?"

"It means that you will post nothing." Francesco gives me a smile. "We will do that for you. Your job is to take pictures of things at strange angles, selfies of you having fun; well, you know what you post. When you see what we post for you, you won't be able to tell the difference. Let's do one now. How about one of those little poems you have in your journal. A new one. The three-line things."

"A haiku?"

"That's what they're called," Francesco says. "We can give you eight minutes, then we need to get you ready for school." He slides his journal out from under the photo of their little family, turns to a blank page, and hands me a pen. "Create!"

Create? With a knife to my parents' throats? Somehow, I start counting syllables. Then I turn the page around so he can see it.

> *I've never ever*
> *Posted my poems. Now I have…*
> *Grown stupid in Rome*

"Good job," Francesco says. "Except this doesn't sound like you." He crosses out *stupid* and hands me back the pen. "You might want to change it before Anjelica sees."

To what? Criminal? Trapped? I need two syllables anyway. Braver? I'm not feeling so brave. Smarter? If I were, I'd already be out of here. I settle on *bolder*.

"*Perfetto!*" He calls for Anjelica to come back.

This time she slaps a credit card onto the table. It has my name, but it's not the one I brought. "Continuing. All expenses will go through us. Do not get greedy." She flashes two U.S. passports. The first one is mine, my picture with my goofy smile. She pulls that back and hands me the other one with a different picture. It had to be from yesterday. It's the first time I wore that shirt.

"This will pass through all but the most rigorous screenings. Notice here…" She thumbs to the next page with a single stamp. "Serbia, not Italy, which means you would have entered this country illegally. Remember that." She hands it to me. "One more thing. You'll take this courier bag wherever you go. And that's all… for now…"

"…because it's school time!" Francesco taps his watch, motions for me to follow him into the living room, and hands me a helmet. "You'll be late if you walk today."

Moments later, I'm zooming on his motorbike, clutching at his waist for dear life. I almost laugh. If they still need me, and with Anjelica's *for now* it seems they will, they won't kill me. Just my parents.

I stop smiling.

Francesco stops a block away from school and momentarily lifts his smoky full-face visor to give me a smile and tell me to be good, which has a whole other meaning than it did just hours ago. Then he zips off ten minutes before school starts.

For the first time this morning, I feel good. Safe enough. But am I really? Exchange Roma could be a setup for some dark and deadly and elaborate crime ring.

No. It actually can't. First, they'd need to fool all the participating schools on two continents. Second, Aunt Debbie, who still has her FBI connections, checked out the program. But did she check out the Rossis?

I want to find an un-cloned phone and call her so badly, but no. She and her family had dinner with my parents and Sofia last night. I have to assume that Sofia's been busy, tapping into every cell and landline I might call. And I have to pretend that everything is perfectly fine. Starting now.

Devin is standing at the top of the front steps outside the school building like he's been waiting for me or Bright or Nicolas or whomever else we met Saturday night. "*Ciao!* Tess!"

I wave, take one step up, and miss. I fall forward and catch myself with my hands, but not before I make a total fool of myself. All I can do is shrug.

I wait for Devin to laugh, but he gives me the biggest hug instead.

I've never needed one more. I could cry, but I'm the one who laughs.

He backs away, his eyebrow arching even higher. This time he blushes. "Sorry. Inappropriate, I'm sure."

"Probably."

"Though I've heard it's proper to welcome one home after a trip."

An adult, making his way past us, shakes his head at Devin.

"Well then," Devin whispers, "I suppose that means I'm to be

70

speaking Italian now, but total immersion is impossible. And my accent? *Orribile!*"

"*Anche orribile.*" I point to myself. "Try speaking Italian when you had no business checking the intermediate proficiency box. Don't tell, though, or they'll kick me out."

I wish.

"*Il nostro segreto.*"

I ache to tell him my secret. Tell anyone. But I stick out my hand, shake on it, and manage a genuine smile.

I've heard about out-of-body experiences, and now I understand. I'm here, watching myself act perfectly normal on the outside, with my insides tumbling and twisting and not even hinting, to anyone, that my whole world has turned upside-down.

If I could know for absolute certain that Devin's not part of this nightmare, maybe he'd be an ally and help me find a way to get out of this. But no. Not until I can trust him. With my life. But how can I get there?

The right words have never been more important.

CHAPTER TWELVE

INSTEAD OF SPILLING TO DEVIN, I DO THE ONLY THING I CAN right now: I head with him to the classroom and find a seat. Then I pretend to search deep inside my bag, shuffling the shadowed, gray contents to find a single, rational thought. One comes. I am safe here for this moment, for this school day. And a fleeting sense of normalcy returns.

Our teacher, Signorina Emma, announces that it's Get to Know You time, not that I fully understand her, but it's what every teacher does. First, we're supposed to give our names and where we're from. Easy. But then we're supposed to say something we enjoy doing *and* give a random fact about ourselves. At least, I think that's what she said. She might as well be speaking Sanskrit through a triple-thick mask. My head isn't exactly in this right now.

I'm about to feign a coughing attack and run to the hall to get the translation for sketching, but others are half speaking, half pantomiming, with Signorina Emma and fellow students helping fill in the words. I can do that.

Except my mind is still fleeing from Viale Europa, and the only random fact I can think of is that I spent the morning as a common thief. That and the one solid memory from visiting here when I was four. I can still picture my slightly older cousin Vittoria pushing me so hard and high on a swing that I flipped off backward with such force, I landed on my feet.

When it's my turn, I change "cousin" to "uncle" because I know that word, and I mostly pantomime the rest. No one seems to care. At least something is going right.

When we break for lunch, Signorina Emma has me stay back for a minute. Even with her warm smile, this can't be good. She waits for the room to clear before she beckons me closer. Then, I think, she says that she understands my situation.

My heart races. That could mean she knows about the Rossis. Or she's working with them. I have no clue how to respond. I just nod and try to clear the chatter from my mind so I can listen hard and maybe understand whatever she says next.

She pats my arm. "*Il tuo italiano non è avanzato come gli altri di questa classe.*"

My Italian isn't as good as the others in this class. I breathe. Almost laugh.

I gesture around the room and try to ask if I can stay here. I don't want to be kicked down to the Basic Proficiency class when I've already made friends. "*Io resto qui? Possible?*" I put my palms together under my chin.

She squeezes my shoulder. Rattles off too many words. But I think she's saying that I looked particularly panicked when it was my turn. Try harder, and I'll catch on faster.

I love her so much right now. I thank her.

"*Ti terrò d'occhio.*"

Something about an eye. She'll keep her eye on me? As in watch out for my well-being or watch me for the Rossis? I don't go there. I just thank her again, but I'm keeping my eye on her too.

Everyone looks like a coconspirator right now. Even Devin and Bright and Nicolas, who are waiting in the doorway for me.

Don't break down. Don't break down. I take a breath, keep my smile, and tell them what I thought Signorina Emma said. About my Italian. Not watching me for the Rossis. "*Sì?*"

"*Sì,*" Nicolas says. "You heard her right."

"You were listening?"

Bright laughs. "We all were. I needed to know if you were the teacher's pet or if you were in trouble."

"In trouble, me?" I smile. She has no idea what kind of trouble I'm in.

We go through the lunch line and take our food to an outdoor table under what should feel like a perfect sky. A few others join us. I wait for everyone to start chattering in Italian, making me feel like I've come in the middle of a conversation and no one cares enough to bring me up to speed. It turns out that Richard, the guy I dubbed as the Bean that first night, and Sydney, aka Red, are even better at Italian than Nicolas. The others are somewhere between him and me. And with Signorina Emma out of earshot, we default to a mix of languages.

Bright starts analyzing our personality types by the shapes of our faces, and we're arguing that with only nine different face shapes and infinite personalities, it's impossible to categorize every person on Earth. I hope so. Sofia and I have the same shape.

Bright spews out some rationale that no one's buying.

"If you don't stop," Nicholas tells her, "we'll start calling you *Signora Frode*."

Madame Fraud. In spite of it all, I'm so swept up in the laughter that, for those few moments, the world is right. I need to learn how to compartmentalize my nightmare if I plan on staying sane.

Especially now.

The topic switches to host families. All the phones come out. Great. I have nothing to show except selfies of me, all alone. No wonder Sofia never sent me the photo of us together. I start to explain in half-English how Anjelica and Francesco are camera shy, but Devin grabs my phone.

I reach for it, but he's a good five inches taller than me, and he leans way over in back of Bright, who uses her body to keep him there. Fine. They'll see that—

"Camera shy?" He keeps thumbing. "You've easily got a dozen pictures."

"I what?"

He hands back my phone. I'm no longer alone in all the selfies; the ones with my pizza at that first restaurant, then with the next pizza in Naples, at the Colosseum, with gelato, with the scarf over my eyes at the Capuchin Crypt, with that painting in Piazza Navona, on the Spanish Steps. There's a man and/or a woman in all of them with me.

Except the other two people are not the Rossis.

Richard, the Bean, speaks up. "*Timido della telecamera? Non!*"

He's right. The Rossis don't look camera shy. I need some explanation. "After they took these—"

Signorina Emma picks that moment to come by. "*In italiano.*"

Which works because my gaze is drifting to the left. I try to straighten it out, though I can blame whatever story I'm about to tell on my ignorance of the language. I try to say they were embarrassed to take more pictures after these, but I might have just said that the giraffe is eating the hedgehog. When no one makes fun of me, I take a breath and really look at the photos.

The Rossis photoshopped a mystery couple into some of them. In at least two, the couple's expressions are the exact same. They probably stole the images from Facebook or Insta or somewhere.

I wonder if anyone else has been as lucky as I am with their host families. Or is part of a crime family themselves.

If I were to suspect anyone, it would be Nicolas. He may be a goofball, and I have a feeling he's a practical joker, but among the four of us, he's been the quietest. The less you talk, the fewer slipups you make.

If that theory is right, though, I should trust Bright the most. On the other hand, no one like her has ever tried to be friends with me. Is she targeting me? She's been an actress, likes to get up in everyone's business, and is really good at getting people to talk. But wouldn't a mole be more unassuming?

Then there's Devin. He seems straightforward and quick to share whatever's on his mind, which wouldn't fit the profile. My

Spidey sense tells me that he's either the best actor or he's not involved in this canister business at all. Or maybe this morning's hug has swayed my opinion. Who knows anything?

Maybe I do. Or did. Those red-flag moments—Sofia at the airport, the Perfume Woman, the Creepy Guy, the tower room— have proven real.

Less than an hour before class lets out, Signor Matteo pops into the classroom to welcome us again and something, something, something. My attention span is shot for the day. Until he asks me to come with him.

My attention returns. He also has my heart rate up, my ears ringing, and is about to get my full confession if he promises to keep my parents safe and me out of jail. Unless the police are already waiting in his office.

The walk there seems to stretch on forever, each footstep bringing me closer to my demise. He ushers me inside and has me sit across the desk from him. No police. At least there's that. He grows very quiet, though, shuffles a few papers, and lands on my application to the program. A spark of hope. Maybe they did admit the wrong person. They're kicking me out, sending me home. Please.

"*Ho saputo che hai una zia e dei cugini a Roma.*" Signor Matteo smiles, and not like someone about to give me what he'd consider bad news. "*Parlami di loro.*" Tell him about *whom*? He repeats it so that I understand.

I nod and tell him that I have a great-aunt and cousins here in Rome and—I hold in a gasp. What if the Rossis are threatening them too? "Are they okay? I mean *stanno bene*?"

Signor Matteo apologizes and assures me that they are fine. Then he speaks slowly enough that I get the gist of what he's saying. When exchange students like me have relatives in town, he needs to make sure we don't ignore our host families in favor of our relatives.

"*No problema.*" I explain that Arsenio found out about Exchange Roma, called my dad, and said how *fantastico* it would be if I came. They'd all finally get to know me. I met my great-aunt Zia Elena, Nonno's sister, only that one time when I was four. Arsenio; his wife, Florenza; and their daughter, Vittoria, who's now in college, did come to the United States three years ago for my grandparents' funeral, and...

How do I explain in Italian that they barely made it in time for the funeral, spent only two days, then left? They had business to get back to and, as my dad said, "Apparently, no grief to work through." Then again, Zia Elena and some others supposedly blamed Nonno for the rift in their family. I barely know this side of the family at all.

A quick laugh escapes my lips. "*I Rossis. Conosco meglio già.*" Which is absolutely true. I already know the Rossis better, faster, than anyone I've ever met. I may not know their favorite movies or music, but I know who they are deep down.

Signor Matteo nods. "*Hai intenzione di vederli?*"

Plans to see my family? Not yet. I mangle the fact that I'm staying with them for a week after Exchange Roma. They're not in town right now.

Where are they? "*Shopping di,* uh, antiques?" The question mark because I don't know the word, but more because I'm not exactly sure what they're doing. I got that impression, though.

"*Antiquariato.*"

"*Antiquariato. Alter*—cities—*città in Italia. Per il loro...*business, work...*laverio?*"

"*Lavoro. Brava.*" Signor Matteo excuses me. No police, no jail, just a smile and a mention that his door is open if I need anything. I need to know if he's watching me. If Signorina Emma is. Or if the other people in my class are.

Mostly, I need to get out of Rome. But the universe isn't listening, I'm not talking, and the school day ends.

Bright and some of the others get picked up. Even though the Rossis expect me to find my way with the nav app, and even though they may be tracking me, they didn't command me to come straight back.

Instead of turning left from the school grounds, I follow Devin, a whisper of an idea forming. If I work this right, I'm hoping I can accomplish two things. First, I want to confirm whether or not Anjelica and Francesco have me bugged for sound. If they do, I'll know to be more careful. The second will be harder. If I learn for absolute certain that I can trust Devin—and my gut tells me it's possible—I might be able to make him an ally. Lord knows I need someone.

"Show me your host family again," I say.

He swipes to a picture of nine people. "This is my favorite. Me, of course. My parents, my sister and brother, my host parents, my host brother Roberto. And that's their daughter Gianna, who's in London as we speak. She's who I exchanged with." Behind them is the requisite backdrop of the Colosseum. "My family, obviously, came for a brief holiday before we went our separate ways."

"Is your host family nice?" I ask.

He smiles. Nods. "They're all right. Yours isn't?"

Crap. Why did he ask that? My expression? Tone of voice? I glance right, left. If they get the wrong idea, they could kill me. Literally. *Act normal, Tess.*

"They're awesome tour guides," I finally say. True. "Saw my backpack and bought me this bag so I'd feel fully Italian." Not entirely true, but if they hear that, they'll like that I'm trying.

But that's not how I want this conversation to go. "Let me see that again." I grab his phone away. Totally out of character. So's being a thief. I point to the photo. "Both your families are literally picture perfect. Impossible. Have they been photoshopped?"

He laughs so hard. "Sorry." Harder. "Truly sorry. It's just that most people wouldn't say, 'Hey! You have two photoshopped families!' Not straight away. They'd have asked what they're like, what they do, all their deep, dark secrets even."

I throw up my hands. "No clue why I said that. I barely slept last night." I make sure to look straight ahead. "Blame it on weird dreams."

"Got it. It took me four days to fully acclimate. You should be better tomorrow."

"I hope." Then I ask the predictable questions. From his answers—his host family is funny and smart; they were kind to his little sister, who kept peppering them with questions; they showed him their emergency cash hiding place—I have to believe he's living with people who won't kill him in his sleep tonight.

A group text comes to our phones. Bright wants everyone from our class to go out after dinner. Bars, I'm thinking. But after several immediate yesses, she gives us her host family's address. Devin asks if I plan to go.

"Hopefully." Anything to get away from the Rossis. Though I'll probably have to get wired for sound. I give a laugh. "New family, new rules. You?" I ask, fishing for more info.

"Same. My family seems wonderful, but I get the impression that they need their rules because I also get the impression that Gianna has a bit of a wild streak."

On the surface, his family sounds normal, but it's too soon to tell.

As I turn down the next street to find my way back to the Rossis, I have to laugh. Even if Devin is safe at his house and neither he nor his host family is homicidal, what could I say to him to be one hundred percent sure? My whisper of an idea goes silent.

I blindly follow the nav app, barely seeing the streets I found so charming just yesterday. Several buildings away from the Rossis, I study the key to the apartment. Why would they give me a key if I'll never need one? Unless that's what they've wired for sound. But it's too sleek, too solid. Maybe they've stuck something on my phone. Though, it'd be easier to plant a bug in the lining of my...

Courier bag. Double crap. And they wouldn't need to have someone following me 24/7 unless they're doing that too.

Or maybe I'm just being overly paranoid.

But two steps into the apartment, it's obvious. I'm not.

CHAPTER THIRTEEN

It's that horrible perfume again.

Anjelica and Francesco are sitting in the living room with the woman from the plane, the same one who opened the gate for me this morning.

"Tess," Anjelica says, "Signora Roma."

Signora Roma laughs. "*È questo il mio nome adesso?*"

"*Per lei,*" Anjelica says.

They made up that name just for me. Mrs. Rome.

Signora Roma beckons me over, and I go across the room like some programmed puppet. She takes my hand in hers and tells me I did very well today.

I nod and maybe smile, but my insides are churning.

She goes on to tell me in mixed Italian/English, so that I understand, that I acted normal enough, as any girl in a new situation might. If I continue acting that way—at school, out of school, everywhere—I'll be okay. And when my time in Rome is over, I'll go back home and live a happy life. My parents too. She switches to English. "As long as you tell no one about any of this. *Capisci?*" Her hand squeezes mine.

Yes, I understand.

"*Capisci?*" she says again with more force. Her grip tightens.

"*Capisci!*" I say it harsher than I mean to.

But Signora Roma just laughs. "*Lei capisce.*" She lets go.

I stay frozen for a moment, then pantomime that I'm going upstairs—fine with them—but I turn back from the first step to ask permission to go out tonight.

"Hey, do whatever you want." Anjelica grins. "*Va bene anche alla stazione di polizia.*"

I can even go to the police station? Is that what she said?

"But there are consequences for everything."

That's what she said.

"Like asking stupid questions about a family being photoshopped."

And there we have it. They're listening in. And thinking about it, the way Anjelica commanded me to always carry the bag, the device is in there. I want to throw a tantrum or cry or sleep until all this is over, but my parents are waiting to go into work until I FaceTime them.

I head upstairs, take a breath, and channel Carly's best smile when they pick up. "Hi!"

"Hi, yourself!" says my mom from the kitchen, the knife block still pushed slightly forward. "I see you got to school and back in one piece."

I manage a laugh.

"We dropped Sofia off at the Metro two, three hours ago. Offered to ride with her today, but she's meeting friends just a stop down. I wish we knew who. If they're good people."

Yeah, Mom, doubtful.

"Carly was here for dinner last night. Maybe she knows."

"I'll ask," I say.

"Thanks. It feels so irresponsible not knowing. But I get it. Sofia's determined to be as independent as possible."

My dad comes into the picture. "Sort of like you. Except she's very chipper in the morning, Miss Groggy Head."

I give him the expected laugh.

"I wish she'd wear off on me," he continues, "because this morning it was hard to lift my head from the pillow." He takes a long sip of coffee.

My mom looks at him. "You too?"

Yes, both of you, I want to say. That's what happens when someone drugs you. Instead, I tell them about school. The get-to-know-you session. Bonding at lunch. Making more friends. And I send them a picture of the syllabus so they can live vicariously through me each day.

I'd rather have a syllabus of whatever nightmarish plans the Rossis have next. It might be more helpful. Or completely terrifying.

I move to something happier: how I'm going out tonight.

"That's great," says my mom with barely any enthusiasm.

"Why?" I ask. "What's wrong?"

"Oh, nothing," she says. "Just the thought of you running around

Rome at night. But you do have your host parents. And they will look out for you. I'm confident."

"They're already looking after me."

I hang up from them and call Carly. She texted hi earlier but didn't say why. If it's about my parents, I need to know. But it's just that she said yes to the internship.

I try to get all excited, but my words come out flat. "Sorry," I say. "Hectic day, so tired. Can you do me a favor and pretend you heard the enthusiasm in my voice?"

"OMG! Tess! Thanks for getting so excited for me. It's an honor!"

I laugh. "And could you do one more thing for me?"

"Jump up and down? Turn cartwheels? Become a full-fledged pediatrician by the end of the summer?"

"Ha. Well, all that and…"

Yes, Carly will ask to meet Sofia's exchange friends. The Rossis can't kill me over that.

By the time Francesco calls me down for dinner, Signora Roma is gone, but her perfume lingers through the aroma of fresh tomato, garlic, and onion from his meat sauce. He is a good cook—I have to give him that. And both of them, together, are experts at making our entire dinner seem like a mom, a dad, and a kid talking about their days.

Though they don't really need to ask about mine. Between the photoshop comment and talk about face shapes—which, looking back, happened with my bag on the lunch table and my phone buried deep inside—they hammer home the point that they can hear everything.

I have no clue what they do all day besides sit around and monitor me. If anyone asks, I'll say that Anjelica is an engineer and Francesco works in tech, which isn't exactly a lie. I get the feeling that she engineers all the plans, and he takes care of the spy-on-Tess business. And what they do for money—outside of criminal activity, which, I assume, is their main source of income—is none of my concern. Unless, for some reason, I can cut off their funding and make them shrivel up and go away.

I head back upstairs after dinner and actually drift off, but something wakes me. I roll over, and Anjelica is leaning in the doorway. Privacy is nonexistent here.

"Rise and shine. Go party!"

"I don't think I can."

"You told them you'd be there, and believe me, you don't want anyone questioning what's going on here." She hands me a slinky tank dress she bought for me today. "It picks up the green in your eyes. Wear it." She switches back to Italian. Tells me to say nice things about my host family tonight.

I almost can. The dress looks more perfect than anything I own. Almost too perfect. In fact, it's like everything they've done is perfect, as if this isn't the first time. Oh God. If they've done this before, where's the other person? Why didn't they turn the Rossis in? Unless they're...

I can't go there. Somehow, I will spend the foreseeable future acting like everything is normal. Without having a nervous breakdown.

About a dozen people show up at Bright's host family's penthouse, which is at least four times larger than the Rossis' apartment. Figures. Though, except for the view of the Colosseum lit up at night, I do like the simplicity of the Rossis' more. With vases and candelabras and figurines and ornaments filling every space, my eyes have no place to rest.

Even so, the conversation is lighter than the surroundings. And lighter than the wrecking ball that sits in my chest.

The laughter starts when we overrule Sydney and Richard and decide to speak in English. "Of course," Devin says, "feel free to speak in either language. We'll keep up. Or try." He bumps his shoulder into mine.

I grab a piece of salami from the vast antipasto platter that sits on a huge coffee table in front of us. There's an equally large tray of cookies right next to it. Bright's host family, she says, does a lot of entertaining and namedrops the restaurant that catered this. Catered? I thought the funky blue *Roscioli* embossed on the napkins was the host family's last name.

I laugh and listen and talk and joke like I would at home, if I had a group of friends this large. It's mostly just Carly and me then sometimes a few others. No question, that needs to change when I get home. If I get home.

I grab another piece of salami as if that will push those thoughts aside.

"Don't they feed you?" Bright asks.

I haven't stopped noshing on meats and cheeses from the tray. I manage a laugh. "No food for Tess, they say!"

"Really?"

I shake my head. "Truth?" Though I'm not about to admit that

I could barely eat dinner. "It's me. I must have the worst case of jet lag ever. My body can't figure out when to sleep or when to eat. And Francesco is the best cook. Made amazing spaghetti Bolognese tonight. From scratch." There. I said something nice. "So please, if I go for more, slap my hand. I need to adjust."

They all start waving everything from mozzarella balls to biscotti in my face. I shut my mouth tight, determined not to eat anything else, until Nicolas comes at me with an Italian wedding cookie, sprinkles and all. "You know you want it. Just a nibble."

My resolve sags. "I've never had one of these." I take a bite.

"Thus ends two nevers for you in one day," Devin says.

Breaking and entering? Stealing? "What's the other?" I manage.

He pulls up my haiku. Francesco posted it with a picture of me looking right into a camera. In my tower room. It's either photoshopped or they're watching me there too.

"Why do you look so shocked?" Bright says. "When you post things, people see them. That's how it works."

I eke out a laugh. "But never did I ever think my stupid haiku would be the center of conversation."

And that turns into a modified game of Never Have I Ever.

Bright starts. "Never have I ever told someone they were ugly."

We all burst into laughter.

"What?"

Nicolas gives her a little push. "I find that hard to believe."

"That's not why I'm laughing," Devin says. "I'm laughing because I can only assume that you think one of us or multiples of us are ugly, which is why you chose that confession."

Bright pushes him. "You found me out, you ugly Brit, you. Your turn."

"Fine." He shakes his head. And again. "I'm struggling. Someone else go."

"Me," Nicolas says. "Never have I ever pranked my brother by pouring water over his head while he was sleeping."

Bright stares at him. "Well, that's specific."

"Yep." And Nicolas's grin grows. "Because it wasn't water. It was chocolate milk."

The Never Have I Evers start flying. Richard, the six-foot-four Bean, never played basketball (except in gym class). Several people later, Lashay, who's wearing some punk band's T-shirt, has never been to a real concert. Suraj, who's lived in India, London, and is now in Atlanta, has never eaten airplane food. And I'm next.

I shake my head. "I already went thanks to…" I shoulder-lean into Devin. "You started this. End with something really good."

"Right," he says. "And I cannot believe I'm admitting to this—"

Red-tipped Sydney pouts. "Well, I admitted that I've never been kissed," she says. In that same instant, Devin gets up and kisses her. Quickly, but still. I almost wish that would have been me. Or not. My life is too complicated now.

The blushing and hollers and hoots die down, and Bright wedges herself next to Devin, tugging on a strand of hair. "You know, lover boy, that doesn't get you off the hook. What have you never ever done?"

"Besides kiss someone on impulse? I believe that's good enough."

"It would've been if you'd admitted it before." Bright pokes his chest. "Still your turn."

He shakes his head. "It is a bit pants, so don't pelt me with prosciutto, but I keep circling back to this. And yes, I'm stalling." He takes a breath. "Never have I ever…reused a tea bag."

"That is so British," Sydney says.

"It's so you," says Bright.

Nicolas grabs a handful of grapes. "And this is so not prosciutto." He pelts Devin, one grape at a time.

We laugh and joke and just when the wrecking ball leaves my body, I get a text.

Giornata impegnativa domani

Devin leans over. "Busy day tomorrow? What do they have planned for you?"

"With them, you never know." I add in a laugh, and everyone treats it as a joke. Thankfully. The Rossis heard that.

The party breaks up, but four of us are staying in the same area, so we share a taxi and keep laughing. And they're still laughing when I get out at the top of my street.

Not two steps later, my phone rings. Aunt Debbie. FaceTime. This late? Why? The wrecking ball settles back in. "Aunt Debbie?"

"Hi to you, too, sweetie!" She's clearly at her office, her back to her desk, the picture of her, Uncle Dale, Todd, and Ben over her left shoulder. And she's clearly not panicking. "You okay? Did I get you from something? Oh wait. Sorry. Time difference."

"It's okay. I'm getting home from a party, and well, the phone just startled me."

"And this startled me. Well, it didn't startle me, but I was so surprised that you left me a gift." It's my stuffed animal from home, the one that Carly took out of my suitcase. Beanie Cubbie. He's on her keyboard. "Tell me. How did you get him up here, past security?"

How did Sofia, you mean.

"Wait. No. Don't tell me."

Good. She does *not* want to know.

CHAPTER FOURTEEN

WHEN I GET INSIDE, ANJELICA BECKONS ME TO THE KITCHEN table.

I brace myself for whatever she has to say about Beanie Cubbie.

But she's staring at her laptop, that same look on her face from this morning.

Dread turns to heart-beating panic.

"You're just in time. Sit. Watch." She swivels the screen toward me. Trees, bushes, houses—

It's Carly's street. Not a photo, but a video from a car moving, driving. Shot from the passenger's side. The view moves to Sofia behind the wheel, wearing my black jeans and my blue shirt, the ones I left behind. "Tsk, tsk, Tess," she says.

I turn to Anjelica. "What is she doing?"

Anjelica just points.

They drive several minutes more, icy waves pulsing from my

stomach, through to my head, down to my feet. Again. Again. The car stops on a street I don't recognize. Makes a U-turn. Parks at the curb. The shot focuses on a corner in the distance then zeroes in on a little red car. Like Carly's. It gets closer, closer, closer. Sofia taps a cell phone.

Pop! Pop! Pop!

The red car's tire blows. Swerves. Its tail knocks into a tree. A car coming the other way can't avoid it. It slams into the front.

"Carly! No!"

"Carly, yes." Sofia smiles. "So sad. Maybe you shouldn't have told her to question me. And most of all, she shouldn't have gone rogue."

"What—"

But Sofia's already racing toward the crash. To make sure Carly's dead? No. She grabs Carly's phone. Because...

The realization prickles my scalp. Our FaceTime. Carly took that screenshot of the Rossis. They must've overheard our conversation. I should have made her delete it. I should have insisted. It's my fault. It's—

Anjelica points to the screen again. Carly's hand is moving. "Look at that. Your friend is alive. For now." The call ends.

My head trembles. Uncontrollably. I reach to my temples, but Anjelica starts running her hand through my hair. Motherly. Calming. Then she takes a handful and yanks it back.

"It's obvious," she says, "that Sofia wasn't alone. Our tentacles stretch everywhere. We can get to anyone you love. Anywhere. Understand?"

I nod.

"So, be *una brava ragazza. Okay?*"

"*Si.*"

She excuses me to go up to bed. I don't dare call my parents. I don't dare try any of my friends. All I can do is lie here and tell myself to be the good girl Anjelica wants me to be. Not a hero.

Throughout the night, I get a rash of messages from my parents and from my friend Tamika, who's the point person for our group right now. Carly was in a car accident; she's in the hospital with cuts and bruises and a broken arm—surgery tomorrow—but she'll be fine.

I wait until morning to text back. And I add one to Carly, because that's what I would normally do. First a big hug gif. Then: The kids will love you. Dr's helper. Surgery. Broken arm. It'll make them feel better. You'll make them feel better. Feel better.

I think about adding a sorry gif, but I don't want the Rossis to read anything into that. I do the only safe thing. I take out a massive mental eraser to push the accident out of my mind for now. If everyone else I love is to stay alive and in one piece, I need to be a good girl and a better actor than whatever got Bright to Broadway.

I manage enough of a smile and come downstairs to breakfast: *cornetti,* the Italian version of croissants, with butter and jam and a *caffe latte* or hot chocolate, my choice. So normal, as if they're treating Beanie Cubbie and the crash as parts of a movie we watched last night. I eat, go upstairs, and gather my bag, leaving plenty of time to walk today.

When I get back down, though, Francesco has his motorcycle helmet under one arm. "*Non c'è tempo per camminare oggi.*"

I look at my watch, look back at him. I have plenty of time to walk. I open my mouth, but he's already heading toward Anjelica, who's jabbing at a copy of my syllabus. "Listen closely. They will take you to Villa Borghese today."

"You remember?" Francesco says. "Outside the museum? The little canoe we paddled out onto the lake. I was rocking the boat. It's up to you to rock that boat today."

Anjelica puts a second piece of paper in front of me, a map. "Inside the museum, right here on the second floor"—She lands her finger on a small square toward the end of a hall—"is an office. The woman who works there—"

"Your sister-in-law?"

"Does it matter?" She gives Francesco a look before she turns back to me. "The woman goes to lunch from two p.m. to three p.m. At that time, you will find your way into the office and steal a worthless copy of a painting. You will replace it with this. It's identical enough."

Anjelica reaches back to the counter and hands me a framed picture, slightly larger than a standard piece of paper. The Renaissance dude in the painting has long brown hair, a billowy white shirt, and some sort of fur slung over his shoulder. Everything is in shades of brown and other neutral colors. Even the bluish landscape out the window in the upper right-hand corner is muted. The brightest thing is a gold caption plate at the bottom, like something a museum might attach: RITRATTO DI GIOVANE UOMO. Then the artist's name: RAFFAELLO SANZIO DA URBINO (RAPHAEL).

"Stop looking at it, put it in your bag, and memorize this." Anjelica shoves the map in my face. "You should be able to guess why."

"I'm not taking the map with me."

"You're not taking the map with you."

I study it for maybe 30 seconds before she snatches it up, turns on the gas stove, and sets the paper on fire. She watches it burn until it nearly scorches her fingers, then she tosses it into the sink and washes away the ashes.

Francesco holds out a sweater. "It can be a little chilly inside the museum."

I take it. But if they think they can buy my loyalty with a bag, a dress, and a sweater, they're wrong. And if they think they can keep threatening me and the people I love while I nod like an automaton, there will come a point...

I try to put the sweater on, but my elbow gets tangled. "Even this sweater is against me," I mutter half to myself. "Why do I have to do this? Why can't you ask the sister-in law or, I assume, your brother?"

Anjelica pushes her chair back. Stands. "We have different ideas of where things belong." Then she swivels her laptop toward me so hard it nearly flies off the table.

"I'm sorry. I shouldn't have questioned you."

"You're right." But it's not Anjelica's voice. It's Sofia's. "I'm ba-ack! How easy it was to borrow your aunt's access card, put on a wig and, well, you get the picture." She gives a laugh. "And how easy it would be to..." She turns the knob on our gas stove, but the burner flame doesn't ignite. Then she holds up the box of long fireplace matches. "...kaboom."

Her whisper slices like a knife down my spine. I close my eyes before she disappears from the screen.

Francesco has come back with a helmet for me. "She's having the best fun with this." I should have time to walk, but he insists on giving me a ride, which gets me to school early.

Already, though, a small group of the people from last night are joking about Devin's kiss and, when I come up, they pretend to tempt me with food.

I laugh along with them. Or fake it enough so they don't notice.

But Devin looks at me funny. "Are you okay?"

"Yeah," I say. "Why wouldn't I be?"

"I don't know. Something seems off. Your laugh was...strange."

"Who are you?" I say. "The laugh police?"

He looks like I slapped him in the face.

"I'm sorry. I didn't—"

"I know." He starts to walk away. "Jet lag."

"Devin, wait." I'm not sure what I can say, but I have to say something. "It's just that my host family. They seem..." I shrug. I can't say much more. They're probably listening.

"Seem what?"

"I don't know. Bothered by something. Business, maybe? It just got to me."

His face softens. "So terribly sorry. Will you be okay there?"

This time my laugh feels genuine. I mean it's all so outrageous, what else can I do? "Don't worry. I'll be a good girl, and things should be fine. They gave me this sweater today." I twirl, and the oversized, loose-crochet knit twirls with me.

He gives me a squeeze around the shoulders, and we walk in. He doesn't race ahead to Bright or Sydney, who are talking. Surprising. The three of them—others from last night too—would soar to the top of the super-popular, high-achieving, picked-for-everything group at my school, much better equipped to handle all this shit. Maybe I'm being super paranoid, but why are they including me?

They can't all be tentacles of the Rossis, but I also can't fully eliminate anyone unless and until they slip up. And yet, I keep believing Devin is safe, and I don't know why.

At home, he'd be swarming all over the likes of Bright or Sydney, but no. Outside of that kiss, which we all know was a joke, he's basically spending time with me. That should have me suspicious, but my gut says to trust him. I'd like to trust him, love to trust him, but I can't, not until I'm three thousand percent sure his host family is nothing like mine. And neither is his London family.

The morning creeps by. Then, what should be a really good lunch—chicken with tomatoes and olives over a creamy risotto—tastes no different than sawdust.

We get to the Villa Borghese Museum about 1:50 and, immediately, I run into a huge problem. Anything bigger than our phones—besides paper notebooks—goes into bag check outside the museum. If I'm so soft and weak, why do the Rossis believe that I can pull off the swap?

Think, Tess.

I have time. They shuffle all three of the program's classes into a room to watch a film about the museum, its history, and its collection. I pay attention only in case a single shred of info will shed some light on what I'm about to do. How. Why.

No such luck.

Finally, at 2:15, they send us off to explore on our own. At least there's that. I don't need to break away from a docent, but I will need to break away from my friends. I realize that if one is especially okay with giving me space to do this task, I'll have reason to distrust them.

I walk out quickly, and a whole group follows. That's the good news. But now I need to lose them. Even when I divert to the bathroom, Bright and Sydney are right behind. As soon as they're locked in their stalls, I dash out.

Devin and two other boys are waiting for us, looking at the map of galleries.

I hate exploiting the girly thing, but I have less than forty-five minutes and can't think of anything else. I pull Devin aside. "What's the game plan?" I ask him.

"We're starting at number eight on the map and going backward."

"Great. I'll meet you as soon as I can."

His eyebrow raises.

"Female stuff," I add.

"Right." He gives me a look like, "oh yeah. Hormones. So, that's why you snapped at me this morning." Let him think that.

I pray that the people monitoring the entrance will buy it too. When I get to the guard, I type into my app: I need to get a tampon from my bag. Can I please go and come right back in?

The grandfatherly type reads the Italian translation, gives me a wink, and sends me out.

I get my bag from the cloakroom attendant, find a deserted spot outside, and shove the picture from Anjelica into the back of my now-unbuttoned jeans. They gave me the sweater for a reason. It billows enough while I'm walking to hide my suddenly square butt.

I give the Rossis credit. They may be turning me into a criminal, but between this sweater and Signora Roma opening the gate yesterday, they are providing tools for success.

I recheck my bag and the smiling grandfather waves me through the metal detector.

Metal detector!?

Please let it be a plastic picture frame. Please, please, please.

I hold my breath, walk through. No alarms.

Now, the office. If their map is right, it's past the bathroom, up a flight of stairs, and down the hall to the fifth door on the right.

This place is so much easier to navigate than the Smithsonian Portrait Gallery back home. And so far, no guards up here at all.

I knock on the office door. No answer. I slip in and close the door behind me.

The office is unassuming with two desks and the normal amount of clutter. There, on the wall, hangs the reason I'm here.

The picture is the exact one stuffed inside my pants. Even the black frame looks the same, except the one on the wall is metal. I swap the two pictures, shove the new one into my pants, too hard. The sharp corner scratches my butt. If I'm bleeding, at least my excuse is a little true.

I straighten the replacement picture on the wall. It hangs between two larger posters, each showing a dozen pieces of artwork that, according to the captions, were thought to be destroyed during World War II. The Rossis have two of these prints hanging in the apartment. The Raffaello picture must also have been lost.

But what if these works of art weren't destroyed? What if they're hidden somewhere in Rome, or really anywhere in the world? They could be worth millions or billions. For someone like my lovely host parents and their equally lovely daughter, that would be worth killing for.

I pull out my phone to take a picture of the posters. No. They'll see it. Instead, I start to copy the names of each work of art on a piece of paper from the printer.

Then I hear voices in the hall. What do I say? What do I do? Stupid. Stupid. Stupid.

These are posters. Probably available online. I should have swapped and left.

Now, I can only flatten myself against the wall and prepare to hide behind the door. Then if someone comes in, I'll dash out like a gust of wind. I'm ready.

The voices grow closer, louder.

They walk past. A different door closes. I breathe a sigh of relief and peek into the hall. It's empty. I race downstairs, away from Gallery 8, away from the front door, toward the bathroom.

There. Ten feet away. Nine. Eight.

A hand grabs my shoulder. Pats my back. Knocks on the picture. Busted.

CHAPTER FIFTEEN

THREE HORRIBLE THOUGHTS FLASH THROUGH MY BRAIN. Police. Jail. Dead parents.

I turn, panic pounding at my temples. But it's Devin, staring me down.

"Devin! You scared me to death." I manage somewhat of a smile.

He doesn't smile back. "What's going on, Tess?"

"I can't tell you."

"Or you'll have to kill me?" He gives a strained laugh.

"You have no clue."

"Try me." He tugs up his beltloop.

"Please. I need five minutes." I point to the bathroom door.

He gestures for me to go.

I lock myself in a stall and first check for cameras. But even in Italy, they can't go around recording women in bathroom stalls. If they do, the world would be outraged. But another day.

Right now, I need to know exactly why the Rossis forced me to steal this. It's not to prove their power. They already have enough power over me. They've shown that they can get to my parents, Aunt Debbie, and Carly. I'm thinking there's something hidden inside the frame. A key? Money? A valuable painting? No to the last one. Museums don't put valuable paintings inside common, insert-picture-here frames.

I swivel the brads on all four sides and pull. Behind the backing is a piece of paper, or a sheet of something thicker and softer than paper. It's a handwritten letter with an occasional odd space, addressed to someone's children. I'd have my app translate it, but if the Rossis are watching my phone in real time...

Among the dozens and dozens of words in Italian, I mentally translate a few, notably war and death and Raffaello, the artist who originally painted this picture. But I have to believe the words may not be as important as the odd spaces. It's almost like I'm looking at an encoded message. And it's possible that the canister, with its random cutouts, acts as a decoder.

I sit there for a long minute, trying to figure out a next move, because whatever's in this letter could bring some answers. First, I need to keep a copy of it. I can't risk going back upstairs to the office. I definitely cannot put one on my phone. And no to making a copy at school. Anyone could be watching. I have only one idea.

I leave the bathroom, the letter tucked in my notebook, the picture back in my pants. Devin is waiting for me.

I try to joke: "Doesn't this look a little suspicious, you, hanging outside the women's bathroom?" But the joke falls flat.

"I am waiting for an explanation."

I can't explain with this picture in my pants. "I promise. Give me five more minutes, and I'll meet you in, well, which gallery?"

"Number three."

At the exit, thankfully, without a metal detector, the grandfather gives me a wink and a smile. Then I go through the routine of getting my bag from the attendant, putting the stolen print in, and rechecking it.

Without the picture, I can almost float. But hanging over me is an empty cartoon caption that needs to be filled with the right explanation for Devin. One that won't get anyone killed.

I'm able to buy even more time because Bright and company are buzzing around him. When he moves toward me, the others move as well. I'm bombarded with, "Where were you?" and "We missed you!" and all I can do is continue the lie.

"Tampons? You've heard of them."

The girls nod. The guys reel back. Except Devin. He knows it's a lie. But soon we're one big, happy group. And they tug me to a picture by Titian called *Sacred and Profane Love*, which doesn't give anyone the feeling of the sacred or profane.

"Unless," Nicolas says, "you're offended by a mostly nude woman and a naked baby playing with some water. But wait…"

He's decided that we need to re-create the picture. As he's setting up, he shoves his phone at me to be a photographer. It's unlocked.

I do a quick search for Francesco's and Anjelica's phone numbers. Not in his contacts. No messages from their numbers either. The only messages with an Italian number are from his host family. That's pretty much rules him out as a Rossi spy.

I glance up, and Nicolas is looking at me, not with any suspicion, but to make sure I'm ready to capture this moment. Using a bench as a prop, he has Richard imitate the fully dressed woman on the left, has Bright kneel down behind the bench—she's the baby—and he takes off his shirt and poses like the woman on the right.

Then comes the photo shoot and the hysterics. It's the best compliment that they waited for me to do this. But with my insides tumbling and my mind racing—what the hell do I tell Devin?—I can't enjoy it.

It's not until we're dropped back at school, where they dismiss us forty-five minutes early, that he has me to himself.

I think I'm ready. I hope I'm ready. I took the time on the ride back to formulate a plan.

I wait until we're far enough away from school before I start. First, I swipe on my phone's playlist, crank up the volume, and drop it into my bag next to the balled-up sweater.

"You know," he says, "there's no distracting me with music or with anything. When I want something, I figure out a way to get it."

"I'm sure you do," I say, "but this isn't a distraction. It's a precaution. Like what I'm about to ask you."

He's arching his eyebrow.

"Some questions. They won't mean anything to you, but they'll mean a lot to me."

"You. Asking *me* questions. Brilliant."

"When you find out why, you'll not only understand, but you'll wonder why I didn't ask more." We stop at a small green space with a bench.

"Here goes," I say. "Why are there like no photos of you on Insta or wherever?" I followed a dozen people last night hoping the Rossis won't target Devin if I ask him to help me.

"I take horrid selfies. A demonstration."

The way he holds his camera somehow makes his nose appear twice as big. Unless that's his way of fooling me. I use his phone then mine to take another with both of us. His nose is weirdly the same. I immediately delete the one on my phone. Could be too late, though.

"There are plenty of me on my friends' accounts." He pulls them up, swipes through a few. "Do I pass?"

"So far." I take a breath. "Next question. What do your own parents do for a living?"

"Father does some, well, public relations work for the government. And Mum was trained as a nurse, but now she likes to throw a lot of parties. Single-use tea bags and all."

I smile at that, just for a flash. "How about your host parents. What do they do?"

"Right, then," he says. "The grilling continues. Piero, I call him AdDad, is president of an advertising agency. Flavia, aka Dance Mum, teaches ballet. She used to perform professionally."

"You're sure?"

He explains that on a tour of the office, AdDad showed him commercials, videos, and posters for his clients, mostly in the food and hotel industry. Then they picked up the younger brother at the ballet studio, where Dance Mum was teaching a combination to the older students. "She holds herself like a ballerina and they have framed photos of her on stage."

I breathe that in, but he mistakes it for skepticism. "Google them if you want."

"Can you please? On your phone? I promise I'm not trying to be a pain."

"Sorry, but you're failing." He sighs and types the dad's name first, then the mom's. He confirms that's who they are; that's exactly what they look like.

I want to ask if he's really, truly, objectively sure, but I'm pushing it as is.

"Question four. Their daughter who's living at your house. What's she like?"

"Gianna is nice. Seems quite smart. Has a fascination with opera. Gutted that she can't sing well enough to perform but aspires to be the artistic director at La Scala, the opera house in Milan, one day. She was hoping to be placed in New York City to visit the Metropolitan Opera, but the Royal Opera House in London was her second choice. My parents promised to take her to a performance. They bought tickets straight away."

He adds that Gianna is teaching his brother and sister Italian. And they're trading slang and curse words in their respective languages. It was Gianna's birthday yesterday, and his parents woke up at five in the morning to set up balloons and bake a cake so she'd have a celebration first thing.

I have to believe that if they woke up at five, no one drugged them. "Thanks for humoring me. Next question?"

His "of course" is dripping with sarcasm.

"And it's just us. I promise, everything is confidential."

"You're starting to infuriate me, Tess. Or maybe, you're freaking me out."

"Good." I stop and look directly at him. "Think about every conversation you've had with your host family. Have they said anything strange?"

His eyebrow arches.

"Wait. Don't joke. Don't try to change the subject. Exactly what you were thinking?"

"Fine. The first day, AdDad admitted he gets a terrible case of the trumps—the farts—when he eats strawberry gelato. No other milk product, no other flavor; just strawberry gelato, which was a problem when one of their biggest accounts wanted him to taste four of their best-selling flavors and he had to—"

I laugh. We both do. It feels good. But back to business. I grab his hand and pull him around the corner.

Devin holds on longer than I do. "Have we finished with the questions?"

"That one, yes." If there had been something strange in a bad way, he wouldn't have leaped to that example so freely and easily. I look straight at him. "Do you trust me?"

He doesn't look back. "I'm beginning not to."

"Please, I beg you, this is really important. Trust me enough to do something for me." I lower my voice and stop right in front of him, closer than any normal friend should. In case anyone is watching, I give him a hug and before he gets the impression that I'm making a move, I start talking. "When we let go, I'll give you my notebook. About halfway in is a loose, handwritten sheet of thick paper. You can't miss it. I need you to take it to the shop across the street and make a copy." I'm sounding too much like Anjelica, but I can't stop now. "Put both back in my notebook. And try to act normal, like I'm not freaking you out."

I pull back. "You rat!" I swat him on the arm before he can get a word in. "You slept through the lecture? Fine, go copy my notes. And give me some money. I'll get us gelato while I'm waiting. Not strawberry, in case your host dad is contagious." I laugh.

I beg him with my eyes to go along with it.

He digs a ten-euro note from his wallet. "Thanks. Make mine a *stracciatella*, the one with the chocolate shavings."

I watch him go, turn toward the gelato shop, then glance back to make sure no one follows him in. So far, so good.

The shop is a small place, just the gelato display case and three tiny tables. No one else is here except the person behind the counter. And no public restroom for the privacy I'll need to put the letter back into the frame.

The server scoops our gelato to the beat of the music coming from my bag. Then I take our cups to the table farthest from the door. It's perfectly clean except for a pen in the middle. Kaleidoscope barrel, purple gel, nice. I ask the person working if it's hers, but she tells me to keep it. It's my lucky day. If only.

By the time I turn around, Devin is back. We sit, the employee gets interested in her phone, and the store's window is high enough that no one, except Devin, will see what I'm doing. With the stolen picture on my lap, partially shielded by the flap on my bag, I undo the frame, position the letter back in, and reassemble it without giving my gelato much chance to melt. I take a bite, fold the copy of the letter, and put it in my shoe, underneath the sole's lining, along with the list of missing World War II artwork.

Devin eats slowly, not taking his eyes off me.

I finally take a bite. "You're right. This *stracciatella* is really, really good. Thanks."

He nods. "Now what?"

Most of me is totally ready to trust him, but... "Last question. I promise."

He basically gives me an eyeroll.

I don't blame him. "What is the worst thing that you or anyone in your family has ever done? Total truth. No judgment. Zero."

"You want me to air all my family's dirty laundry? Maybe you should air yours."

"Believe me. I'm about to."

He nods. "I wasn't supposed to know this, but I have an older cousin who went to drug rehab. Then we found out she was also selling. That was bad. My sister got suspended for a day, but it wasn't actually her fault. She shouldn't have slugged the kid, but he kept harassing her best friend with anti-Semitic slurs. My parents, back in college, got detained by the police for demonstrating against racism, but in my book, that's not a bad thing either."

"It's a good thing." I take a bite. Another. "When we finish our gelato, we'll go outside, and I'll talk. Answer any questions."

"Right."

I wouldn't believe me either.

CHAPTER SIXTEEN

"First," I say, "let me show you something." Using his phone, I do a search for Francesco and Anjelica. Half of me is shocked—half, not surprised. We find pictures of the couple—same names—who were photoshopped into my selfies. "Don't they look nice?" I say.

"They looked all right in your pictures yesterday."

I pull up my selfies again. Tell him to compare the two phones.

"Wait. What?" He sees. Maybe now he'll believe everything.

We leave the shop and start walking down the street. If anyone is following us, they're not close enough to hear. Also, the music must be drowning out our conversation; otherwise, Francesco would have already zoomed up and whisked me back to Anjelica, who'd hurt someone else I love.

I'm ready to start explaining, but Devin stops me when I'm only two words in. "Who are you looking for? Are we being followed?"

"It's possible." I take a breath. "I do know that I'm being tracked, which is why I had you go into the copy shop. And this bag has a listening device, which is the reason for the music."

"Are you some kind of spy?"

I'd laugh, but this isn't the time for jokes. "From the beginning…"

I start with the plane, the Perfume Woman. "I'm jumping ahead, but I've seen her twice more. The Rossis told me to call her Signora Roma when she was at the apartment yesterday."

"Sounds like an alias."

"It is. Then there's the Creepy Man. He doesn't have a name yet, but he was also on the plane." Thinking about it, he could have been our driver in Naples, but I skip ahead to the encounter in Piazza Navona and seeing him with Francesco at the Pantheon. "If only I'd wished something else when I was looking up to the oculus."

"What did you wish?"

"Something like, 'Please make me stop imagining bad stuff. Please let me have fun.'"

"Sounds like your wish, possibly, came half true."

I look at him. "I'm not exactly having the time of my life."

"Not that half. The bad stuff, I gather, you're not imagining it anymore."

I nod. "True."

"But go on. What is it that your host parents are doing? Have they hurt you?"

I shake my head.

"Then what did I copy? Why the secrecy?"

I hold up my hand. "Here goes." I skip over stealing the canister. It's enough that Sofia threatened to blow up my house today.

"She wasn't joking?"

I shake my head. "Dead serious. So were Anjelica and Francesco. Unless I do what they say, she'll murder my parents. And everyone I love." I tell him about Aunt Debbie and Carly.

"Why are you waiting?" He whips out his phone. "Call the police!"

"And what? Tell them I stole a picture, no matter how worthless? Do you know what the justice system is like here? Have you not watched that documentary about the American girl in the Italian prison?"

"No."

"Well, I did. And it scared the shit out of me. Besides, if I don't show up where and when I'm supposed to, my parents are dead."

"Ring your parents. Tell them to leave."

I shake my head. "There's more." I fill him in on my suspicion that all the phones have been cloned or bugged. I show him my fake passport. "So, maybe there is a way out of this, but right now, I need to do whatever they say. And eventually, it will stop." I smile up at him. "Or you might find me permanently at the bottom of the Tiber River."

"Don't even joke about that."

"What's the point if you can't joke about things? It's how I was brought up. When we rushed to the emergency room last month—my grandmother slipped in her kitchen—the first thing my mom said wasn't, 'OMG! How are you? I'm so glad to see you!' No. It was, 'Mom, you've never looked worse.' And my grandmother laughed...or tried to. Her gashed head and broken ribs made it hard."

Devin nods. "Okay, but that still doesn't solve anything. I, for one, would like you to stay alive and have some fun."

"Both would be good. Right now, I'm just hoping they're done with me. That I'll wake up tomorrow morning, come out of my bedroom—which is an isolated alcove up a steep set of spiral stairs—and, poof, they'll be gone. Disappeared. Forever."

"Where's the justice in that? Shouldn't they be stopped so they'll never be a threat to anyone again?"

"Self-preservation first, Devin. Which is why I need to know what's in the letter. Hopefully, it can somehow get me out of this."

With the way he looks at me, we both know that hoping won't make it happen.

"So, here's what's next," I say. "You'll go back to AdDad and Dance Mum, and you'll tell them all about your day at school. You'll pretend this conversation never happened and that the world is full of sunshine and rainbows except for the fact that you dribbled gelato down the front of your shirt." I wipe off most of it with a napkin.

He holds on to it and to my hand. "And you?"

"I'm going back to the lovely apartment to show them I can follow directions. I will pretend it was a wonderful day at school and at the museum. I will have dinner, and I will sleep, and I will see you tomorrow in class. Just like any normal person would do."

"I don't know if I can keep up my end," he says.

"You said you want me alive? Do it." With that, I turn and head toward home, wretched home.

CHAPTER SEVENTEEN

THE DOOR TO THE APARTMENT IS UNLOCKED, BUT NO ONE'S THERE. Though, with class out early, they probably didn't expect me yet.

I climb the stairs, sit on the floor at the far side of the bed, and fight the urge to open the picture frame to try and interpret some of the letter. I have no doubt they've planted a camera in here. That picture of me they posted, the one with the haiku, is probably a screenshot from a motion-sensor videocam.

I pull up the picture—an extreme close-up—to figure out where I might have been in relation to the camera. No clues. I'm guessing it's hidden in the alarm clock, lamp, mirror, vase, flower picture, crucifix, or the monkey. I run downstairs, dampen my shirt, change out of it, then lay it over both the lamp and the alarm clock on the night table. If I've covered a camera, they'll move it. If they don't, next object.

Then I sit back on the floor, savoring the moments of quiet, moments I haven't had since I've been here. Too soon, footsteps echo up the stairs. Anjelica's.

I move the soles of my feet together and do butterfly stretches.

"Yoga?" she says.

"I took some classes with a friend."

"What's your favorite pose?" she asks like she's testing me.

"Not downward dog. One day, our instructor made us repeat it so many times I almost puked. I'm more of a mat girl. Child's pose, bridge pose. You know."

"*Hai bisogno di allungarti dopo tutto quel ballo. Sì?*"

She's back to Italian. I'm thinking that's good, but I don't understand. "*Ripeti, per favore?*"

"*Musica? Ballare?*"

Okay. Music and dancing. She assumes the music led to dancing. And I let her. In broken Italian, I tell her that my friends and I were eating gelato, and we decided to have some fun.

"*La prossima volta fagli suonare la loro musica.*"

I nod. Next time, they'll play *their* music. But today, mine worked.

Anjelica points to the shirt covering the lamp and alarm. "*Perché?*"

When I explain that it's wet, she nods and tells me to take it off before I turn on the lamp. We wouldn't want to cause a fire. But she leaves it there. Just takes my bag downstairs.

About ten minutes later, she calls me to join them.

Francesco, at the table, finishes his sketch of an ostrich and puts his journal back under their picture. Then the three of us sit, the bag in the middle like a large centerpiece. Or an explosive device.

They don't say a word. Neither do I.

Finally, Francesco breaks the silence. "*Hmm. Cosa c'è dentro?*"

He knows, very well, what's inside. So do I.

He pulls out the sweater, nods at me.

"*Grazie,*" I say. And I mean it. I would have been sunk without it.

Next comes a zippered bag I'd brought from home. I transferred the contents of my purse—my wallet, passport, all the small stuff—to that. He investigates and closes it back up. Then my notebook. Thankfully, I really did take a lot of notes. It kept me sane all morning.

He thumbs through every page. "*Buono!*"

Then my key, my case of pens and pencils, and finally, the picture. Francesco taps the frame. "*Metallo. Buono!*"

Yes, the frame is metal. It's the picture they wanted and not the one they gave me. Even so, I hold my breath as he takes off the backing.

"Ta-da!" He puts on a big smile.

Anjelica, not so much. She points to the lower right-hand corner. A small piece of the paper, no bigger than my baby fingernail, is bent. She stares at me. "Next time, no dancing."

Under normal circumstances, I'd argue it was probably that way to begin with, but I take my gift of her excuse.

Then it hits me. She said, "Next time." They're still not done with me.

She gets Sofia on a video call. "Sorry, daughter of mine. Put the matches away."

"Well, bloody hell. I had it all planned. The wailing, the sobbing. My survivor's guilt." And she laughs, lines crinkling around her eyes exactly like on Anjelica's face. Is she really still in high school? Or did they manage to fake that as well? One thing is for sure, she is Anjelica's daughter. They look so much alike.

I take note of that observation. I need to take note of them all. Even something insignificant could be more important than it seems. I'd write everything down, but that would be another piece of paper inside my Chucks. And if it rains, these shoes aren't waterproof.

I need to move the papers. And I refuse to make Devin my personal safe-deposit box. I've dumped on him too much already. It's my battle to fight. To the end.

I get another shiver. Involuntary. It sends my mind to something I said to him, just to make a point. That I'd need to do whatever they ask. That this will eventually stop.

The thing is, if it does stop, for real, I'll be no use to them. How easy it would be to fall victim to an "accident." Carly did.

Sure, I joked about winding up dead in the Tiber, but this time I fully feel it.

I will do whatever they ask, but I can't just sit back and wait. Not anymore.

CHAPTER EIGHTEEN

I STAND AND STRETCH. ANJELICA AND FRANCESCO BARELY NOTICE. They're chattering with Sofia so fast I catch only randomness— words for *music* and *smart* and *able*. If they're talking about me, I'd rather hear *stupid* and *obedient* and *gullible*. Survival words.

But some of their next words include, it sounds, Italian for *torture* and *agony*. "*Si,* Tess?"

I play dumb and shrug, which makes Sofia call me stupid. When I don't react, she runs out of camera view and comes back flashing our fireplace poker. She waves it like a sword then puts it down, and between chuckles, she says something about *shish kebab ragazza.* "*Si,* Tess?" she repeats. "You would look good." And they all laugh.

So, I grin as if she praised me instead of suggesting that I become a human skewer.

Their laughter, though, dissolves into silence. "Oh, Te-ess?" It's Sofia again.

Anjelica has me sit back down. "What were you doing here?" In the picture I'm off to the side, away from people in Gallery 3, before we went to the other room for the photo shoot.

"I might have been recovering from nearly getting caught."

"So sad," Sofia says. "And why didn't you take pictures of this?" It's Nicolas's re-creation of the painting.

"I did, but on someone else's phone."

They're waiting for a different answer.

Fine. "I wasn't exactly in the mood to take all the pictures."

Sofia shakes her head and ends the call.

"Next time," Anjelica says, "force yourself." Then she lays a hand on mine. "*Continua così e starai bene.*"

Keep it up and I'll be fine… Passive-aggressive, much? Unless they're just words to keep me from freaking out so hard that I'm useless to them.

The only thing I can control is me.

I can't control my posts, that's for sure. Anjelica shows me today's: the predictable emojis, Nicolas's re-creation she lifted from someone's account, and a haiku. "*Il mio primo haiku.*" It's her first haiku.

My new friends and I
We can't stop joking around
Wish you could meet them

I praise her just to please her. But truly, besides the lack of punctuation, lack of originality, and the fact that I would never have wasted a syllable on *We*, it's not complete trash. Once I'm free, I'll set the record straight. For now, I can't say anything. As much as I've decided to take back some control, I can't do anything except wait for the next task. Or maybe I can.

My fingers itch to text everyone: Where's the party tonight? I need five minutes of privacy. Bright's house, Devin's house, anyone's house. Anywhere except this hellhole.

How did I get here?

This time, I don't mean into the program, which is still a question. And I don't mean Rome. I'd thought it was going to be exciting.

But how the hell did I end up with the Rossis? Luck of the draw? Or did someone say, "Hey! She's easy to manipulate!"

Does it really matter? What matters right now is getting five minutes alone.

As if my wish found its way to the heavens, my phone pings. Nicolas to the group: My turn. Party here 2nite

Anjelica leans over to read, as if she didn't have another way to eavesdrop. "*Gruppo sociale, eh?*" She tells me to go but warns me not to have too good a time. And not to trust anyone. You never know. She and Francesco crack up.

But the joke's on them. Before I go, I casually cover the vase and mirror with my new sweater.

Francesco drops me off at Nicolas's house and tells me to text if I need a ride home. A few people are out front, including Devin.

It would be a very Devin thing to stride up and introduce himself to Francesco—manners and curiosity—and when I take off my helmet, he does move forward. Then he checks himself.

Bright, though, rushes up. "Tess! Next time you do that, you need to shake out your hair like an actress in a movie. It'd make such a statement. Try it now!"

"*Si, si!*" says Francesco.

Like a good puppet, I do. I get my share of applause and take a bow. Francesco, helmet still on, gives a wave and is out of there.

Bright shows me the video she took. "You did it just like a movie star."

Nice, but even nicer, I have a real picture of Francesco. Okay, so he's not recognizable. But I have the license plate. Except, if they made a fake passport, they could easily make a counterfeit plate or steal one from any motorcycle on the street.

But wait. There's the single chain-link tattoo on his left wrist. Unless that's fake too.

"Here," Bright says. "I'll send it to you."

"No."

"No?"

"My parents'll freak if they see me on a motorcycle," I lie. "I have a relative who almost died."

"Oh no!" She gives me a quick hug. "But really? You let them scrutinize your phone!?"

I give a laugh. "Of course not. But if I forget it's there, and I'm swiping through my pictures at home, well, you get the idea. You'll send it to me later. It'll be a good reason to keep in touch."

Bright shrugs. "Whatever."

Whatever could save your life. Look what they did to Carly.

"Avoid whatever will get you in trouble," Devin says, apparently trying to save me. "That's my motto."

"Devin Kessinger-Scott!" Bright leans into him, hands on her hips. "Avoid having fun? Upon my word!"

"Upon my word? When did you turn into a Jane Austen Brit?"

"You're turning me," she says. "But really, avoid fun? Just no."

He shakes his head. "Have fun, yes. Merely avoid getting found out."

"Much better." She gives him a longer hug, and she makes sure to sit right by him in a place where I can't.

Nicolas has me follow him into the kitchen. "You know she has a huge crush on him."

"It's obvious."

He scratches his shoulder. "Is it...obvious about me with her?"

"You're crushing on her?"

"Then it's not obvious." He grabs a huge bowl of tiramisu and a platter of cannoli, and I pick up the other dessert tray: chewy chocolate amaretti; spumoni slices; and cookies with pine nuts, with sesame seeds, and with powdered sugar in the shape of an eight.

"You know," I say, "maybe you shouldn't be so subtle."

"Like I should put a laxative into Devin's food to get him out of the picture?" He laughs.

I shake my head. "She'll want to nurse him back to health," I say. "Sorry, and I hate to say this, but I think Bright has you in the friend zone."

"Shit. Not that. It's an impossible trap."

"Tell me about it," I say.

"You? With Devin?"

"No. No. Just friends."

"Damn. If you could steal him away, maybe she'd drool over me. Can you try?"

If things weren't lethal, maybe, because if we get together and the relationship crashes, there'd be nothing to stop him from talking too much. And getting both of us killed. I give Nicolas a smile. "You never know."

More than an hour passes before Devin can finally break free from Bright. It's not that she's had him cornered, more that everyone has been staying put with a game that Sydney calls Around the Circle. "Go around the circle and tell us your most embarrassing moment." Or "Go around the circle and tell us the top two things on your bucket list." Or "Go around the circle and tell me the last thing you'd ever do."

When it's my turn, I'm tempted to suggest that there's no true answer—I'd never become a thief or knowingly put my family in danger—but I blurt out the first thing I think of. "I'd never become a female bodybuilder." Though it would have helped me climb through the window.

The game fizzles in the middle of the fifth question. Devin finally detaches himself and heads to the bathroom. Nicolas nearly pushes me there to run interference.

Perfect. My bag is way across the room and, finally, I might get five minutes of privacy to see if the letter lines up with the partial rubbing of the canister. If Devin will cover for me.

But he pulls me aside first and asks if I've always been such a good liar. "Or was there really a motorcycle incident with your family?"

I shake my head. "If they knew Bright had that video…" I don't need to finish my sentence. Don't want to. And I can't. She's back.

And too soon, it's close to the 11:00 p.m. curfew everyone seems to have. Too soon because I don't want to go back. Too soon because I still need that five minutes—without Devin looking over my shoulder. He doesn't need to know that I broke into the old woman's apartment.

I get a ride back from Richard's host family. Inside, Anjelica and Francesco are all sweetness and light. In the morning, they're the same. I go to school like this little game is over.

For once, I can be a normal person at Exchange Roma who tries to muddle through the language with missteps and laughter and everything. But I check myself.

If the Rossis are making things easy to catch me off guard, I can't let them. I just can't.

CHAPTER NINETEEN

AND THE PARTY'S OVER.

I wake in the morning to a piece of paper taped over the small window in my tower room, light straining to seep through it. It's that picture of me, standing alone at the museum yesterday.

It could be a reminder to force myself to take pictures, but it feels more like a warning. And it's proof that someone at school is watching me.

I examine it for a glimpse of Devin, Bright, Nicolas. Richard or Sydney, even. If they're in it, they didn't take the picture. But I'm absolutely alone.

Who was in that room with me? Who's the tentacle at school?

I limit it to Signorina Emma and the people in my class, the only ones who see me often enough to matter. I've pretty much ruled out Nicolas. Also, Devin. If it were him, I'd be facing unspeakable consequences.

I should be grateful to have one person in my corner, but if I could increase Team Tess, it might be life-changing. Until I fully trust Bright, though, I can't even add Nicolas. He'd probably spill every secret to get her.

I sit in class, running through sure-to-fail team-building ideas until, mid-morning, Bright asks if I'm having cramps or something. Maybe if I stop thinking and start observing, the tentacle will reveal themself.

Shortly after lunch, Signorina Emma sends us outside with a small library of familiar picture books. It's a fun way, she says, to help us better understand the written language without it being hard to digest.

I grab up two: *Il Gatto e il Cappello Matto* (*The Cat in the Hat*) and *L'orso Bruno* (*Brown Bear, Brown Bear, What Do You See?*). They're both old favorites, but today I like them because their large sizes make ideal shields so I can compare the letter with the canister rubbing.

First though, I stop in the bathroom and take the papers from my shoes before I go out to a perfect day—not too hot, with clouds occasionally breaking up the sun. Most people are reading in small groups under the trees, but I choose a spot on my own little island, facing the school building, my back against a large hedge, where I can see anyone approaching from three sides and no one can surprise me or take a photo from behind.

I open to the middle of *Brown Bear* and lay the papers on top of one another. It's impossible to tell if the characters on the letter line up with the cutouts on the canister. I need scissors. Or a backlit window so I can see through one paper to the other. Thank you, Rossis, for that inspiration. In reality, though, I need the canister itself. A partially decoded message won't tell me enough.

With none of those options, I use a pen point to open the holes in the rubbing just to confirm that I'm on the right track. So far, each hole lines up with a letter or a space. But even if the entire message spells out a something coherent like *find money inside the third hypogeum of the Colosseum,* my work would already be done. The Rossis definitely need something else. And they'll need me again.

Brown bear, brown bear, what do you see? I see hopelessness staring at me.

I mentally slap myself. Positive thoughts. Positive thoughts. I'm positive I'd rather be three trees away with Bright, Devin, Nicolas, and four others, who are dramatically reading parts out loud. Laughing. Maybe…

I write a note. Start recording our conversation on your phone. Then I move into their little circle, my courier bag smacking Devin on the shoulder. "Bad bag!" I hurl it way behind me. While the others are distracted by its trajectory, I slip the note onto Devin's lap.

He takes one look, gives a slight nod.

Normally, I'd sit there quietly at first, but normal me left this body a few days ago. I open my book and take the stance of a kindergarten teacher. "*L'orso bruno, l'orso bruno, che cosa vedi? Vedo un uccello rosso che mi guarde.*"

That starts a whole ten minutes of us making up things that

Brown Bear sees. We laugh. We talk. Bright turns on Italian versions of Lady Gaga songs. So, there's singing too.

After school, Devin and I go our separate ways. I don't want Bright and Nicolas following or questioning us. I wander for a bit, then make my way to Devin's house.

AdDad and Dance Mum are both still at work and Roberto is at his summer program. I get inside and, just for transparency, I text Anjelica that a group of us are here. She's surprisingly fine with that as long as I'm back by eleven. And at school every day, she adds.

"I can work with that," I say to Devin.

He laughs then waggles his phone. "Why did I—"

I hold up a hand. "Have anything to eat? You know they'll all be hungry."

He gives me a look. "Right."

"They were like two minutes behind me. I'll let them in."

If the Rossis believe we mostly meet in groups, less chance they'll target Devin. For sure they've heard us talking, I've been to this house twice now, and if someone is tailing me, they saw that hug the other day. Knowing what the Rossis are capable of, I'll never forgive myself if Devin ends up like Carly.

I place my bag with its bug in the middle of the room, open the front door, and pretend people are coming from down the street. "Ciao!" I call.

A man and woman wave, laugh, and say, "Ciao!" right back to me. Perfect.

I have Devin unlock his phone and start the audio of our picture book session. Then I slowly turn up the volume, trying to make it sound like a group of exchange students is coming toward us. I put his phone on a nearby chair. "Food ready?"

Devin peeks in from the kitchen. "Almost?"

I push him out the back door, as far away from my bag as possible. "We still have nearly eight minutes of taped conversation and…" I pull the pieces of paper from my pocket. "I didn't tell you everything."

His face reddens. "You said—"

"I said you'd understand. And you did. But I need more help."

I unfold the paper with the rubbing. Then I fill him in on that first morning at the old woman's apartment. "Full disclosure, I took a kitchen towel too. I didn't want to, but I needed it to wipe off my fingerprints. Don't hate me for doing all that. Please."

His face softens, and he holds on to both my shoulders. "I don't. I couldn't. I am so sorry this is happening to you. So terribly sorry."

I want to lean into him, but the recording is only so long. "Thanks," I say, "but I don't want sympathy. I want ideas. How can I beat the Rossis at their own game?"

"Let me get this straight," he says. "You climbed through the window of some poor woman's flat and stole her canister."

"Don't make it sound like a crime. I mean, it was, but I feel guilty enough."

"Right. Sorry. Was there anything else in the apartment that looked—"

"A picture. It had lots of multicolored squares. Little ones. If it's a flat version of the canister, and if I can somehow get my hands on it, I'll be able to decode the message."

"How can we do that?"

I tell him how she walks her dog every morning. "But not *we*. Me."

"Oh no. I'm in one hundred percent. Maybe you can do this without me, but will the evil parents let you leave at six a.m. again?"

My stomach sinks. "Doubtful."

"I can make that happen, but I need my phone." That's all he'll say.

We only have two minutes left in the recorded conversation, so he feigns that Dance Mum just texted a reminder about their dinner party tonight. "Bugger," he says. "I forgot. You should all probably leave." We say goodbyes in different voices from different parts of the room.

He says a final fake goodbye then turns to me. "Tess, stick around for a minute."

I close the door as if I'd come back in. "What is it?"

"I hate that I kicked them out. Do you suppose people would wake up early to come to breakfast?" He rolls his hand as a cue for me to continue the conversation.

What do I say? Why didn't he ask... "Why didn't you ask before?"

"I wanted to make sure you would come."

I fake an embarrassed laugh. "Me?"

"Yeah, you. Like six or six-fifteen? Time to eat, hang out." Devin rolls his hand again.

"Our field trip tomorrow—the Roman Forum, right? We can slog through on less sleep."

All this while, he's doing something on his phone.

I get a text. Breakfast tmrw anyone? Back here? 6:00 a.m. If u can, call. Don't text—I'll tell u why tmrw

"Really?" I say. "Your host parents are good with this?"

"They're usually up that early anyway. I'll assume there will be leftover pastries from tonight. AdDad has been baking up a right storm. And Roberto sleeps through anything."

I call him.

"I'm standing right here," he says as his phone rings.

"I'm very good at following instructions," I say. "Ask anyone."

He answers his phone, and I tell him I'll be there if I'm allowed. Silently, though, I'm making a short list of why it won't work. I grab his phone and type.

Remember:

They have my phone cloned. Tracker too!

They're listening in, and they EXPECT to hear things!

Sometimes I'm being followed!

How can you make it work???!!!

He types, deletes, types again. Say you need to stop in the loo before you leave.

I do, and he follows me in. I'm standing with my butt against the sink. He's barely a foot away, his legs against the side of the toilet. I can feel his breath on my forehead. Minty.

I stumble to the side, and he grabs my elbows to steady me. Doesn't let go. "This is awkward." Why did I say that?

"Awkward, but safe. They won't expect you to bring your things inside a personal loo, will they?" He looks into my eyes. "And yeah. Awkward." He steps into the shower stall to put a little space between us. "Back to business, now. Points one and two. They will expect you to be here, so we leave your phone and your bag in my room."

"And when they don't hear anything?"

"Easy. AdDad moved all the belongings into my room. You didn't realize. You'll apologize. They'll glower. You'll apologize again."

"They do still need me. But if I'm being watched?"

He tugs up at his beltloop. "I will make this work. Trust me."

My mind believes him.

My gut doesn't.

CHAPTER TWENTY

I BARELY GET INSIDE THE APARTMENT BEFORE FRANCESCO, sprawled on the couch, brushes back his hair and grins at me. Way too big. *"Sento un po' di romanticismo nell'aria?"*

"Que?"

He repeats the same line.

I'm too tired to play this game. "Can you maybe ask in English or help me out? It's not like I've had a normal time here, you know." I clamp my hand over my mouth. Wait for him to call Sofia for her next kill tactic.

But he starts laughing. "I wouldn't talk like that when Anjelica is here," he says. "I asked if you have a little romance brewing, you and your pal Devin."

I shake my head. "Why do you say that?"

"You and he hung out yesterday. You're the one he asked about breakfast tomorrow. Men's intuition." He gives an exaggerated shrug.

"We're just friends," I say. "He's the first person I met from class. And it's not like I'm the only one going to breakfast." I've started to believe the lies so much, it's easy to look straight at him.

"Take it from a guy. He likes you. Just be careful. No one is immune from accidents." He shifts a pillow under his head. "*Capisci?*"

"*Capisci.*" I point upstairs. "*Pisoline.*"

"*Un momento.* You forgot to ask if you're free to go to breakfast tomorrow."

"Am I free to go to breakfast tomorrow?"

"Yes!" he says. "We have no plans for you. But you might want to be available later. You never know... *Sogni d'oro.*"

I wish for sweet dreams. A whole night of them. As vivid as my dreams tend to be, it's been a black hole of dream awareness since that last great day of sightseeing. It feels worlds away, but it's been only three days. The worst three days of my life. And yet, it's like they've awakened a part of me I never knew existed. And never want to know again.

I really am tired, but I check on Carly, who's still at the hospital. Her mom texts that the surgery went well, she's recovering, and should be good as new—knock on wood—soon. I find four pictures of cute animals and send them to her. Next, the requisite call to one of my parents to keep up this façade of normalcy. It's lunchtime back home, which means my dad is easier to reach. My mom has a lot of lunch meetings.

He answers right away. "Tess! *Come va?*"

"English, Dad?" I say. "All this Italian all the time is making my brain hurt."

"That means it's getting exercised."

"But I don't want to pull a muscle." I manage a laugh. "How are things there?" *How's Sofia*, I want to say, but who knows what that might trigger.

"Everything is basically as you left us. Mom and I are working normal hours. Sofia is at school all day then, like you, with a group of friends at night."

Or she drugs you then calls to threaten me. "Sounds great." I tell him about going to the Roman Forum tomorrow, the chef's lasagna lunch, the picture books outside.

"Can't wait to see the posts," he says. "You're doing a great job with those, but that last haiku? Where's your punctuation?"

Really, Dad? "Just taking your advice and trying new things. I'm even getting up too early tomorrow. Devin from my class invited a bunch of us for breakfast. His dad makes unbelievable Italian pastries."

"I understand Florenza does too. When do you see her and the others? Arsenio, Vittoria, Zia Elena? This coming Sunday?"

"They're getting back to me today or tomorrow." Then I end the call quickly because I really, really need to take a nap. And stop lying.

I wake to the smell of garlic and herbs from downstairs. Francesco has made tortellini with a basil cream sauce, which is utterly outstanding. I actually have a bit of an appetite, maybe because it's my day off as a thief. Or I'm getting so used to the stress that my body sees it as normal.

One thing's for sure. I can't be lulled into a state of complacency. I need to be alert and sharp with every step I take. Starting again tomorrow morning.

CHAPTER TWENTY-ONE

I SPENT SO MUCH TIME RUNNING THROUGH THE TRAIN directions that first day, they repeat like a song I've heard since birth. *Spagna station. Take the MEA Anagnina. Switch at Termini...*

Starting from Devin's, though, I'm clueless. But the Rossis expect me, my bag, and my phone to be there. With him.

By the time I'm a block away, I still don't know how to convince him to let me borrow his phone and go alone. He shouldn't take this risk, not for himself or for either of his families, here and in London. But when I spelled out all the risks yesterday, every single one I could think of, he told me he doesn't care. Like he and everyone around him are fireproof.

He hasn't seen someone threatening to slit his parents' throats with a knife.

I can always bail. Just refuse to go. But I need to, and I need an ally. It's not like I can buy a burner phone with the trackable credit card. And the few euros the Rossis let me have at one time aren't enough. They probably researched that.

I walk the path that's starting to become so familiar. This early in the morning, the city is quieter than I've ever heard. It was probably this quiet on Monday, but the buzzing in my head was way too loud. This is my choice today, which makes all the difference.

The sun, low in the sky, peeks around the corners of these narrow, narrow streets and passageways and grows bolder in more open areas. I take the route that passes the Pantheon—closed this early—and the Jewish Quarter. So far, being inside churches hasn't done me much good. Doubtful that passing near the Tempio Maggiore, the Great Synagogue of Rome, will do anything, either, but like my mom would say, it couldn't hurt. I stare in its direction and chant the *Shema*, one of the only prayers I know in Hebrew. Then for my dad, I cross myself. God has to understand I only have the best intentions, that I need to cover myself at every turn.

When I left this morning, Anjelica told me they'd be tracking me. No problem. The problem is that no one else but me is coming to breakfast. Devin better have that covered.

He meets me at the door.

"Am I the first?"

"First and only. Cloris and Lashay didn't want to bother their host families for a ride. Bright, either, which had Nicolas texting in the middle of the night that he decided to sleep in. Then Suraj just said he's glued to his pillow. So is Sydney, who's sleeping off a migraine. And by the time they let me know, you'd have already been on your way."

He lets me in. "But now that no one else is coming, AdDad and Dance Mum decided to go back to bed." And he pantomimes that they really are asleep. "But there are pastries. And I can make coffee. Or leave you to have a nap on the couch."

"Maybe a nap." That way, they won't expect to hear me.

Amid talk of him getting me a blanket, he has me type the old woman's address into his phone. Then he takes my courier bag and hands me a gear bag with the AS Roma soccer club logo. Inside is a pair of bright red AS Roma shorts, a black AS Roma shirt with Roberto on the back, and a red Nike cap to match the shorts. "Little brother size," he whispers.

I change in the bathroom, wind my hair into the cap, and try to convince myself I'm Roberto. Except the shirt isn't quite baggy enough to fully hide my boobs. It's better than being in my own clothes, but if the Rossis have someone watching this place, it might not be enough. I come out of the bathroom, giving Devin my best skeptical look.

He holds up a finger and has me follow him into the kitchen. "Out this door," he whispers, "is a skateboard. Can you ride a skateboard?"

I shake my head.

"No worries. Tuck it under your arm and go through the alley to the street. Roberto does that every morning. Later, but still. You're a little taller so slouch some, which will also throw off your walk. Meet me at the bus stop." He hands me directions plus two ten-euro notes. "By the time you get us each a day pass, I'll be there."

He's thought of everything. Except… "You do know this isn't a spy movie. Real people, including you, can get hurt."

"You as well, Tess. As your friend, I can't sit by and let you hurdle this all on your own. We can outwit them. Two heads, better than one and all that." He pushes me toward the door. "Enjoy life without being listened to."

I step outside, slouching, skateboard under my arm. I'm at once buoyed by the seeming freedom and bogged down with the thought of endangering Devin. And with the weight of this skateboard. Though it would be a good weapon if I need one.

I flinch at the thought. Everything is about survival these days. I've never had to think about survival except once, five summers ago, and just for a split second. I was swimming when a volleyball hit me so hard, it propelled my head into the side of the pool. Instinctively, I scrambled up and out as things were fading to black. That's it. I've lived that kind of easy life where food and clothes and opportunities and love are plentiful. I have not trained for this, and yet, I'm surviving. It must be instincts.

By the time I buy our passes, Devin is there as promised. He's wearing a matching cap and what's probably AdDad's AS Roma shirt.

I skip the joke about us being teammates and get right to my point. "Part of me hoped you wouldn't show. This is my mess to handle."

He shakes his head. "You didn't make this mess. You're a victim. I'm not. I've understood that I can leave at any point. End of discussion."

The bus is on time. The train after that too. Both are so quiet, it's like the world has agreed not to break the silence. Once we're off, I lead Devin down Viale America, right on Viale Pasteur. Except...

"Perfume Woman, Signora Roma," I say just loud enough. "She was the one who let me into the gate."

"No worries," he says, his voice rising above the cars now passing us. "Did I tell you that I run cross-country? And I'm fairly competent at it too."

"Really?" I open my eyes wide. "I didn't know cross-country runners can hurdle eight-foot iron gates. And just the other day, you told me you were talent-free."

"Right," he says, "but I don't like to gloat. You've heard of the Olympics?"

"As in *the* Olympics? Can I see your medals?"

He arches his eyebrow. "They're under lock and key, but I can show you my tacky plastic trophies."

We turn onto Viale Europa, my heart rate ratchets up, and my voice quiets down. "Seriously, though, the gate?"

"I'm tall, I can jump a bit, and I should have the arm strength to hoist myself over."

"And that won't draw attention?" I shake my head. "First, we wait to see if anyone comes out. Anyone, except Signora Roma. Or the Creepy Man."

"Creepy Man." Devin shakes his head. "He needs an official alias. I suggest Il Creepo."

I nod. "Il Creepo, it is. After that, unless I come up with a spare idea, it's all you."

Like last time, we're plenty early, so we walk past the gate toward the church. "I sketched that," I say, "but they took the drawing away from me."

"No evidence of where you've been. However, they don't have a hold on me." Devin takes pictures of the church, the storefronts, the apartments with their laundry out to dry. Then he wants some selfies.

"Remember your nose?" I joke.

"Right. But if you can be this brave, I can show my falsely accentuated proboscis in public."

"Still." I shake my head.

"Why not? No one will see them unless I choose to show them. Even if they do, no way they'll know where we were."

He takes a few, the skateboard covering half my face.

"I don't really look like me," I say.

"Because you're Roberto."

We're across the street just before seven, exactly where I stood last time. The sparse traffic is suddenly less sparse.

"Oh, bugger!" Devin says. "I should have jumped the gate when everyone was still sleeping or getting ready or just not out."

"No worries." I nod toward a man—a foot shorter than Il Creepo—in the courtyard, nearing the gate.

We wait for a car to pass and trot across, skateboard still under my arm. I stop at the side of the gate and turn to Devin. "*Chiave?*"

Devin starts fiddling in his bag for the "key" but looks up when I give a little Italian-type shout of surprise, something I wouldn't have known just days ago.

"*Buongiorno!*" I say to the man.

"*Buongiorno!*" He holds the gate open for me. Doesn't bump into me. Doesn't say, "Have fun."

We're in.

CHAPTER TWENTY-TWO

WE HAVE NEARLY FIFTEEN MINUTES UNTIL THE OLD WOMAN IS scheduled to walk her dog, assuming her Thursday schedule is the same as her Monday one and assuming that Anjelica spoke the truth, that this is an everyday thing for her.

"Worst case," Devin says, "wasted trip."

We're at the far corner of the courtyard in the shade of what Devin calls a stone pine tree. I lean against its trunk, and he sits crisscross to my right. Being here, knowing the drill, feels so different this time.

The woman's kitchen window is open. The slider, I assume, is locked. Bonus if it's not. I mentally run through the layout of the apartment so that I can get in, get good shots of the picture, and get out. Maybe take a quick look for anything else important.

Even so, the seconds rush by like hours—the minutes, like days. And Devin sits as still as a statue, which doesn't look suspicious at all.

"So," I say to break the tension.

He jolts up before I wave him down. "Sorry. I'm just…"

"I get it."

Devin reaches into his bag and pulls out pastries and bottles of water.

"A picnic? Now?"

"Why not?"

"My stomach is a bit busy," I tell him. "Nerves and all."

"And I'm the poster child for stress eating."

"You do know," I say, "you're not going in with me."

He looks at me like I've grown an extra nose.

"If she gets back too fast, you're running interference. Ask her which way to the church or something. Loudly, like those people who think that speaking a foreign language in a deafening voice helps you understand them better."

"But I'll look like a knob."

"Seriously?" I point to my outfit.

"Yes. Sorry." He holds out two pairs of gloves. He'd obviously planned to use one.

"Thanks."

He shrugs.

"No, really." I give him a quick hug as punctuation.

We sit. We wait. He eats. I don't.

"So. Cross-country," I say. Anything to make the time pass. "What's that about?"

"Frogs." He gives half a laugh. "It's about frogs." He takes another bite.

"You're just gonna leave me in suspense?"

"I didn't think there was enough already." He wipes his mouth with a napkin. "Well, there I was, this pudgy kid, year six, your fifth grade, running with a questionable lot. We thought it would be funny to let loose a couple dozen frogs in the classroom. My mum was furious when she found out, and said, 'If you enjoy communing with nature that much, then commune.' And she signed me up for cross-country."

"That's it? That was your punishment?"

"After we spent three days scouring the classroom with tooth-brushes. My muscles, brutally sore, made that first practice absolutely excruciating."

"Serves you right," I say. "Wonder what your mum would think now?" I check my watch. "Three minutes." It's like my blood knows to start pumping to my arms and legs for the climb. Devin could give me a boost, but that'd only attract more attention.

He sets his phone to stay unlocked. Even a few seconds can mean a lot. I slip it into my pocket, tuck both pairs of gloves into my waistband—no need for a bag this time—and stand to stretch my calves, hamstrings, arms, shoulders. Then for distraction, I practice flipping the skateboard into my hands.

Like clockwork, the old woman appears in the slider window with the leash. My body can't decide whether to relax or tense back up. Doesn't matter.

She hooks up the dog and, within a minute, she and her companion walk out the gate.

It's on.

CHAPTER TWENTY-THREE

I DON'T WASTE TIME WITH THE INSIDE DOOR. THE SLIDER IS locked too. I turn to tell Devin not to watch what will be an unparalleled awkwardness of me climbing through the window, but he'd watch anyway. Before I can turn back, I bump into one of the patio chairs. At least I catch myself before I fall on my face. And at least, this time, I hoist myself into the window on the first try.

I go to steady my hands inside the sink, and I'm up to my wrists in soapy water. I do not need to drag my body through suds, so I angle myself to use the counter as leverage. The soggy gloves may leave puddles there, but sogginess doesn't leave fingerprints.

I scuttle in, scraping myself again, but there's no time to nurse any wounds. I do take a beat to slide the water back into the sink and wring out my gloves before I shove them back into the waistband. Then I grab a kitchen towel—a match to the one I stole—and dry the drips on the counter and the floor. This time I leave the towel there.

Sitting on the coffee table where the canister used to be is a vase decorated with an old-time map. Could be important. I fish out Devin's phone and grab pictures of it from every angle. Then, a quick series of pictures of the whole room, including the old-school prints on the wall.

My target is nestled between a portrait of a different Renaissance dude and angels coming down from the heavens. I change the plan. If this 2-D version (I'm nearly positive) of the canister is as easy to steal as the picture at Villa Borghese…

I tug on one glove and attempt to grab the picture, but it's bolted to the wall. Instead, I line up the camera as perfectly as I can and do a photo burst. I reposition myself and do it again.

I still have time to check the other two rooms in the apartment for anything else that looks important. The bathroom has the usual: powder, soap, shampoo, lotion, towels. Three seconds and I'm out of there.

The bedroom, my hiding spot from last time, is more cluttered than I remember. Then, though, I was intent on escape. Now, I have extra time. And a warning system.

The single-sized bed in the middle of one wall is flanked by wooden nightstands, each with a lamp. The nightstand on the side nearest the door has a collage of different photos—mostly of the dog—held in place by a square of glass that fully covers the nightstand's top. The pictures may not be important, but still, I move the lamp to the floor with my gloved hand and take pictures with the other.

On the far side of the room is a wardrobe instead of a closet. Unless the woman stores her clothes elsewhere, she has about the same amount that I brought with me to Rome. And just five pairs of shoes lined up on the wardrobe's floor. On the shelf above are hats and purses. If I had time, I'd rummage through everything, but I'm already pressing my luck. I take a couple of pictures, close the wardrobe.

I move to the nightstand on the other side of the bed. The lamp here has such a wide base that it covers nearly the entire glass surface and whatever is pressed underneath. It seems to be another map. Same as the vase? Different? I hoist up the lamp.

Devin's voice floats in from outside. *"Buongiorno, Signora!"*

She's back.

The lamp sticks for a moment, dislodging the glass a couple inches. No time for the second glove. I hold the map down by its soft edge, soft like the letter's paper. Then I center the glass the best I can, burst a few photos, replace the lamp, and turn to leave.

Devin is asking the woman something about coffee. I have a few more seconds.

The dresser comes up to my chest. On top is a lace mat with a comb, brush, and a small jewelry box with a variety of earrings and necklaces. I take a quick picture of that and, also, of a framed photograph. Time to get out of here.

Then I freeze.

The photograph. I've seen it before. The big house. The grounds. The swing. The people. It's my Italian family. Not the Rossis. My real family. Arsenio. Florenza. Vittoria. And Zia Elena…who's holding hands with a little girl. Four-year-old me.

She's the old woman with the dog. This is *her* apartment.

I need to get out of here. How would I explain this to Zia Elena? The others? My parents?

I unfreeze. Devin is still talking. I open the front door with a gloved hand, slip out, turn away from the entrance. I climb up the stairs toward the second-floor apartments—

Clip-clip, clip-clip!

It's Signora Second Floor. Do I let her see me again? Or take the chance that Zia Elena will recognize me? I don't move.

Then I do. Unless Zia Elena is one of those gifted detectives on Netflix or Hulu or wherever, she'll see me as a kid, a huge AS Roma fan. But I'll get a good look at her. I walk down the seven stairs. *"Buongiorno, Signora."*

She smiles back. *"Buongiorno giovanotto."*

It's her. And by her response, she assumes I'm a boy.

CHAPTER TWENTY-FOUR

DEVIN IS BEHIND THAT TREE, AS IF HIDING MIGHT BETTER protect me. Or if he's smart, himself. When I'm within his line of sight, he lowers his hand, with a half-eaten *cornetti*, to his side and pushes off the trunk.

I signal for him to stay. Why chance bumping into Signora Second Floor?

After she leaves, we follow. It's not until we're past the gate and three buildings away that we start tumbling over each other's words. I motion for him to go ahead, but he motions back stronger.

"First, thank you so much for stalling her," I say. "I really needed it."

"You found something?"

I nod, but just hand him the soggy gloves. "Soapy water in the sink. Basically, I took lots and lots of pictures."

"Could you give me fewer details?"

If I tell him about Zia Elena, we might not get to his side of the story. "Still processing. You go."

He nods. "I hear the gate clink shut. It's the woman. I was mostly watching for you, so I almost missed her. But I managed to call in plenty of time. '*Scusi! Scusi!*'"

"You said something about coffee?"

"I asked where the best coffee shop was, very slowly. Then I made her repeat the directions." He shakes his head. "I didn't think you'd ever come out. And now you tell me you were leisurely taking pictures?"

"Don't get mad."

"Sorry. It's a post-freakout reaction." He puts an arm around me, gives a squeeze, then lets go. "It something I do. My parents hate it too."

"I usually have a post-freakout cry, but I'm not in the mood, so either this whole adventure has snapped me out of it or I'm still freaking out."

"Why? Worried the towel is a sodden mess?"

I wait for a man and woman to pass. Then I swipe to the last picture I took. "That's the woman you talked to, right? The same one in this picture."

"A younger version, but yes. Who is she?"

"Meet my great-aunt, Zia Elena. And my cousins: her son Arsenio, his wife Florenza, and their daughter Vittoria. And this little girl is me."

He stops. Turns to me, eyebrow as high as I've ever seen it. "Your host family made you steal from your blood family? They've got some connection!?"

I nod. Shake my head. "I don't know." We move down the street again, everything passing as a blur. No matter how hard I try to find some explanation, I can't. "On the bright side," I say, "I may have an answer to another question."

"Which is…"

"How I got accepted to Exchange Roma. I wasn't qualified to—"

"Not qualified? You're at least as qualified as I am."

"Have you heard my Italian?" I give a sad laugh. "Suddenly, it's so clear. Somebody wanted me here. The Rossis wanted me here. Me. Not just anybody."

"You do know what that means."

"Tell me." I need to hear it from someplace outside my own head.

"The only way they'd manage that is with an accomplice inside the program."

"A tentacle. They do." I tell him about the picture of me inside the museum, and my doubts about everyone in our class but him and Nicolas.

"Our classmates don't have that type of power."

"But someone must." My mind leaps to that first day when Signor Matteo called me to his office. "You had to fill out a long admissions form, right?"

Devin nods. "Ticked all the academic, physical, and mental health boxes. Half-expected to reveal exactly when I was potty-trained."

I force a smile.

"Well then. We'll joke later," he says. "What about the form?"

"Emergency contacts. My parents listed themselves first, of

course, but they also listed Zia Elena and my other cousins in the optional part, local contacts."

We get to the train station in time to catch the one we need. Again, the last car is empty. I head to the back but ask Devin to stop midway and put his head in his lap while I change into my own clothes. "I'm done!"

He takes off his cap and adds it to the bag. "To dispute the current theory," he says, "why would the Rossis need you in particular? Mightn't they work with any one of us? It's not as if they had you visit your aunt then steal the canister from under her nose."

"Could be their idea of a hilarious coincidence. An extra level of amusement they didn't have to pay extra for." I think about it for a moment. "No logic in that. How would anyone know that I'm related except for the application? Now, I'm positive. The Rossis have someone inside the program."

We list every adult we can think of, from the teachers to the chef to Signor Matteo to whoever might be his bosses, and we only come up with more questions. Time to let it go for now. Instead, we swipe through the photos I took.

Outside of what we came for—about a dozen good ones of the picture with the squares—there's not much. It is interesting, though, that the vase map and the nightstand map are from the same place. Ostia Antica, the remains of an ancient harbor city just outside Rome.

AdDad is in the kitchen when we get back. Devin left him a note that the party fizzled, and we'd gone for a walk so as not to disturb. AdDad says we should pick another time when he can have a house full of people to cook for. Then he makes me eat, tells me I'm looking too thin, and has me assure him twice that I'm all right.

Why couldn't I be living here? Anjelica and Francesco haven't once been concerned about my personal well-being, except for the nap when I first arrived. Chances are, that gave them the opportunity to rifle through all my stuff.

Devin's host family leaves for the day about twenty minutes before we need to. As they go out the door, they warn us to be good. With a wink. If only they knew.

While Devin prints a few of the square-picture photos, I take out the letter from my shoe. It's already beginning to smudge. The plan is to cut out the little squares that seem to represent the canister's cutouts and, hopefully, read the letter's message.

I shake my head. "I suppose it's impossible to take a perfectly square-on picture of something like this," he says. "I thought you nailed it."

"And yet, I didn't." Even so, we cut out several of the black squares at the top, bottom, middle, and sides. Some letters come through in full, some partially, some not at all.

"If only you'd stolen the picture itself."

"Right. Because I am a common thief."

"Sorry. I—"

"I'm joking. And confession, I tried. It's bolted to the wall, and with the size of that frame, it would never have fit into Roberto's bag." There's not much else to say. "Let the eavesdropping continue!"

I fetch my bag from the other room, already rehearsing an

apology for the silence in case they don't believe I took a nap. If they were reasonable people, they'd accept a reasonable excuse. As in, "Do you want me to look like a deranged old woman attached to her bag like it's a lifeline? That wouldn't be suspicious." I wish someone would just steal the thing.

"You know..." I say to Devin while we're walking to school. Maybe he could be the purse-snatcher. Yes, the Rossis would replace it and fast, but still. "What if—" I check myself. Those two hours free from their eavesdropping nearly made me reckless.

"What if, what?"

Later, I mouth. "What if they assigned group project partners, and they made me and Bright research, like, the financial market. We'd be sunk, but how funny would that be?"

We riff on the hilariousness of similar scenarios all the way to school. Might as well have fun while I can. I'm not expecting much on our field trip to the Roman Forum.

We ride the school's buses to a large area with lots of ruins, lots of green space. This used to be the hub of Roman life: markets, courts of law, gladiator matches, government elections, and everything you'd expect in a society. Physically, the columns and buildings—remnants and functioning structures—are remarkably intricate. Typical of Rome.

But after such a long morning already, I wish I could go back to the bus and sleep for a year. Our guide is so amazing, though, I'm waking up.

He focuses on the power struggle inside the ancient Roman senate with the likes of Julius Caesar, who's not just a Shakespearean character. I never truly thought of him as having been a living, breathing human, caught up in all the drama. Until now.

As our guide continues, a thought nags at my stomach. All this talk of secrets and lies and underhanded dealings makes me believe that maybe, just maybe, there's one big, ugly power struggle happening between the Rossis and my own family. And I'm the poor pawn caught in the middle.

CHAPTER TWENTY-FIVE

I GET BACK TO THE APARTMENT—I REFUSE TO CALL IT *HOME* now—and steel myself for all sorts of accusations after this morning's failed breakfast party. But when I tell Anjelica and Francesco that no one else showed and yes, I did fall asleep on the couch and no, Devin and I weren't locked in his bedroom and yes, his parents and brother were there, they laugh and leave it at that.

Francesco hands me a plate of bruschetta. "Take it upstairs if you want, but first..." He motions for my courier bag. "Let's see what you bought."

Oh, so they get credit card alerts. I show them the book I bought at the Roman Forum, but they barely look at it before they let me go upstairs. The rest of the night is equally uneventful.

I should take this stretch of normalcy as a gift, but it feels like they've dangled a sword on a threadbare rope over my head. And once again, I can't help but wonder if they're giving me space before they force me to steal a million euros. Or murder the president of Italy. Or blow up the universe.

Even this morning, before I go to school, it's kisses on the cheek and wishes for a great day. Great for them. Hell for me. The threats, sure, but also the unanswered questions.

It's not until after lunch that I manage to get Devin alone in the back of our classroom, away from my bag for something I should have asked on the train yesterday. "How can we expose whoever's working with the Rossis?" I whisper. "Is it one person? More?"

Devin pulls at his beltloop. "Let me think."

"Think about what?" Bright moves in, tugging at her hair.

"I've been thinking about this since yesterday," I say.

Devin looks at me as if I've lost it.

"Suppose you were a slave in the days of the Roman senate. Or rather, make that one of those freed people."

"Me? A *liberta*? One step above a slave? Not even a citizen?" She laughs.

"Yes," Devin says, "we're pretending here."

I nod. "So, your superiors are all over your case. They've heard that you're talking shit about them, and you have, but only to specific people. That means someone in your network is a mole. What's the perfect way to trap that person?"

"Ooh," Bright says. "Good one."

Signorina Emma leans in. And she doesn't look happy. If she's working with the Rossis, Sofia will make an ugly appearance tonight. "*È inglese questo o sbaglio!*"

That's all? That I was speaking in English? *"Si, scuso,"* I say. *"Italiano adesso."*

Now she smiles. Signorina Emma either has the best poker face or my scenario means nothing to her in a Rossi sense.

She gets the attention of the class. Says ours is a good question and starts a discussion about how we might discover whether there's a traitor among us.

Why did I open my mouth? If someone in the room is working with the Rossis, this will get back to them. I'll swear it wasn't my idea. That we were talking about Spartacus leading his escape. The subject morphed to espionage. Done.

After most of an hour, we reach a consensus. The head *liberto* would whisper to his closest allies, secretly and separately, that there'd be a stash of money at a specific location. Each ally, though, would be told a different location. If, by morning, the money was missing from any of the sites, he could identify the mole.

"I liberti avrebbero attaccato?" Signorina Emma asks.

No, we decide, the freedmen would not attack the mole. There's more power in knowing than in taking a revenge that won't solve anything. The guilty party might have loyalists of his own, and that could lead to all-out war. Keep your friends close and your enemies closer.

Good advice if you're positive who's who. But I don't. Any person here could be working with the Rossis.

Devin, Bright, and Nicolas are still discussing the hypothetical as we leave school. I listen just in case Bright incriminates herself, but the conversation goes nowhere.

"Here's the problem," I finally say. "If someone showed up at one of the money sites, it wouldn't prove who was the mole, just that there *might* be one. What if an innocent person accidentally found the money? No mole. No betrayal. Just coincidence. End discussion. Moving on," I say, "Favorite fruity candy. Gummy bears or Skittles?"

I look directly at Devin, and he winks. "If we're not talking chocolate, then Jelly Babies."

And while he describes exactly what those are, I slip his phone from his hand and type.

Up for a repeat field trip?

CHAPTER TWENTY-SIX

I NEED TO GO BACK TO ZIA ELENA'S. THIS TIME, THOUGH, I'll knock at the door, and she'll welcome me in. I have everything planned. Except permission...

Which is why I specifically FaceTime my dad.

"Tess! You were supposed to call Mom today."

"Forgot." I've turned into an expert liar. Though I don't have to lie about my day. I go through everything, especially blaming the hypothetical on Spartacus, hoping my openness shrinks any suspicion the Rossis might have about that.

"Ah! Conspiracies!" He gets that sparkle in his eye. "We wanted to take Sofia to Ford's Theatre. She asked about the Lincoln assassination. Also, if I knew where Presidents Garfield and McKinley were killed. And where Ronald Reagan was shot. She must have a fascination with assassinations, which makes sense now. Rome was filled with them. I'd hoped to play tour guide, but with her busy social life, there's no time this weekend. Oh, well."

Be careful what you wish for. I want to say that so badly.

"Hey!" Thankfully, that snaps me out of it. "TGIF!" he says, his face too close to his phone. "What's the weekend hold for you? Seeing the relatives?"

"Dad. I don't want them to get sick of me. In five weeks, I'll be with them full time."

"Five weeks will turn into four weeks then into no weeks, Tess. I know how shy you can be. Make an effort now or it could be uncomfortable later. I can call them for you."

He's so predictable, which plays perfectly into my plan. "You're right," I say. "Um, well, do you think, maybe… Some people are interviewing older citizens to see how Rome has changed, and—"

"Zia Elena!" He stands.

"She'll let me come over and ask her questions?"

"Of course. Of course. If not, let me know. Maybe she won't understand your Italian."

"She'll understand yours, Dad?"

He laughs. "I can always have Sofia translate for me."

"Did you forget? I'm in Rome. I can have Francesco or Anjelica do the translating."

"Can they, really? Do they speak better English now?"

Oops. "No. Sorry. They speak the same English. I'm just understanding them more, so it seems like they're practically speaking English to my ears. And maybe I'm teaching them more. I don't know."

I have nearly the same conversation with my mom, minus the fumbling. And when I go down to dinner, Anjelica and Francesco are back to English.

"Ah yes," Anjelica says, "our English is much better than when we talked the first time."

I close my eyes, shake my head, then look back at her. "Sorry. I didn't. I—"

Francesco waves me off. "No harm, no foul. He bought it. But she needs to as well."

"My mom?"

Anjelica gives a dangerous chuckle. "Zia Elena. You don't want to say the wrong thing to her. No, not to her." She looks directly into my eyes. "Just you wait. You have no clue."

I have no clue? *They* have no clue.

But I keep a straight face. "That's why I'm hoping to bring friends with me. They speak Italian a lot better than I do."

Francesco has been nearly chuckling through this all, but he stops long enough to tell me to call her now. "See if you can drop by tomorrow, assuming your friends will be free."

"Though," Anjelica says, "I'd bet your friends will be friend. Singular. Devin." The way she says his name sounds an alarm through my gut.

"You're right," I say, regrouping. "I'll bring only one person so we don't seem like an interrogation team."

I text Devin, pray he plays along. Will you be free tomorrow if I line up someone for our project? The one with the interview? If he doesn't understand—

But he comes back with a thumbs-up.

I turn to Francesco. "I'd call her now, but I don't know if she'll understand me. Devin speaks better Italian, but I assume you don't want him here."

Anjelica sighs and gives me a look.

"No, of course, no one comes here."

They agree to help with the call.

Zia Elena's phone rings only once before she picks it up.

"*Zia Elena? Questa è Tess. Tess Alessandro dall'America.*" I confirm that I'm in Rome and having a great time. Francesco whispers from halfway across the room to help me understand her and say all the nice things a girl like me should. And I almost want to cry.

Zia Elena gets so excited. She tells me not to eat much for breakfast. She wants to feed me. And every word sounds so sweet and caring, like any grandmother I'd ever want. I'd run to her for protection, but the Rossis could storm in and hold a knife to her throat. The rest of the family's too. I need to make everything right, but all I can do now is ask about tomorrow.

Francesco reminds me to get her address.

First, she tells me to call when I get there so she can open a gate for me. I purposefully don't react. She continues to explain if the gate is open, come right in, walk through the courtyard and into the building. Down the hall will be a doormat with a picture of a dog. That's her apartment.

I look at Francesco. I look at Anjelica.

Their grins couldn't be wider.

"Twenty-two Viale Europa?" I whisper.

I was wrong. Their grins could grow wider.

I make sure mine doesn't show at all.

CHAPTER TWENTY-SEVEN

It's Exchange Roma tradition to throw a party for us the first Friday night. Rumor is, they do it to stop us from going clubbing. Though, we could go clubbing anytime we want. In Italy, the drinking age is sixteen.

This year's party is in Trastevere, not far from Devin's host family. Francesco drops me off at the entrance to Piazza Trilussa, where the lights cast an orange glow over everything. The entire piazza is teeming with partiers going in and out of clubs and pubs or just hanging out on the steps, having fun.

I get swept up in the energy and practically dance my way to the club, which is closed to everyone but us students tonight. A bouncer at the door checks me in, and I take a moment to get my bearings. Lights are flashing, music is blaring, and suddenly, Bright is dragging me to the dance floor. It's so loud and she's pulling so hard, she can't possibly hear my protests, that I'm the world's second-worst dancer. My dad comes in first.

He doesn't know it, though. He loves embarrassing me, my mom, and all their friends. I wish he were here if only for that. Then no one would give me a second look when I can't make my body move like, well, like Bright starts to.

I take a step back, but she grabs my hands and, almost like a tactile tutorial, I'm getting the feel for it. My shoulders relax, which causes a chain reaction down my arms, through to my hips. It's like all the tension of the past few days has told my muscles to give in and go with it.

After two more songs, Nicolas and Devin joining us, Bright pulls me over to where the culinary students are tending bar. There's a big vase of flowers on the heavy wooden counter, and she takes out two for us to wear in our hair.

Signor Matteo, who's right there handing out napkins and probably making sure the party doesn't get too wild, salutes and moves the vase to a back table.

Bright tries to order a Negroni, some Italian drink with pretty much all alcohol, but they have a limited drink menu. "And I hear," she says, "like barely no alcohol in any of them. *Non è così Signor Matteo?*"

Signor Matteo won't say if it's true. But he does hand Bright, Nicolas, and me our margaritas. Devin, though, sticks to water.

"What fun are you?" Bright says. "Join us. You have to. It's the law!"

"Perhaps later."

Not me. I plan to drink enough to find out if the wine wiped me so hard last Sunday or if the Rossis slipped me something else. I cannot get so wasted, though, that I'm giving away Rossi family secrets. *"Cin cin!"* We clink glasses. And true to rumors, the drink tastes alcohol-free.

I wish it weren't. I suddenly want to get so fully wasted before the next task that I can't do it. But it would only delay the threat. And maybe anger them enough to cause another *accident*.

I take a bigger gulp. Maybe these do have some alcohol, because the threat's edges seem to soften. And with the dancing, so wild, and the laughter, so infectious, it's almost easy to forget I'm carrying a load that no one else is. And the music is so loud, I can say anything without worrying what the Rossis might hear.

They let me leave my courier bag at the apartment in favor of this party purse, another present that is certainly bugged. Forget that. Forget it all! "Party! Oops!" I laugh. *"Festa!"*

Devin pulls me back half a step. "Tess. This is not you."

"Stealing is? Living with the threat of death is? This is me, trying to have fun for once."

"Did they threaten you today? You, specifically?"

I look right at him. "They don't have to tell me they'll kill me at the end of this. What other choice would they have? I know too much."

"But they have no clue how much you know."

"Know about what?" It's Bright and her supersonic hearing.

I turn to her. "Know how much they're watering down these drinks. C'mon, Bright!"

Devin throws his arms up.

"Keep a stiff upper lip," I say to him. "And carry on. This whole night is brilliant."

He just glares.

Whatever. Bright and I go back to the bar for our second drinks. This time, Signor Matteo hands Bright hers, then he ducks down for a minute before he gives me mine. *"Scusate. Ho lasciato cadere il tuo tovagliolo."*

"Cute," Bright says. "Apologizing for dropping your napkin. Cheers!"

We clink glasses.

This drink tastes different. Bitter. Stronger.

What the hell. I chug the rest. A deep-down warmth starts in my stomach and spreads down my legs before it changes course to my head. I look up. Signor Matteo meets my eyes, grimaces, and gestures with a napkin.

He's written something on the inside of mine.

NOT A DANGEROUS DRUG.
YOU WILL BE FINE. DO NOT KEEP MESSAGE.
DESTROY NOW, PLEASE.

What?

I turn to Devin. "I'm so, so, so, so sorry. Please. Can you get me a water? A big one."

"Perhaps you should get it yourself." He turns away, but I grab his arm and shove the napkin in his hand.

I whisper in his ear. "He's the one. Signor Matteo."

He reads the napkin and wraps an arm around my shoulders. I look up. As far as his lips. Tilt my head. Go in for the kiss. But he shakes his head. "When you're sober." And he goes.

I move to the side of the room in a not-so-straight line and steady myself against the wall.

Bright is shadowing me. "How is it," she says, "that you had Devin wrapped around your little finger from day one? And why can't I? That's never happened before."

"Zere, th-ere's a first time for everything." It's hard to form words, but I need to try. Anything to stop myself from lying down right here. "First night at the party." The lie comes so easy. "You were talking to, to..." I wave a hand. "I dunno. Some peoples. I told Mr. Devin hyphen name, that me, Tess, I get people to do whatever I want. So not true. But he ash't ass-kuh-d me how. And I said that I have some sort of extra-wordly power over..." I wave my hand around the room. "Joking. Big persh, personal joke. And I cannot talk. My tongue"—and I grab onto it—"is shuddenly the shize of a cannoli."

Bright laughs. "Let me guess. First time drinking, hon?"

"No. Second and a half. Don't tell. Maybe I had a little too much wine at my cousin Ben's bar mitzvah lash, lash—whatever—year."

"And the half?" Nicolas says.

"Oh, Nicolas, when did you get here?" I wave my hand. "Doesn't matter. I will answer your question. Dinner. Host-y parents."

"Then maybe you should stop," he says, "or they'll have to call your host-y parents."

"Host-y dad will be cool," Bright says. "Him on that motorcycle the other night? Movie stuff. What's he really like, Tess? Tell me everything."

I want to so badly, but no. Don't trust. Maybe she's a tentacle. Testing me.

Devin is back with my water. I chug the entire bottle. He hands me another.

Bright looks right at me. "You were saying…"

"My host-y parents, Devin. She demands I say stuff about my host-y parents."

"Careful, Tess," he says.

Bright cocks her head. "What do you mean?"

"By all accounts, they're much different than her parents at home. And we wouldn't want to spread rumors."

I slap Devin's arm. "Too funny." Then I turn to Bright. "No rumors, all true. You saw the pix. They are younger. So beautiful. And the helmet. They are surprising. I do not know what they will say next. They are not heli—heli—heli-poc-ters." I shake my head. "They do not hover over my person. What else, Devin?"

He shakes his head. "I've not met them."

"Ooh!" Bright says. "Next party at Tess's!"

"No, no, no, no no, no, no. Unless you want the ceiling to fall on your head. The apartment is under, uh, paint cans and plaster."

Bright laughs. "Speaking of plaster, she is so plastered."

I am, but I know enough to stop talking. "We need to dance." A sentence I never thought I'd say, but it's the safe thing to do.

I down half the second bottle of water and swear it's literally sloshing around. *Start working. Please, start working.*

I dance. And dance. And lose track of time and everything else until they play a slower song, and we pair off. But I'm with someone shorter than Devin. He's over there with Bright. I'm leaning hard on Nicolas. It's all fine, even if Devin starts falling for Bright.

But not now, Devin. I need you to help me. And I like your eyebrow.

Oops. Did I say that out loud? The music's loud. Nicolas does not look at me funny. I look at his ear. Then I pull a strand of Nicolas's hair that is threatening to bump into his shoulder. I want to help it along. "Why do you grow your hair down to here? Trying to be like host-y dad?" I shouldn't have said that. I need to stop talking altogether.

Nicolas laughs. "Because I knew I'd meet Bright, and she likes it longer."

"Really?"

"Nah. I meant to get it cut at home, but I got lazy."

"That is what happened with me and Italian. Verbs, too much trouble. And adjectives, ugh. Right, Ni-co-las? Did you ever keep repeating your name until it sounds very strange? Ni-co-las. Tess. Tess. Tessss."

He laughs. "You sound like a snake."

"You know who sounds like a snake? I mean, do you want to know who is the snake?"

"Who?"

I pinch my lips together. I want to yell that Signor Matteo is a snake for drugging my drink and that the Rossis are dangerous snakes and—

Suddenly, the music is way too loud, and the flashing lights are blinding me, and I just want to curl up and die. But Nicolas turns us around and I catch a glimpse of Signor Matteo, and I find something inside to keep this up. "The snake is an asp."

Nicolas laughs. "The snake is an ass?"

"The snake is also an ass, but I said *asp*. A-S-P. Do you not read Cleopatra? Do you not know your snakes?"

"Nope. Me and Cleo have not hooked up. But thank you for the recommendation."

The song ends, and I find a seat on the floor. A few others join me, and they're talking about something for who-knows-how-many songs. All their words, all the music, how can they hear themselves think?

I need a minute alone to regroup, but Bright insists on going to the bathroom with me. I lock myself in a stall and just sit there, fully dressed, for who knows how long.

"You didn't pass out, did you? You're not about to puke, are you?"

"Wish I could puke water. Gulp, gulp. Too fast." I pull down my panties, and I pee, which proves what I just said.

She's still there when I come out, and she ushers me to the sink as if I might forget to wash my hands. But the initial rush is starting to fade. I suppose, this would be the time when a person might grab her next drink, but with Signor Matteo playing bartender, just no.

Bright is holding her third or fourth or however many. Steady hands, clear eyes, lucid speech. No way he gave her anything strange. "Feeling better?"

I nod.

"Another drink? Just to sip?"

I shake my head. "I can't come home totally wasted. My host-y parents would not like that."

"But you said they're not the helicopters. Or heli-pocters."

I said that? Great. What else did I say? I don't ask. "Maybe not helicopters," I say instead, "but they might ground me if I'm acting stupid. Like parents do."

"Unfortunately." She finishes her drink and puts down her cup.

When we get back out, she and Nicolas go to the drink table. I start dancing all by myself. The physical activity is working to clear my head. But then I twirl—big mistake—and the orange flower from my hair falls to the floor. It's about to get trampled. "I'll save you, flower! You're Carly's favorite! I will save you for her and—

"Oh, Carly! I should have sent you flowers. I should have texted you every day. I should have—" I take a picture of it and text it to her. Then I cup the flower in my hand and head to the bar to put it in some water.

Devin pulls me aside. "You're having another?"

"Puh-lease, Boy Scout. No. Because, hey, did I tell you…" I drop my purse on the ground and move away from it. I look up at him. Those lips. I did that once already tonight, at least I think, and it didn't end well. "Hey," I say instead, "did I tell you about Signor Matteo?"

He nods and pulls the napkin partway out of his pocket. "You also gave me this."

"Great. My memory is…" I wave my hand, can't even find the right word. But I can find a good idea. "You know what I should do, Devin? I should stand on the bar and hold up the napkin and point to the rat Signor Matteo and I should announsh, announ-ce, that he has drugged me. And he is helping the people who want to kill my parents. Maybe I need another drink to get the nerve."

Devin presses on my shoulder. I've apparently been on my tiptoes. "Tess. Take a breath." He goes and fetches my purse. Before I can say anymore, he grabs me, and we start to slow-dance. "What he's doing is wrong," he whispers in my ear, "but it's not a good idea to announce it. And especially not a good idea to get another drink. We have an important assignment tomorrow, and I'm thinking it won't help if you're hungover. Maybe that's what the Rossis wanted. They don't want you to be sharp."

"But Signor Matteo—"

"Will be there on Monday. You can decide what to do then. Enjoy tonight."

He's right. This night has been mostly good: the dancing, the laughing, the whole package. But if I mess up tomorrow, I could mess up forever.

CHAPTER TWENTY-EIGHT

FRANCESCO IS WAITING ON HIS MOTORBIKE, HELMET DOWN, when the party ends. "We told you Signor Matteo would take good care of you."

I grumble.

"Heard you were feeling no pain for a while."

"That's a good thing? What if I slipped? I could have cried about everything. The police could've been waiting to arrest you when you pulled up."

"And yet," he says, "they weren't. We both know why." He drives off, we get to the apartment, and he goes through the door first. It's dark. Just a glow from the streetlamps outside. But he doesn't bother to turn on the lights before he goes into their bedroom.

Why?

Something moved. Something…where? I turn right. Turn left. Pivot behind. Anjelica. In the shadows. With a gun. I stumble back. Back. Back. "Please," I whisper. "No."

But she doesn't answer, doesn't move.

I stay frozen too. Then I blink. "Anjelica…I'm, I'm sorry?"

She still doesn't move. What's she waiting for?

"I… I…" And my eyes adjust to the darkness. I almost want to laugh, or cry. It's not Anjelica. Just that massive floor lamp, backlit by the streetlights.

I blow out a breath, hands on my knees, and I let my adrenaline settle. I blame Signor Matteo for that hallucination. Or maybe I should thank him. I'm on even higher alert now, a place I need to stay.

I flip on a light and take a good look around; otherwise, I'll lie in bed listening for all the bad things to happen. Anjelica must be in the bedroom with Francesco. No one is in the kitchen or the living room. And no one is in the second bedroom. In the past two days, the ceiling has miraculously healed itself and the Rossis have turned it into a home office with a safe that, I'm sure, holds the canister and letter then whatever they have me steal next.

I turn out the light, head up to my tower, and drunkenly, but purposefully, toss my shirt over the vase and its dying flowers. By morning, the shirt is still there. Either the vase is not a camera, or they'll move the shirt while I'm away. I lie there for a few minutes, my head surprisingly clear enough to review today's plan.

Devin and I are due at Zia Elena's around 10:00 a.m. with pastries from AdDad. We'll chat a little before we start asking her questions for our "project." At some point, I'll notice the vase with the map. *"Parlamene."* After she tells me about it, I'll ask about the picture with the squares. Then we'll either ask to borrow it long enough to make a copy or, if it feels right, I'll tell her everything.

I won't admit to stealing the canister, but I will mention that the Rossis have a canister with a similar pattern as the picture. Then Devin—

Oh God! Devin can't come. Zia Elena talked to him. He'll insist, but he can't come.

I'm still figuring out how to convince him when I go down to breakfast. Today, there's a whole basket of rolls and a variety of jams and butters on the kitchen counter. They may be horrible people, but they feed me well, have me in a comfortable room, and make sure I have everything I need. Then again, the witch in *Hansel and Gretel* fed them so they'd be plump and juicy when she cooked them for dinner.

Anjelica and Francesco are humming and almost giggling in the office. I'm hoping they're just overly amused that I'm going back to the scene of my first crime.

Anjelica sweeps in. "*Caffè o cioccolata calda?*"

I need to be sharp today, so I'm thinking espresso, but this is not a good day to see how my body responds to shots of pure caffeine. "*Caffè. Prego.*"

She pours me a cup with milk and sugar, the way I've been drinking it, and she hands me a plate. "*Mangia!*"

I really don't want to. I'll be doing a second breakfast soon. Besides, what'll they do? Kill my parents for my lack of appetite? A laugh escapes my lips.

"*Ah, è così emozionata per oggi!*" Francesco says.

Yes, I'm excited, but in my mind, I'm already tongue-tied. I ask if there's anything I should say to my aunt.

They laugh like it's the funniest thing they've ever heard. Then they start spouting so much so fast that I only catch a few basic words. Numbers, cart, box, leave, disappear, money, and of course, dead. Great.

Devin texts. I'm on your street. Can I come up? He's hoping to get a glimpse of the Rossis. Before I can hide the text—though, what's the point; they'll read it anyway—Francesco takes my phone, smiles, and shakes his head.

"I told him no yesterday. I mean *gli ho già detto di no ieri*."

Francesco texts back that I'll meet him at the corner, which I do.

But before I break the news that he's not coming with me, I pocket his phone. "Sorry," I say. "I seriously need to use the bathroom again. Wait right here."

Anjelica is holding the door open for me. "Really? Bathroom again?"

"It happens." I go in, actually pee, flush, wash, then peek out. They're in the office again. "Okay if I grab an orange for the road?"

"Whatever," she says.

With the refrigerator door as cover, I use Devin's phone to take a picture of their family portrait on the kitchen table. *"Arrivederci!"* If anything happens to me, Devin will have a lead for the police. I hand his phone back, pull his ear close, and tell him what I just did.

"You're quite brilliant," he says.

"Brilliant enough to know you can't come with me." I tell him why.

He holds me close, speaks softly. "Sorry, but I am going with you. First, I was wearing the cap over my eyes. Second, the dog was tugging her toward the house, so she barely looked at me. Third, I mentioned I was leaving to go back home and hoped to return next year after I graduate college. I've been told I look a lot older." He pulls back and starts forward.

I'm not fully convinced, but I toss him the orange and we continue to Spagna station. Maybe he's right. It's not like I remember everyone who's randomly talked to me.

We travel there mostly in silence, me, psyching myself up to meet my great-aunt for the first time in memory. And to pretend I've never been inside her home. Twice.

I call when we get there. And it's such a relief not hiding my face with my hair or underneath a cap and, especially, not climbing through the window.

Zia Elena bustles out, dog in her arms, to let us through the gate. She grabs me so hard and tight that I'm afraid I'll crush the dog. But mid-hug, she puts him on the ground and grabs me again. Kisses both cheeks. "*Tessa. Tessa. Finalmente! Sei bellissima, così come le tue foto.*"

Pretty as my pictures? I don't need to fake excitement. "*Questo è il mio amico*, Devin." I hold my breath, but Zia Elena doesn't show a single flicker of recognition.

She grabs him just as hard. "Devin. *Così bello.*" She moves us together, holds our chins in her hands. "*Bello, bello!*" Maybe she thinks everyone is beautiful.

Zia Elena pats her thigh, and the dog comes running. "*Questa è Panna Montata.*"

I look to Devin. "Does that mean anything in English?"

He holds up his app. The dog is named Whipped Cream.

"*Panna Montata.*" And I gesture eating some with a spoon. "*Deliziosa!*"

We all laugh, my cheeks warming in the moment, but guilt sneaking in. How could I have stolen from someone who loves so strongly, loves me so hard?

Devin hands her the pastries he brought, and when we go in, she arranges them on a platter and brings them to the living room along with a whole antipasto tray and a pitcher of fresh-squeezed orange juice. She has coffee brewing in the kitchen. Plates, forks, and napkins are already on the table with one other object. That vase.

"*Mangi! Mangi!*" Zia Elena hands us plates, and when we don't take enough for her satisfaction, she piles on more.

She asks about my parents, and yes, they're fine and send their love. Then she turns to Devin: *I detect a British accent. Are you from London? What do your parents do there?*

Before he answers that last question, she turns back to me. "*Mio fratello, tuo nonno, ero così triste quando è partito per l'America.*"

"She said," Devin says, "that—"

"Her brother, who's my grandfather, it made her sad…"

"When he left for America."

It takes us a minute to translate what she says next—that after he left, she saw him only once, briefly. She refuses to fly, and he refused to come back to Rome again. "*Due persone stupide e testarde.*" Two stupid, stubborn people.

I lean over and show her my locket with the picture of him and Nonna inside.

"Giusto!"

"That was his name," I tell Devin.

Zia Elena puts a hand to her heart, looks up, crosses herself, then pulls me in for another hug. Devin uses the translation app to capture the next bit. That Giusto was such a good boy, but his opinion of what was right came before his family. It should be family above all.

My guilt over the canister grows, but just as fast, gives way to a sudden curiosity. If I knew why Nonno went against the family and what disgusted him enough to leave forever, I might have a better handle on what's happening.

Before I can open my translation app to ask, Zia Elena shakes free from her nostalgia and, in a more businesslike voice, asks what we want to talk about for school.

I'll save my questions for another day. Right now, it's more important we get a copy of the picture.

CHAPTER TWENTY-NINE

DEVIN GETS PERMISSION FROM ZIA ELENA TO RECORD OUR conversation. Then he launches into our list of prepared questions. What was it like as a little girl? Was school much different? What were your hobbies? Are they the same now?

Zia Elena pulls Panna Montata onto her lap and says that she knits. Really? Outside the yarn in the canister, I've seen no trace of knitting. Maybe she gives away hats or sweaters or blankets and keeps her needles and yarn in the dresser drawers, the only thing I didn't search.

But it does give me an opening. I point to the vase on the table and ask if she also does decoupage. "*L'hai fatto?*"

"*Si, si.*" She did make that. And using Panna Montata as a model, she starts describing the process when the door behind me opens.

"*Ciao! Nonna! Cugina!* Tessa!" It's Vittoria. She hugs and kisses Zia Elena first, then she wraps me in the biggest hug.

Vittoria wants to speak English and be our translator. "Okay? No problem?"

No problem at all.

She apologizes that her parents are looking for one thing or another in villages around Pisa, Livorno, and Genoa.

"If I may ask," Devin says, "what, exactly?"

Vittoria translates for Zia Elena, who chuckles and throws her hands in the air.

"No pay attention to her," Vittoria says. "She no understand what they do."

"My dad said they're antique dealers."

Vittoria smiles. "I say their name, *i localizzatori*, the Locators. There are things from your memory, you look all the places, but you can't find? They find things. Is a good business."

"What are they looking for now?" Devin asks.

She shrugs. "The photographs, the jewelry, old coins, books, maps, goblets, teapots. Don't know today. Before, the best they find, a jewelry box."

"Filled with jewels?" he says.

"Ah, no, no, no. Jewels will be best. But *papà* said there was a key."

"Key to what?" I ask.

Vittoria shakes her head. "Is very mysterious, no? You find such a box and you want to know, *si*?"

This is everything I dreamed, the Rome I expected. I want to live forever in this moment. But I'll never be able to until the Rossis are out of my life. That means I need answers.

My bag is sitting next to my feet. I stiffen like the vibration on my phone startled me, which startles Panna Montata, who jumps off Zia Elena's lap and trots to the other room. "Sorry. My phone. I'm ignoring it."

"Good plan," Devin says. "So, have either of you visited Tess in the United States?"

They look at me.

"I guess I didn't tell him that you were there, what? Three years ago?"

"*Si*, Chicky."

Devin looks at me. "Chicky?"

"You're the only one who calls me that, Vittoria." I turn back to Devin. "My mom makes these wings we call little chicken, and Vittoria thought my mom was calling me little chicky." I jump again. "Sorry. Anyway, Vittoria spent the entire rest of their time there calling me Chicky."

"Perhaps I should start calling you that."

I smack Devin on the arm.

"That's a definite no."

I pretend my phone buzzes again. "Third call. Sorry. I'll be right back." I grab my whole bag and go out to the patio, closing the sliding glass door behind me. I drop the bag on a chair, take my phone into the courtyard, and pretend to talk for a minute. Then I gasp and run back inside closing the door behind me. "I think," I croak out, "I swallowed a bug."

Zia Elena gets me a cup of water while I try to cough it up. Or pretend to. This act must be working because Vittoria is whacking me on the back and Devin is standing there, looking mostly helpless. I take a few sips, give a couple more coughs, then nod.

"Better," I say. "And I'm sorry. This classmate called three times, and I thought it must be an emergency, but no."

"No problem, Chicky."

"Vittoria!" I mean to give her a nasty look, but I break out laughing instead. "Whatever. Call me Chicky if you want."

"Chicky, chicky, chicky."

"Changing the subject…" I point to the vase. "When you barged in, Zia Elena was demonstrating how she made this. But what's on it? A map?"

Vittoria nods. "A place she love. Special place as a little girl." She translates that into Italian.

Zia Elena smiles. "Ostia Antica *è il suo nome.*"

Then, Vittoria translates, Zia Elena would often tag along with her parents to Ostia Antica. She and her sisters, Agostina and Rosa, would run around with their mom while their dad was busy with something or other.

I'm dying to ask—if this place is so important, why cover up the map in the bedroom? But I can't ask if I've supposedly never been here.

"So," Devin says, "if that map is a copy, do you also own the original?"

He read my mind.

Vittoria translates, Zia Elena answers, then Vittoria tells us it's just a map. All the memories are here.

Zia Elena holds a hand to her heart at that point. *"Ricordi d'infanzia."* Childhood memories.

"Are those also childhood memories?" Devin says. "The pictures on the wall?"

That's my cue to ask the most important question. I go there, stopping first at the pictures from the Renaissance era. Then to my target. "I've been staring at this one. It's so different. Almost looks like a game."

Vittoria can't quite hold in a laugh. "Often, we believe same."

"How do you play it?"

"Is not a game with rules. This picture. Nonna, she made it."

"Zia Elena, you are so artistic!"

She shakes her head like she understands me, but then she looks to Vittoria, who is already translating.

"*Non. Non. Non sono artistico. Solo buone idee.*"

"Good ideas, yes. And artistic." I turn back to her, give a shy smile. "Could you make one for me? Or can I scan it and make a copy or…" *Please, please, please.*

Vittoria doesn't translate. "Sorry. We keep on wall. Nonna's rule."

"Can I take a picture at least?" Maybe, by some stroke of luck, I'll get it right this time.

"Your phone is outside," Vittoria says.

Devin stands. "I'll do it."

There's little more I can ask, so I head outside to get my stuff.

Vittoria follows, pulls me into the courtyard. "Listen hard." Her voice has a completely different tone. "Do you think is coincidence you live with your Italian family? Do Nonna and I think is coincidence you ask about the picture and map? Or *il contenitore* is gone?"

I have no words.

"If you think we are so simple…" She shakes her head. "When is the time you will get us *il calice*? From your family."

"What? And which family? My family back in DC? The Rossis here?"

"*Si*." Vittoria smiles like she means to confuse me.

I am confused. "Okay, then," I feign instead. "I'm beginning to understand."

Her face softens like, suddenly, we might have a deeper connection. "Then you hear the stories? *Il colonnello*, he try to keep Giusto home. He tell Giusto about *il calice*. Giusto still not stay. Tell him, 'You come back, *il calice* still yours.'"

I nod like I've heard all this. And I don't interrupt her. I need to remember every word.

"Giusto return when *il colonnello*, he was dying." She leans closer. "Tell me. Did he then give Giusto *il calice*?"

I give a slight nod for her to continue, but Vittoria mistakes it for a yes.

"Did Giusto sell to get money? Was not in his house after he died. Not in your house."

They searched our house?

"Who knows where is it?" she says. "Your papa, your mama?"

I shake my head.

She pinches my arm. "When we need, you will help. *Capisci*? But now you stop the sneaking. Forget the map, forget the picture, forget the box, forget the key. Stay away unless… Oh! Not necessary for *il calice*. If you know the *parola d'ordine*. The word?"

What word? I give a half smile and shake my head. Let her translate it either way: no, we don't or no, we're not telling.

But she gets closer to me. Closer to my face. Closer.

187

Until I take a step back. "Look. I didn't ask for any of this. I just want what my *nonno* wanted when he came to America, to enjoy life. *La dolce vita.* He barely talked about his life in Italy, so if—"

She gestures to the patio door. Devin's coming. She leans in and whispers, "What you want no matter. When arrives the time, we work together. No is request. *Capisci?*"

Devin waves. "Your grandmother said she was tired, Vittoria."

She pastes a smile on her face. "*Si.* She wake up before the sun. Now, more sleep. She will tell you goodbye, Tessa, but when she is ready for her *pisolino*, she does her *pisolino*. I will send her your goodbyes. My parents, they come back in three days. They want to see you then."

She kisses Devin's cheeks. Then mine. Without another word, she goes back in.

CHAPTER THIRTY

Devin heads toward the gate. I don't.

I'd say I'm processing, but I can't even do that right now. Vittoria sounded so much like Anjelica. And Sofia. *I will help them,* she said. It wasn't a request. It was like another knife.

"Tess?"

Before that, Vittoria was saying that my parents and I have what? Some sort of word. A password maybe? Also, *il caliche.* I repeat it so I don't forget. *Il caliche. Il caliche. Il caliche.*

"Aren't we leaving?" Devin doubles back.

I shake out of it, grab my bag, and march past him, straight out the gate.

"Is it my imagination," Devin says, "or am I sensing a strange vibe?"

I don't stop, don't acknowledge him, don't care if I'm going the right direction. My soft place to fall has turned into a chasm of granite.

He grabs my elbow.

I shake loose. But I do stop.

"What is it? The picture? Disappointed you didn't—"

I look up at him. Start to speak. Don't.

He's tugging on his beltloop. "Sorry, but you're freaking me out."

I move to a bit of green space. Trees, a couple benches. But people too. Not safe to toss my bag and leave it.

I back up to a hedge and drop my bag to its base, my foot looped through the strap. I whisper nothing, but he picks up the cue to bend his head closer.

"They're working with the Rossis. Or against them. Or think I am. Or something. And they knew I'd be living in that hellhole of an apartment." I can barely get the words out. "My own family." For the first time, the tears come.

Devin doesn't say anything. Draws me in. Holds me. I clutch at the back of his shirt. We just stand there. I look up. He kisses me. I kiss him back. And for the moment, everything bad fades. Until it doesn't. Underneath, it's still there.

I pull away slowly. Take a breath, a quivery one. Touch his chest. "Your shirt's wet and sorta snotty." I try to laugh, but at least I've stopped crying. "You can let go now," I say.

"Not until you've told me what happened."

I sink back into him. Into a hug that's more genuine than this morning's hugs and kisses. From. My. Family. Even after I tell him what Vittoria said, he won't let me go. He just nudges my bag fully under a bush and we sit on the ground far enough away.

"Maybe this is a good thing," he says, still in hushed tones. "You now know that everyone is looking for this *il calice*." According to the app, it means chalice or goblet. Suddenly, the Rossis' love for glasses—or goblets—all makes sense.

"Or they're looking for a word inscribed on it."

"Right. But it's important or your cousins wouldn't be wandering the country to find out if your *nonno* may have pawned it. And Vittoria is pressuring you because they've had no luck."

"And that's a good thing why?"

"There may be potential to turn this new information into some sort of plan to figure out their game." He pulls out his phone. "First, we list everything we know."

But we don't know anything, not for sure. Some goblet maybe has a password. And maybe, if we get the canister and the letter together, it will spell out a message. Devin, though, is typing more than that.

I lean over, almost into my snot stain. I grab a leaf to wipe it away. He puts an arm around me, our thighs and shoulders touching so we can hear one another's whispers. I want to kiss him again. Harder.

He looks at me. I look right at him. He runs a finger down my cheek.

I desperately want to lean in, but I pull back. "You were right last night. We need to wait."

He's still looking at me. Deciding. Deciding. He finally nods and shows me his phone.

Canister/2D picture = decoder?
Letter = message
Il calice = password = for what?
Map = where we need to find the next thing?
Box with key to?

"How do you know about the box and the key?"

"The way Vittoria was baiting you earlier, it was obvious. Besides, you just told me."

We play back the recording Devin made of the "official" questions and answers in case something Vittoria or Zia Elena said means more now. But nothing stands out except for the objects Vittoria listed: photographs, jewelry, old coins, books, maps, goblets, teapots, and jewelry box, which may or may not be the same as the box I'm supposed to forget.

"If the Rossis make me steal all these things, I'm done. Maybe a professional thief or a magician could escape arrest, but me?" I shake my head. "Until Vittoria got all nasty, I wanted to tell her and Zia Elena about the Rossis so badly. With all the hugs and love, I thought maybe they could be my heroines."

"It's good you kept quiet or…"

"My parents might be dead already."

"And you wouldn't know as much as you do."

I'd scream if it wouldn't attract attention, but it comes out as a grunt. "I hate, hate, hate to think my own family set me up. Sent me to the Rossis. How can anyone want something so desperately that they resort to death threats?"

By the time we get back to the station at the Spanish Steps, we have no clue how to beat them at their game. I lean into Devin. "I hate this, but I should probably sit back and let the Rossis make the next move. Then maybe we can connect the dots."

But when I get back, I can't help myself. I go right up to Francesco. "Are you working with my family?"

His laugh is deep and full. "With them? No, no, no. Against them."

I just look at him.

"It's like this," he says. "When the pieces started falling into place, both families understood how valuable it might be to have you in Rome. And you have been a big help to Anjelica and me. Best part is, your *zia* Elena and her family have no clue how you've helped us. Or that you have at all. Trust me on it. Or not." He walks out of the room.

I stand there for a minute, hoping he'll tell me more. But he goes into his bedroom and closes the door. I'll have to wait for that next move, I guess. I head upstairs, Vittoria's menacing tone still ringing in my ears.

The truth is, she may have been intimidating in the moment, but she was a kitten compared to Anjelica and Sofia. And she gave me so much more information than I've gotten here. Not only with *il calice* and the password, but saying that it's not a coincidence I'm here with the Rossis.

Two ways to translate that. Zia Elena's side set me up here. Or the Rossis did. Even if there's a third and fourth translation, one answer is obvious now. How did I get here? It was a masterful job of recruitment. One of the families, maybe both of them, are convinced that I can lead them to *il calice*. Everything else is just details.

Francesco comes up the stairs and sticks his head in. "One more thing. Feel free to ask your parents about what Giusto received or was supposed to." He waggles the page of his sketchbook with the goblet drawing. "We won't listen in. Much."

Not happening. Not unless Sofia invades their bedroom, this time with a gun and—

I can't tempt fate like that.

> *Dear, dear Universe,*
> *Ignore that thought from just now,*
> *I'm a bit broken.*

Post that, Anjelica. I dare you.

CHAPTER THIRTY-ONE

ANJELICA ACTS AS MY ALARM CLOCK IN THE MORNING. "*È DOMEN-ica, giorno del vaticano. Alzati e risplendi!*"

I groan. I do not want to go to the Vatican with them. I don't want to go anywhere with them. Or with anyone, for that matter. I got back late after a much-needed night out, eight of us at Bright's house well after midnight. For chunks of time, my brain wasn't overheating with all the things. I didn't even ditch my bag.

"*Ah, dolcezza. Hai i postumi di una sbornia? Una* hangover?"

A hangover from a Coke and a San Pellegrino? Then again, because everyone wanted me to do a reprise of drunk Tess, I pretended for their amusement. And now, I'm thinking, for the Rossis' amusement as well.

I don't answer. Let Anjelica believe what she will. She leaves for a minute then comes right back up. "We've decided you need a day off. Quite a shock after yesterday, huh?"

Not the way she thinks. But I nod.

She tells me they're going to see the pope, as if that will absolve them. They'll call after so I can join them for lunch. "*A meno che tu non stia andando a fare un picnic.*"

Something about a picnic. I won't be going on any picnic with them, but I thank her. Not that she deserves my thanks, but I'd rather make her and Francesco feel good about their occasional acts of kindness. Maybe they'll multiply. Or not, but a person can dream.

Anjelica pats me on the shoulder. I dive back under the pillow to wait for her to leave, but apparently, she's doing something in here. Just for a minute. Then her bare feet pad down the stairs. Finally, twenty minutes later, the front door closes behind them.

I take that as a cue to roll over and check the monkey. They hadn't bothered to uncover the vase, so last night it was the monkey's turn. I picked him up and, pretending to be drunk, I talked to him like he was an old friend, told him he looked cold. That must have given them some laughs. Then I tried to cover him up, but my shirt wouldn't stay put, so I moved the monkey to the night table then put my bag on the shelf in front of the crucifix. "To keep your spot warm, monkey, so you won't be cold next time."

My shirt is still on the monkey, and the monkey is on the night table, but my bag is off the shelf with the crucifix. And while they may have gone through my things before, this is the first time they've noticeably moved anything.

The crucifix. Figures they'd use that as a spy cam. So sacrilegious. I need to cover it with something else in an unsuspicious way. Not immediately. They'll expect my hangover to keep me down for hours. There is, however, the matter of needing to use the bathroom.

When I come back up, I'm shivering. Or making it look that way. Eyes half open, I pull a handful of clothes from the wardrobe, shove my head into a sweater, then tug it back off. I do that with a T-shirt then another and finally settle on a sweatshirt. I roll the discarded clothes in a bundle and jam it on the shelf in front of the crucifix.

If I've guessed right, they'll be totally infuriated that they can't watch me. Too bad, so sad. If I've guessed wrong, I'm in deep trouble for what I'm about to do, especially if they have the whole apartment wired for video. I get the feeling it isn't. They're almost always down here when I am.

First stop, the office. If they still have the canister, it's in the safe.

They won't exactly dust for fingerprints, but I tuck my hand inside my sweatshirt and give the handle a tug. Locked. And I can't begin to guess the combination.

The shallow desk drawer contains a small pad of paper, pens, paper clips, and rubber bands. I hold the pad of paper sideways to the light. My dad made me watch this movie, *North by Northwest*, where the main guy lightly rubs a pencil over a pad of paper and discovers where the woman is heading. She pressed hard enough that her writing left an indentation. Not here. If I'd watched more movies like that with my dad, maybe I'd know what to do next.

Instead, I trust my instincts. In the living room, there's nothing behind the pictures and nothing tacked to the undersides of the sofas and tables. Then again, small things like that would be in the safe.

Even so, I check their bedroom night tables and wardrobe,

and the pockets in their clothes. There's not even a grocery list. Everything must be in the safe or on their devices. I don't dare mess with the devices. They probably track log ons too.

I won't find anything in the bathroom that I haven't already seen unless Anjelica is hiding something in her tub of moisturizer. So, I end up in the kitchen where they don't seem to care what I open or where I look.

I get an orange from the refrigerator, pour some coffee they left for me, put a roll on a plate, and sit down. In Anjelica's seat. For spite. Not Francesco's.

He's been nice to me. As nice as a threat can be. And we connected a little with our sketching.

I slide out his journal from under the picture to see what he's drawn since the ostrich—Anjelica was kidding him about occasionally putting his head in the sand—but it's the last thing in his little book. I close it up and place it exactly where it was with the sugar packet covering half the O in *Diario*. For two seconds.

This time, I start at the beginning. Many of his sketches were inspired by things Anjelica said while we were sitting here. Others, random scrawls and squiggles. That shelf of goblets, which suddenly makes sense. A few grocery lists embellished with more doodles. I'm almost to the ostrich and have mentally given up. Sketch of a library. Next page. Open book with squiggles. Next...

Pay dirt!

This page is basically a flowchart, an illustrated list of everything they're making me do. Or will make me do. It starts with the canister. Then the picture. An arrow points down to seemingly random letters.

B F H L A…

I assume the ellipsis means there are more in the sequence. Next is what looks like a map, but it has a big question mark over it. Then a box with a key lying inside. Sitting on top of that is a goblet inscribed with the letters *p.w.* Password? It's *password* in Italian too. Vittoria's *parola d'ordine.*

That verifies it. *Il calice* has some type of password. Not for a computer file, though. People didn't have computers when Nonno left Italy. I try to put myself into the mind of *il colonnello.* He might have used a code word, as spies do, to identify their contacts. But that's movie stuff. Not that this whole business couldn't be.

Concentrate, Tess.

It's hard, though, when all the answers seem to drift overhead like a cloud just out of reach. But every new thought seems to lure it a millimeter closer.

Okay. If Francesco's picture is complete, Vittoria and her family have everything except the box and *il calice.* Unless they don't have the letter from the museum office.

Switching families… The Rossis used the canister to decode the letter, which probably led to *B F H L A,* etc. What they don't have is the map Vittoria said to forget.

Sorry, Vittoria, I can't forget something that's decoupaged on a vase, printed on soft paper, and is part of Francesco's flowchart.

Wait. How do the Rossis know all this? Do they also know about Zia Elena's map? Doubtful. Otherwise, they would have made me steal that too.

I shake my head. If the Rossis and my Italian family would work together, they'd probably have everything they'd need. Except *il calice*. Which, apparently, I'm supposed to have. Or my parents are.

A smile creeps over my face. I may be the only one who can get what both sides want. And if I stay that valuable, everyone stays alive.

CHAPTER THIRTY-TWO

It's like I've had a mental shot of espresso. Suddenly, I realize that even now, without *il calice*, I have value.

My value to Zia Elena's side is the letter. Before I'd even consider giving them a copy, I need to know what it says. I could translate it with my devices and immediately delete, but one tentacle or another might be monitoring in real time.

My value to the Rossis, besides being their personal bitch, must be the map, assuming the nightstand map is THE map. Maybe it was once in a book—Francesco's drawing—but I haven't seen a book with that kind of paper in Italy or ever. I need to compare both versions of the map.

I don't have them. Devin does. But the more it's just the two of us, the more reason for the Rossis to cause another "accident." I can't go to his house. Or I could without my phone and bag, but if the Rossis come home, I'm dead. Now what?

I reach for my phone like it might have a solution. It actually does.

Hours ago, Nicolas texted Devin, Bright, and me. We're going on a picnic! No excuses!

So, that's what Anjelica meant earlier. Lunch with them unless I'm going on a picnic.

In the next text, Nicolas lists everything he's bringing. Devin added to the list and said to meet at his house—there's a good park nearby. Bright texted back with a head-explosion emoji. Apparently, she's the one with the hangover. But she'll come. JUST DON'T SHOUT.

Before I respond, I shower and dress to make it seem that I've been sleeping until now. I get permission, then I'm off to Devin's fifteen minutes earlier than necessary.

AdDad meets me at the door and greets me like we're family. I've been there enough. Devin is in his room, AdDad says, and I'm free to go back as long as we keep the door open. He winks.

"You're early!" Devin gives me a quick hug.

I gesture for something to write with. "I thought I might fall back to sleep if I stayed in bed any longer." Doesn't hurt to feed the story.

While he talks about last night, he hands me his phone.

I type. Print pix of vase map & map on nightstand pls

While he's fetching the printouts, I write part two of my request. Also need to translate letter. Can I use yr computer?

He raises his eyebrow. "Already did."

"You what?"

He tugs me out of his room, away from my bag. "Eventually, you would have asked. I thought I'd be expedient." He goes back to trigger the printer again.

202

This time I follow. I point to the computer, shake my head. Pull him out of the room. "You cannot keep that on your computer, Mr. Expedient."

"Who'll see it? My family here doesn't bother my things. And my computer is always with me at school."

"Until it's not. Just five minutes away from it, and Signor Matteo might see everything. Or plant some sort of spyware so the Rossis can. You saw the napkin Friday night. You know what he did to me and what Sofia did to Carly." I stand there until he deletes then empties the computer's trash bin. I search his computer for one of the words and nothing comes up. I'm not one hundred percent sure it's gone, but it would take some expertise to find it.

"Satisfied?" He hands me one copy of the printout.

I am not satisfied that he has another. But he shows me how he maneuvers folded papers through a two-inch rip in the lining of a jacket he won't wear, he says, until he gets back on the plane. And no reason for anyone here to go through his things.

I sit on the edge of his bed, the maps next to me. They are definitely the same. Now, the translation of the letter. I get through the first three lines when AdDad announces that Nicolas is here. Without a word, Devin walks out and closes the door behind him.

To My Children,

All of you are receiving this same message, but not all of you are receiving the same letter. One day, this will make sense to you.

Today, however, I have a question. Do you remember the song we used to sing, the one about Raffaello?

The prince of painters, Raffaello, he painted
    such glorious scenes.
The men, the women, the babies.
The angels, the graces, and the most holy.
Our beautiful, wonderful Raffaello.

I often sang that to myself when the war was turning bleak. One day, after I learned of my new orders, I added a verse.

The prince of painters, Raffaello, he painted
    such glorious scenes.
There came along those to take them away
To places they shouldn't have been.
Our beautiful, wonderful Raffaello.

I often think of our own Raffaello, my firstborn, who fought valiantly but met with his untimely death during a war which has triggered many feuds within our family. Knowing I played a part in this makes it all the more difficult to do what I must.

In my mighty position in the army, I was able to collect a goodly share of spoils from the war. Italian spoils belong in Italy, not Germany. I put these spoils in a safe place, under lock and key, to remain until the world has forgotten about their existence. This was to be your inheritance, one which would allow you and your children and your children's children to want for nothing. Now, however, for as long as the feud continues, you will receive nothing.

When death has silenced my ears from your fighting, I will bequeath each family one of four objects that, when put together, will lead to the whereabouts of my treasure. The fifth piece, our dear Raffaello's, is with our trusted and inseparable friend, the shopkeeper I call The Mountain. You must always keep your object in your family until one glorious day when you or your descendants find a way to reunite peacefully.

Given time, that is my hope. Should that not happen, let this personal war ruin your lives, and let the treasure forever rot where it lies.

With love and hope,
The Colonel

Maybe it's just a story, but it sounds so real that—
An icy shudder runs the full length of my body.
If everything in the letter is true, I may be related to the Rossis.

CHAPTER THIRTY-THREE

I SLIDE FROM THE BED TO THE FLOOR, PRESSING ON MY TEMPLES, hoping to put the pieces of my exploded brain back together. And trying to bury myself inside any bit of logic that proves I am not related to them.

Maybe I'm not. If the Colonel's letter belongs to Anjelica's sister-in-law or someone else in that office, I'm not blood-related to the Rossis. And… I don't really believe that.

First, the Rossis *and* Zia Elena's side are clawing to get all the objects in the letter, which probably makes us one big, dysfunctional family. Second, Anjelica's brother could have hidden the letter in his wife's office for safekeeping, which still has me related to all the Rossis. Third, and totally objective, the woman at the airport juice bar mistook Sofia and me for sisters. Genes don't lie.

Genes are strong too. The Rossis made me steal. I stole. And I was pretty good at it. But gene pool or not, I refuse to let those acts define me. I'm still who I am. And I'm not a criminal.

I make peace with that for the moment and concentrate on the facts.

The Colonel, for certain, was Nonno's dad. He had five children. According to Vittoria, Nonno was to get *il calice*. Zia Elena got the canister. Or the map. How does she have both? And who got the letter?

Focus. Facts only.

I now know that Nonno's brother, Raffaello, died in the war. By process of elimination, he was to get the box. That leaves two more siblings. A sister, Agostina, died semi-young. Let's say she got the map and left it to Zia Elena. That leaves the letter and the last sister. Vittoria said her name, Rosa. I have no clue what happened to—

Rosa. Signora Roma. They could be the same person.

Suddenly, every bit of logic says that my parents and I are being held captive by blood relatives who may be no better than black widow spiders who kill and eat their mates once they're done with them.

Francesco is right. I need to talk to my dad, because if some goblet can get us out of this, and if my dad has *il calice*—

My breath fully leaves my body. My dad. Arsenio. All those phone calls, all those conversations encouraging me to apply. Staying on me until I did.

Dad. Tell me you did not put me through this hell.

I desperately try to shake that idea, but having been blindsided by the Rossis and Vittoria and Signor Matteo...

I push through and summon more rational thoughts. If my

parents owned some important goblet, they would have sent me here with it. Or they would have come here themselves without the charade of having me attend an exchange program. A vacation might have been cheaper. Besides, they worry about me way too much to put me in this kind of danger.

I open my locket. "Nonno, if you're listening, help me find *il calice*. Please." I close my eyes as if I might get a vision, but all I see is darkness. I sit with that for a minute.

Once enough of this panic feathers away, I open my eyes to the maps, both of Ostia Antica, where Zia Elena would go with her parents. The nightstand map first. I study it from the center to the right to the... How did I miss this before? A line of small, careful handwriting down its side.

6 PASSI A OVEST—2 PASSI A NORD

Six steps west and two steps north, but where's the starting point? From the map, it seems, Ostia Antica has acres and acres of potential hiding spots, the reason no one has found...whatever, which must be an impossible task without every piece of the Colonel's puzzle.

The Rossis still need more than this map, so my crime spree will continue. When it does, how I'd love to get up in Anjelica's face and tell her everything I know, prove to her and Sofia and Francesco that I, Tess Alessandro, have some power. But there's still the matter of getting my parents to safety.

I slide the printouts, plus the papers from my Chucks, into the lining of Devin's jacket. Except one. I keep the Italian version of the letter in case, somehow, I can access the canister.

Then with "my phone call" done, Nicolas, Devin, and I head to Villa Sciarra, a historic mansion built in the 1500s on grounds where, legend has it, Julius Caesar hosted Cleopatra on her visit to Rome. The house, with its pale pinkish hue and multiple stories, may be impressive anywhere else, but it's not as large as Villa Borghese, and the grounds aren't as rich. Best part, though, I won't need to break in and steal anything.

We go past a fountain to settle under some trees not too far off the road so that Bright can find us when she gets here.

In one shopping bag, Nicolas has brought all the nonfood items for our picnic. In the other, containers of olives, grilled veggies, and cold pasta. Mostly, he brought Stromboli, two types. The dough in one is filled with salami, prosciutto, olives, sun-dried tomatoes, and cheese. The other is vegetarian because, on some days, Bright claims she is. We set that out on the blanket and save whatever pastries Devin brought for later.

By the time we've almost decimated the food and have set up a game of Jenga, which was at the bottom of Nicolas's bag of nonfood items, Bright finally shows up in dark sunglasses. She jumps right into the game and grazes Devin's shoulder each time she pulls out a piece, as if that will stop the wooden tower from tumbling down.

"If I knock it over," she says more than once, "it's because I should be sleeping this off."

It's obvious she wouldn't have come if I weren't here. And probably why she's so friendly with me. She either sees me as her way to get Devin or she wants to prevent me from making some huge move. Or prevent him from the same. Too late.

I smile about that. Also, for a second reason. If Bright were another tentacle, the Rossis would have demanded she get here on time.

Bright tugs at her hair with one hand and pulls out a Jenga piece with the other. And the walls tumble down.

"Oh man!" says Nicolas. "We should have run odds on this. I would have bet so hard that you'd be the one who did that, Bright."

She pushes him. "You shithead. No faith in me. Ever."

"No faith in you in this condition." He lifts her sunglasses up then drops them back down before she can get mad. "Another round? But I promise. I won't pick you to—" He looks up just as I get a tap on my shoulder.

It's Francesco, fully helmeted. He waves to my friends and beckons me.

My stomach drops. My bag is right here. I told them where I'd be. What did I do? "Back in a minute," I manage. And I follow him to the street about a hundred yards away.

Anjelica is leaning against the motorcycle. "Having fun?"

"I was."

She laughs and hands me ten euros attached to a note. "Surprise. This is legal. On your way home, stop here and get a copy of this. And you can keep the change." They speed off.

It may be legal, but for whatever reason, they don't want to be connected with this either.

Devin gives a great smile when I'm back within sight. That doesn't get past Bright, who leans her head on his shoulder.

He pats her head then stands. "Everything okay?"

"Yeah. They asked me to grab a book for them at a bookstore. It's walking distance from here, and they're running late."

Bright scrunches her nose. "How'd he find you? It took me like forever to track you down."

I hold back a smile. Finally, one little slipup. It's their fault that Bright seems suspicious. I can justify any answer I give her, but I can't go rogue—not until my parents are out of danger. "Maybe," I safely say, "I give better directions than Devin does."

The guys finish up the remaining bits of lunch, then we dive into the *bombolone*, Italian cream-filled doughnuts, before we head out.

The used bookstore has three copies of the title they want—it's on Ostia Antica—but Anjelica gave me only enough money for one. Which one? I start paging through the first.

Bright grabs my sleeve. "Buy it already."

I launch into another lie, how my mom once bought a used book, which had hilarious comments plus a twenty-dollar bill as a bookmark. "That's why I'm looking."

In the end, the books are identical. And when I get back, the Rossis don't even squirrel it away. They thank me and set dinner out—apparently *cacio e pepe* is a Sunday-night thing for them—then, like a normal family, we watch funny videos until well after dark. They are in as giddy a mood as I've seen. I say good night, and as I'm halfway up the stairs, Anjelica is still gushing. "Cornelio is a genius! Sunday in St. Peter's Square, we were blessed."

I smile because when all is said and done, I have to wonder exactly how blessed their afterlives will be.

I lie back on the bed and check in with my parents, where everything is going swimmingly, or so they think. Aunt Debbie and Uncle Dale are back after a long weekend in Delaware. Carly is recuperating at home. Sofia is an angel. "I'm sure she's something, Dad."

I'm about to click off, but that one ridiculous, paranoid thought won't leave me alone. I need to know that my dad has no role in this nightmare. I weigh each word before I speak.

"I've told you about my BFF Bright," I start. "Well, she was arguing that sometimes parents have kids to make them their built-in servants."

My parents start to protest, but not overly so.

"Also," I say, "she sometimes thinks she was born—and really, I don't feel like this, so wait till I'm finished—but she was born for cocktail-party conversation and not because her parents really wanted a kid." Actually, that wasn't Bright. It was another girl in our class. "Do we know people like that?"

"That's so sad." My mom looks at my dad, who's also shaking his head.

"If I knew those people, I'd divorce them from my life immediately. And now, I just want to give you a hug." He reaches out a hand. "Sofia's great, but it's not like having you here."

It's not their words, but their whole beings that reinforce what I knew to be true, that they sent me here because they wanted the best for me.

"One more thing," I say, again being careful. "I should have asked Zia Elena yesterday, but why, exactly, did Nonno leave Italy?"

My dad rubs his chin. "We've talked about that."

"Not in depth. Just that he left for a reason, something bad."

"Which is why he didn't like to talk about it. There was one specific instance. His father was dying, and Nonno decided he needed to see him one last time. How he dreaded that trip!"

My dad gazes off at something. He finally looks back. "I was about ten years old then, but I can still see him packing his bags and shaking his head. 'It's impossible to look in the face of that thief,' Nonno said, 'and pretend everything is okay.'"

"What did his father steal?" I ask.

"I asked him then. And he just said, 'I don't want anything from that thief. I don't need anything from that thief of a father.'"

Great. And now I'm a thief... *Nonno, forgive me.*

"I wish I'd paid attention whenever he talked about his child-hood," my dad continues. "I especially wish I'd pestered him and Nonna with all the questions before they died. And I'd kept pester-ing until they answered. So let that be a lesson to you. Even if I don't have answers, ask the questions. In fact, while you're there, make sure you pester Zia Elena, but nicely. She has answers." He gives his classic wink. "And report back to me."

"You can count on it." Once I hang up, my questions fly in three thousand different directions, but I settle on the newest one. Why did the Rossis have me buy a four-euro book? I'm hoping it's because they're stumped. They have no next move. And I'm done. Free.

But I'm not delusional.

Unless they plan to vanish into thin air, no way are they finished with me yet. And I can't be finished with them until they send me in search of the next piece of their family's puzzle.

No. It's *my* family's puzzle.

CHAPTER THIRTY-FOUR

IT'S THAT FIRST MONDAY MORNING ALL OVER AGAIN. EXCEPT it's Tuesday, it's not as early, and I'm not shocked silent when they force me to the kitchen where Sofia, onscreen, hovers over my parents. This time, though, she has no knife, no lighter, no nothing, at least from appearances.

"They had such a nice meal a few hours ago. I made them tortellini with pesto. They loved it! And they loved the drug-laced tiramisu even more. See how happy they look."

"Thank you for making them happy," I say.

"Ooh. Good job. Sarcasm without a sarcastic tone." She lifts her hand into the picture and drips fluid from an eyedropper into a bottle.

"Bravo, Sofia. What's next on your murder-weapon hit list?" But she's already gone.

Anjelica grabs my hair, though.

"Okay, I get it."

She pulls harder, digs her nails into the nape of my neck. I don't give her the satisfaction of wincing. When she finally lets go, I pull a tissue from my pocket to wipe away the blood, and I rub a squirt of sanitizer across my neck. The alcohol in it stings like hell, but I just smile.

"And that," she says, pointing to the bloody tissue, "was without even trying."

Francesco takes a step between us. "We need to make sure you get the point."

"I got it the first time and the second time and all the times."

"Maybe you're not as slow as we thought." Anjelica yanks me to the bathroom, now with her nails digging into my wrists. No blood, though.

The lipstick writing on the mirror lists a university library plus the title and Dewey Decimal number of a different book about Ostia Antica. Once I've memorized it, she wipes it away. "Do not check it out. Have it to us by seven o'clock tonight. You'll have plenty of time after school."

I wait several seconds until it's clear that she doesn't have anything like a bag or a sweater to help me smuggle a book through the sensors without them going off. "Am I allowed to bring friends with me?" I finally ask.

"Devin again?" she says.

"I said *friends*, as in multiple."

"Probably a good idea." She runs a fingernail across the front of her neck, like she's scratching it. She's not.

At lunch, I pull Devin aside. "Busy after class? Got an assignment." We've nearly finished putting together a plan to steal the book just as Bright pops up. Nicolas behind her.

"What are you two plotting?" She looks directly at Devin.

"How to convince you to come with us this afternoon," he says. "University library."

Time to lie again. "My cousin wants me to prove that libraries here use the Dewey Decimal System. I mean we could just go to this library, but it'd be cool to say we started our college search in Rome then buy a sweatshirt or something from the school store to prove it."

I actually might. I used the fake credit card only that once at the Forum. And Anjelica and/or Francesco have used mine, I've found, to buy my sweater and little purse, plus toiletries and snacks that I might ordinarily use. Sort of. I don't like pork rinds, but I "bought" them for a friend who got our coffees. Lies, lies, lies. But Bright's in. Nicolas too.

It's all fun and laughs on the walk, but my adrenaline spikes as we reach the university grounds. I need to get this over with. Bright, though, insists that we stop at the school store first.

"And your wish," Nicolas says, "is our command." He taps her with his pencil wand, and she pushes him away. But with a huge smile.

"Maybe your command, Nicolas." I laugh. "For me, it's business first." I veer toward the library, and Devin follows, which means we all go.

"It's just two seconds, a bunch of pictures, and we leave," Bright says. "Right?"

Nicolas puts an arm around her. "What do you have against libraries except that there's so many foreign words in this one?"

She pushes him away then bumps back into him.

When we get inside, predictably, the three of them follow me like we're glued together. I already planned for that. I stop and gasp.

Nicolas pats me on the back. "Did you inhale a fly?"

"No. An idea," I say. "Totally un-gasp-worthy, but I got inspired yesterday. As long as we're here, I'm gonna look for books on ancient ruins. For my personal project."

"Ooh! Me too!" Bright says. "But not ruins. Research! I mean it'd be better if we were in Milan, but I'm definitely doing mine on the fashion industry." She finds that Dewey Decimal section on her phone and heads over there.

Then Nicolas goes in search of mythology books. Devin heads a fourth way but doubles back to the nine hundreds.

The section on ancient civilizations is toward the far back. So many titles. I scan the spines, inching closer to 937.6, but Anjelica, in her twisted gameplay, did not give me whatever numbers come after .6.

"She's probably enjoying this," I whisper to Devin.

He nods. "But two heads and all that."

He starts combing through the 937.6 books on the top shelf, and I go through the lowest one. Then we move to the two in the middle. I shake my head. So does he.

Before we start checking one another's shelves, I move my bag five sections away from us. "This time," I say, my voice still low, "tilt out one book at a time so we don't accidentally skip any of them." We both do. Nothing again.

And *nothing* will have Sofia dripping poison into my parents' mouths and them waking up just long enough to writhe in agony.

"What if it's checked out? Or missing forever?" Devin sounds as panicky as I feel. "What do we do now?"

I close my eyes and press my temples, trying to obliterate the terrifying buzz that's invaded my brain. *Think, Tess, think.*

My mind clears just enough to think out loud. "For my other, um, missions, Anjelica and Francesco were completely calculating and gave me what I needed. The bag, the sweater."

"Nothing today?" Devin asks.

I shake my head. "Which means I don't need anything. The book has to be here, which means no one checked it out. And if you don't want someone to check out a book…"

"You hide it," Devin finishes.

We take out each volume, looking between them, behind them, inside them. Top shelf, nothing. Bottom shelf, still nothing. He takes the top middle. I take the bottom middle, my fingertips shaking a little more with each book I put back.

Next book, no. Next book, no. Next—

This book is on Abraham Lincoln, and it's not 937.6. It's 973.6. I open the cover and, immediately, there's a separation in the pages about one-third of the way through.

Tucked inside is another book about the size of a paperback if paperbacks were only twenty-five pages or so. I nudge Devin and have him touch the cover. "Feel familiar?"

He shakes his head.

"It's the same paper as the letter. Also, the nightstand map." I sigh. "Except for this." The security sensor strip is firmly and fully attached to the inside cover.

"We've known that would be a problem," he says. "But the book is so small, perhaps, if you photographed the pages—"

I shake my head before he can finish. "They're expecting me to steal it, I'm sure. It's part of their power play."

"I suppose that calling to ask is out of the question."

"They'll want to lock this in their safe if only to make sure that Zia Elena never sees it. But what don't they want her to see?"

I turn the pages. Folded, and bound into the middle, is the same map that Zia Elena has. With two differences. No handwritten directions. And it's the only part of the book that's not soft paper. It's as if Zia Elena took out the map and replaced it with a decoy. Go Zia Elena!

I turn the remaining pages in case there's something else. Nearly at the end, sideways near the binding, is one handwritten marking: **G-7**.

That could be map coordinates and the starting point for those paces. If it were C-1, I'd change C to a G and the one to a four and really make life hard for them. Then again, they probably have something that would detect the changes and *Ciao!* to a decent life. Or any life at all.

I slip the book inside my journal. Not only does it fit perfectly, but I can easily stretch the journal's elastic band so that everything stays put. Now to escape.

Devin moves to another section and picks up a book on traditional Italian pastries. Just steps away, he grabs another that's displayed face out, its cover with a Maserati and a Ferrari.

I need to say something so the Rossis know I'm not hiding from them. "Your project, Devin? Cars? Food? Which one?"

"I'm working a plan for a chain of drive-through bakeries."

"Where only Maseratis and Ferraris are allowed?"

"Brilliant! Pastries for the ultrarich! That's my project!"

Bright and Nicolas are near the 100s, waiting for us.

"About time," she says. Then she grabs Devin's car book. "Ooh! I'll bet you have both of these back in London."

He smiles and shakes his head, his eyebrow rising. Really? What else does he have? Polo ponies? A country castle? Later, though. We need to get out of here.

We near the entrance, and I reach for his pastry book. That's the plan: me, in deep conversation, mistakenly walking out with a book. And when the sensors sound, I'll go, "Oh, I'm so absent-minded!" I'll hand my book to Devin, who's standing on the library side of the sensor, then we'll get out of there.

Devin, though, moves both books to his other hand where I'd have to make a play to get them. Normally, it'd be sweet, but this is no time for chivalry. And he's lagging back to let Bright catch up, which she does immediately in full chat mode.

Nicolas moves up to me and starts talking about which Roman gods he might use for his project. We near the exit and he's saying Vulcan something and Vesta something and, suddenly, we're way too far in front of Devin and Bright.

I stop. Turn.

"What?" Nicolas says.

I point to a guy. "He looks like someone I know, but it can't be. He's in Wyoming now."

Wyoming? Where did that come from?

Doesn't matter. Devin is now just a quarter step behind as we reach the exit.

Ever so slightly, I swing my bag back so that it's as even with him as I can make it. Three steps, two steps...

Here goes. *Bzzz! Bzzz! Bzzz!*

I'm ahead of Devin, who's just beyond the sensor. I stop. Point to myself. *"Sono io?"*

"Oopsies," Bright said. She and Devin both have books. "We were just talking away!"

Devin laughs. "Looks like it." Then he gets all serious to the library attendant who's rushed forward. He hands her the books and gushes out an apology.

I should have walked ahead, but I didn't. Nicolas and I are still standing way too close. The attendant comes out. *"Hai anche dei libri?"*

We shake our heads. Nicolas pats himself down. No more books. I point to my bag and asks if she wants to look.

I should have walked away. But I step toward her, open my bag, pull out my journal, and tell her this is the only book I have. I point to the word *Journal* on the cover. *"Il mio diario."*

"Si, si. American?"

Nicolas, suddenly our spokesman, explains how we're on an exchange program, that I'm from DC, Bright is from New York, he's from Chicago, but Devin is from London. And for the person who's often the quietest among us, he gets even chattier. If I didn't know better, I'd think he was hiding something. Then again, he could have put a book on Roman gods down his pants. I had a picture down mine the other day.

They finish their conversation and we're out the door.

"When did you get so chatty, Nicolas?" Bright asks.

"I was worried for you and Devin," he says. "Did you see that documentary? The American college student, falsely imprisoned here?"

Devin laughs. "I didn't, but Tess did, and apparently it scared the snot out of you too."

We get to the school store, and we shop around for the better part of an hour. Bright insists we each buy a sweatshirt then further insists that none of them match. "We don't want to look like a team especially if one of us is a kleptomaniac." She gives Devin a shove.

"Look who's talking," Devin says.

I'm grateful for the joking. I'm also grateful for the sweatshirt. It's turned drizzly. And by the time I get back to the apartment, my shirt underneath is the only thing that's dry. I hand my bag to Anjelica.

As usual, she pulls out my notebook and my journal. *"Dov'è il libro?"*

I open my journal.

"Molto intelligente!" She also compliments me on getting Devin all distracted. Apparently, they were listening.

I don't bother to tell her that it happened organically. The more clever they think I am, the more they'll respect me. Maybe. Doubtfully.

Anjelica tugs at my sweatshirt sleeve and tells me to take it off. I have no clue whether she thinks it's hers because I used their credit card or she's mad because it proves where I was.

Whatever. If she wants to take it from me, she can have it. I'll choose another battle, one that means something.

It turns out, though, that she just wants to dry it for me. "*Una mano lava l'altra.*" She gives me a truly genuine smile.

One hand washes the other? I smile back as if I appreciate the sentiment, but I really want to ask when this policy—"I do for you, you do for me"—started. I stole a canister. She did nothing for me. I stole a letter. She did nothing for me. Sure, she gave me things I needed to succeed, but afterward, nothing. What makes the book different?

I freeze. And I know. This is the calm before the storm. The next task must be absolutely devastating.

I need to get ahead of this.

CHAPTER THIRTY-FIVE

My alarm keeps chiming, and I can't seem to turn it off. I finally open my eyes enough to stop the noise. They must have drugged me again, because I can't remember it's Wednesday until I check my phone. Then it takes me another long beat to remember where I am and what's going on today. Devin is bringing the nightstand map to school to show me where G-7 lands.

The big danger is keeping it hidden from Signor Matteo and any other tentacles there.

Funny, but Signor Matteo doesn't seem like the dangerous type. He doesn't have the same killer look behind his smile that the Rossis or Signora Roma or Il Creepo have. Whatever. He's still a snake.

And there he is, the first person to greet me right outside the school building. I drop my bag and pull him aside. "Why are you doing this to me?"

"Doing what?"

"Spying. Drugging my drink. Whatever else I haven't seen. What do they have on you?"

His cheeks go pale. "I do not understand."

"Yes, you do, so talk," I say. "It's safe. They listen through my bag, way over there."

He shakes his head and adjusts his glasses.

"Fine. I'll call in an anonymous tip to the police. That you roofied me, gave me the date rape drug. And that you've molested at least five girls. Do you understand? Or do we need a translator?"

"No, no, please." He holds up his hands like a pair of stop signs. "Is like this," he says. "One time, Cornelio, he help me out of trouble."

Maybe that's Il Creepo, but the name doesn't matter. I motion for him to keep talking.

"He say, 'I do this and you will help me one day.' Then he come to me with your picture and tell me that you are a special guest of his family. That we will make room for you in school this summer. Make room for you and his niece Sofia, exchange partner. And I will watch you."

I just nod.

"I do not want to make trouble for you. I make sure what I give you not harm. But please, I have two children. Girls. Like you." He's near tears.

I look up. Someone moves from a window. Great. If he's not the only spy here, I might have just made life unbearable for him and his daughters. I need to fix it.

"Keep doing whatever they ask you. But if it's harmful, find a way to alert me, okay?"

He nods.

Now, the fix. "Today, you will see me with a piece of paper at lunch. You will tell them. Understand? They will appreciate you. Then if I need help later, you will help me. Okay?"

The fear in his eyes grows.

"No, no. I will not hurt you. I will not hurt your family. I will not go to the police about you unless I have no choice." I point to myself. "They threaten to hurt me and my family too. And if I really need you, I hope you'll help, but only if it's safe. *Capisci?*"

"I understand." He smiles and puts an arm around my shoulder. "*Grazie.*"

I go to sit at the side of the school, but the grass is still damp from yesterday. Instead, I lean against a tree, figuring out what I could possibly draw that might jolt the Rossis into slipping up and filling in some of my blanks.

It takes a few minutes of no ideas before I fish out the good-luck purple pen I found at the gelato shop and a piece of green printer paper I salvaged from a recycling bin. In the middle of the page, much more crudely than my usual, I sketch the canister, picture frame, and book with the letters O. A. Above, slightly smaller, a star, key, and purse. Underneath, a car, flag and, in the larger size again, a map.

I shove that into my bag, throw the pen into the trash, praying I'm not throwing away any luck I have left, and stroll toward the school's entrance. When Devin sees me, we go back around the side, I slip out the drawing, then I launch my bag farther back on the grounds.

He gives a laugh. "Aren't you afraid they'll see the wear and tear?"

"I'd come back with something equally funny, but no time." I show him the folded piece of paper. "At lunch, when we get up for food, I'll be dropping this near my place. It goes against your breeding, I know, and remind me to ask you about your Ferrari later, but do not be a gentleman. Do not pick it up for me." I explain why.

He nods. "My turn." He opens his notebook to the pictures of both the maps. "I looked at these again last night, and well, notice one crucial difference."

I don't at first, not until I look for G-7. On the vase map, the number and letter guides along the top and the side are in numeric and alphabetical order. On the nightstand map, though, the C is where the G should be, and vice versa. "Well then," I say. "The Rossis can't use any old map of the place. They need the nightstand map. Or what we know about it."

"And you're not about to tell them."

"Only when I need to."

"Wait. What?" he says.

"I mean if I need to. If they force me."

He nods like he believes me. And he expects me to go on, but if I talk too soon, I might chase away a sudden sliver of a plan that hangs, again, like a cloud, just out of reach. This map info, though, has moved it a centimeter closer.

We head to class, my mind circling. With the book in their hands, the Rossis probably believe they now have the map. But if they go to Ostia Antica and search near G-7, they'll hit a dead end. So, they need *the* map and, according to Francesco's sketch, they also need the box with the key. Plus, a password for it, which my parents may or may not have.

I spend half the morning imagining three thousand scenarios, each using the map info as a bargaining chip. The ideas range from finding a way to threaten the Rossis, to begging for mercy, to pretending that I want a piece of whatever riches they find at the end. But every single plan ends with the same conclusion: Just because I give them something they need, *una mano lava l'altra,* there's no guarantee that Sofia will leave without killing my parents.

CHAPTER THIRTY-SIX

I NEED TO GET SOFIA OUT OF THERE. PREFERABLY IN HANDCUFFS, but I'll settle for out of my house, on a plane, out of the country with an ocean between her and the United States.

That will take more than switched letters on a map. It'll take even more information. Ideally, the decoded letter.

If the Rossis were reasonable people, we could strike a deal, the map for ten minutes with the canister. But I'm too smart to trust that they'd carry out their part of the bargain.

I revisit my mental list, which has turned into a chant. The canister reveals the message hidden in the letter. The map and the book lead to G-7 in Ostia Antica. The word on *il calice* and whatever's in the box…

I shake my head.

Even if I miraculously found *il calice* and this Mountain man who has some box, there's another hurdle. Ostia Antica is the size of nearly one hundred football fields. One hundred fifty squares on the grid. It could take days to find the exact location within G-7. And even if I get lucky, how the hell can we excavate an important historic site without being arrested? All that swirls in a vicious circle and won't let up.

Today's class topic is food, yet I barely pay attention, not even at lunch. They've arranged an extra-long buffet to reflect the evolution of popular Roman cuisine from ancient times through now, Signor Matteo tells us. He has us gathered around for a culinary tour of sorts. Soon, he wraps it up and opens the lunch line.

I catch his eye then go to my table to "find" the drawing I dropped. Signor Matteo strolls by, phone in hand. I barely notice him taking pictures. He's that smooth.

I crumple up the paper and start to throw it away, but I slip it into my bag in case this "evidence" might prove valuable. Or at least lifesaving.

When I get back to the apartment, Anjelica is drumming her fingernails on the table. She swivels the screen toward me. There are two pictures. A full shot of me holding the paper and a close-up of it in my hands.

"*Spiega questo!*"

"Is it okay if I explain in English?"

She huffs out a breath. "Are you never going to learn Italian?"

"Really? Is that what you want to know?"

"My. Aren't we getting huffy?"

Sarcasm will do me no good. "Sorry. I'm really, really tired."

She motions for me to go on, and before I can say another word, Francesco joins us.

"We're about to get a juicy story," Anjelica says. "Let's see her talk her way out of this."

If Signor Matteo ratted me out...

I can't get defensive—not until there's something to be defensive about. I stick to what I rehearsed. "We were in the lunchroom, which you already know somehow. Maybe you've embedded a camera and a microphone in my forehead."

I get a real laugh from that one.

"Anyway, the topic of the day was the evolution of Italian food. Signor Matteo had us gather around the buffet line to explain what we'd be eating."

"Thrilling," Anjelica says.

"When he was done, he invited us to get in line—stayed up there to serve the *Bolognese*—but I went back to my seat to get a tissue. My friends saved my spot." I'm careful to keep their whereabouts clear so Anjelica and Francesco can't possibly suspect them or Signor Matteo. "You saw what I found by my seat." I dig into my bag. "I was going to throw it away but thought you might ask about it."

Francesco takes it from my hands. "Could be anything."

"That's what I thought at first, then it scared me. Who else knows what I'm doing?" I point to the middle row.

Francesco and Anjelica look at one another then don't know where to look, as if they're rattled. Finally.

Francesco recovers first and pulls up something on his phone. "Not Matteo. Even his bad sketches are better than this." He nods toward me. "Hers too."

Good. I didn't implicate Signor Matteo or myself.

"If he had his daughter draw it…" Anjelica shakes her head.

"No," Francesco says. "His daughter would be a prodigy. She's only three. The other one is a baby."

Whew.

"Or…" Francesco combs through my bag, puts it down, then looks directly at me. "Just because you can draw good, doesn't mean you can't draw bad. Where's the purple pen? Did you throw it away?" He's bluffing. He hasn't searched my pouch since I found the kaleidoscope pen.

"You've seen all my stuff," I say. "No purple pens, no purple clothes, no purple anything."

"Then you borrowed one," Anjelica says.

"I swear. I did not borrow a purple pen. And seriously, if I planned to do something like this, I'd use a generic pencil so you wouldn't grill me like this."

She looks at Francesco, the floor, the ceiling. Gets up in my face. "Who? Who knows? Him? Him? Her? All of them?" She has pictures with me, Devin, Nicolas, and Bright. Someone was watching us Sunday at the bookstore. It doesn't matter now.

I shake my head. "After what you did to Carly? No. I swear."

Angela eases back. "How is Carly, by the way? I understand she needed surgery on her arm, poor baby."

I'd simmer over, but I refuse to let her get to me. "She's doing better, thank you." And despite the turbulence in my head, I give a big grin.

"What are you smiling about?"

"I'm sort of at peace. I've learned how to compartmentalize things. I can be tortured, and I can have fun in the same day. My friends are the fun part. Why would I do anything to jeopardize them? Answer that."

Francesco gives a laugh. "We've created a monster."

I interlace my fingers and sit back with an even wider grin. "Is that all you need from me today?"

"Possibly," Anjelica says. "Dinner at eight, as usual."

That's my cue to escape upstairs, my little haven in this madness. I lie back on the bed and allow myself a real smile. Although I might not be able to trust Signor Matteo fully, there's now a better chance I can use him if I really need to. But my smile fades. Doing that could jeopardize his family. I'm like King Midas, except I might have the touch of death.

I sit up and make my calls. It's nearly 11:00 a.m. at home. I try Carly first, but she has only a few minutes before physical therapy. Next, my mom. We have the usual chat about school and friends, with me hiding all the bad stuff like an expert. She doesn't. Her worry crease has deepened. "Are you okay, Mom? You look really tired."

"I'm fine. Truly. Sleep's been a little interesting since you left."

"But you said it was the best sleep ever last week."

She nods. "True, but some mornings it's like nothing can wake me up. And I'm having very strange dreams. But don't worry. I think we just miss you, and it's playing with our minds."

"We? As in Dad too?"

She gives a laugh. "He accuses me of elbowing him in my sleep.

I accuse him of stealing my pillow. We've turned it into a game. Except nights like last night make me want to take a nap."

"Then hang a sign outside your cubicle: *Nap in progress. Disturb at your own peril.*"

She gives a laugh. "I should, but really, I'm fine. Maybe I'll meditate for fifteen minutes."

"Meditate?"

"Aunt Debbie suggested it. That, aromatherapy, or lemon balm, some sort of tea she swears by. Couldn't hurt." She laughs.

I do, too, but if she's agreeing to even one of Aunt Debbie's "new-age, holistic, alternative, mumble-dee-jumble" suggestions, no matter how tame, it's bad.

Whatever Sofia has been giving my parents cannot be healthy. I lie back on my bed and try Aunt Debbie's breathing, but no amount of meditation, no amount of compartmentalizing, no amount of anything will help me find that calm right now.

I march downstairs toward the bedrooms. "You heard that conversation with my mother," I say loudly enough that Francesco and Anjelica can hear from wherever they are. "Or if you didn't listen in, feel free to play back the recording."

Anjelica appears in the office doorway. "I have no clue what you're talking about."

Francesco moves right next to her, forming a wall as if they're blocking my view. Too late. I already caught a glimpse of the canister.

I stand as solidly as they do. "What is Sofia using to drug my parents? Tell me."

Anjelica chuckles. "It's harmless, really. It's not like she'll be medicating them for more than another week or two. After that, slight withdrawals, and done!" She snaps her fingers.

"How do you know it doesn't mess with their prescriptions? How do you know they aren't recovering addicts? How do you know you haven't sent them on a lifelong spiral back into that dark space?"

"Are they?" Francesco asks, partially closing the door behind them. "Did we?" His tone sounds so caring and considerate, and yet, he's as guilty as Anjelica and Sofia. Maybe that makes him more dangerous.

I start to answer, but I don't. He knows I'm bluffing.

"I believe," he says, "you're overtired. Why don't you go take a little nap? You'll feel so much calmer."

"So you can drip poison into my mouth? No. I'm fed up with the threats. I'm tired of being your accomplice. Get your own damn things next time."

Anjelica moves into the kitchen and takes on the calmest demeanor I've ever seen from her. "I guess there's no need for you to exist, then." She flexes her fingers and pulls a butcher knife from the drawer.

I didn't mean to take it this far. "I didn't—"

"You didn't mean it," she says. "Well, isn't that the epitome of backtracking. Go upstairs and let us decide exactly what to do with you."

My heart beats faster, harder. I glance at the stairs, then I stare down the knife blade. They still need me.

The adrenaline pumps through my arms, my legs, and right into my voice. "You know what you're going to do with me? You're going to listen."

"Okay, then." Anjelica waves the knife with one hand, loops her other arm into mine, and forces me to sit at the table. As if choreographed, she and Francesco sit on either side of me and pull in their chairs.

I try to gulp in air, gulp in something to get myself out of this. Or not. I'm ready. "We have a problem. Or actually"—and I smile— "you have a problem. I know more about this game than you think. You had me get your canister. You had me get your picture. You had me get your book with a map and the map location."

That gets a reaction, at least from Anjelica. I'm keeping my eye on her and that knife.

"So now you really understand I'm not bluffing. I know lots of things." I take another breath. "Like I also know you don't have the map."

Anjelica laughs. "You just told us we do."

"I said you have *a* map. Check the book again. Touch the pages. Touch the letter from the Colonel. Now, touch the map. You know in your heart that your map is different, ordinary. It won't work the way you think. I can get the one that will."

"Then it can only be at one place." Anjelica waggles the knife. "It's at Elena's."

I smile. "Right. You know exactly where I've been and who I've talked to. And, true, my cousin Vittoria did mention something about a map."

236

"Exactly," Anjelica says. "Which means you have nothing. We can always kidnap and torture her instead."

I shake my head. "If that's all it takes, you wouldn't have made me your bitch."

"Well, listen to you," Anjelica says. "You're becoming one of us. However…" She clutches the knife, yanks my hair, and saws off a five-inch chunk from the nape of my neck. "You're not there yet. This is still our game. And you're still our pawn."

"Am I?" I manage even though every fiber of me is quivering.

I need a moment, so I force a smile, look left, right, then straighten in my seat. "The fact is, suddenly, I'm more valuable to you than you are to me. Except for one thing. There's the matter of Sofia and her daily ways to kill my parents."

"And we love it so much!" Anjelica says.

"I'm sure you do, but from where I'm sitting, it seems you love the prize at the end of this game even more. True?"

Anjelica twirls my lock of hair then looks at Francesco, who gives the slightest of nods. "Go on," she says.

I push my chair back and move to the other side of the table where I can see both of them at once. "If you want my help, you need to do something for me, right here, right now. You're going to book Sofia onto the first flight back from DC." I put on a sad face. "She's been so homesick and can't bear to stay a minute longer. She put up a good front, but it's starting to crumble, just like your plans."

It's like I'm channeling her and Anjelica. She and Francesco, the two of them, sitting there, seem to be experiencing the hell they put me through. Good.

Anjelica takes a breath. "Why can we trust you?"

"Keep tracking me with my phone. I have nothing to hide there. Keep my money and credit card. I'll use yours. You can see whatever I buy. Oh yeah. My passport, the one you gave me. It shows I'm illegal. And my guess is you have incriminating evidence that I'm a thief. So many ways you can bring me down. But then you wouldn't get what you want."

Anjelica gives a laugh. "You may say you're not bluffing, but you are. Remember how we got to Carly? That wasn't necessarily Sofia's doing. We can still get to your parents."

My knees start wobbling, but I can't back down now. "I understand. But I can destroy the map. And I can disappear with the last piece of the puzzle."

Francesco moves in the chair next to Anjelica. "Now she *is* bluffing."

"I know." Anjelica leans forward. "Prove you're not."

"Right. Like I'm just going to hand you the map. And I'm just going to tell you where you can find the password for the box." I shake my head. "No. That gives you free rein to murder me and my parents."

They don't answer.

A sudden thought comes. "You do know that I have another bargaining chip. It's obvious that you want the same thing as the woman with the little white dog on Viale Europa. And if Sofia isn't on a plane within twenty-four hours, I'll give her all the pieces."

"How do we know you haven't done that already?"

"How do I know my parents will be alive tomorrow? Besides, I assume you're aware that Arsenio and Florenza are on a wild-goose chase for that last piece, right? They've been to Bologna, Pisa, Florence…" I may be making up the cities, but they sound solid to me.

It must seem plausible to them too. They put their heads together and whisper in Italian.

I'd be able to hear and understand enough of what they're saying if I weren't busy kicking myself. It was too soon to do this. I should have waited until I found the one thing that has eluded them all, *il calice* and its password. And now if I don't find it, I'm dead. Or at least, fighting for my life as an orphan.

My shoulders shudder. My head buzzes harder. I can't stand still while this jury of two is deciding my fate. I move toward the office.

They stand.

Right. The canister. I reverse step. Need them to trust me. I don't want to live like this, not for another day and definitely not for what I hope is a long life. And with what I just said, it won't be a long life if I can't find the password.

I move into the living room, glancing out the window then back at them, waiting for their verdict. How much is there to discuss? *Please don't ask me for the password. Please. Please. Don't make that my condition. I'll give up the map, but…*

I won't need the password. Ever. I just need to keep up this bluff. As soon as Sofia is out of there, I can alert my parents. I can run directly to the authorities. With Signor Matteo as my translator and my witness. And pray that will be enough to keep me out of prison. Then again, I'm already in one.

I come back to the table. Sit. Sigh. Smile. Big.

That gets their attention.

Anjelica leans forward. Stares me in the eye.

I don't waver.

She opens her computer and pulls up the airline site.

Francesco gets on his phone in a texting fury and lets me look on. Sofia agrees to pack up and go, my parents unhurt.

Anjelica shows me the flight confirmation. It departs at 6:45 a.m., DC time, tomorrow with a connection in Newark. "Done, but you'll do one more thing for us."

She flashes a broad smirk. "Nonnegotiable."

CHAPTER THIRTY-SEVEN

IT'S LIKE WE'RE DOING A POWER DANCE TO SEE WHO HAS THE most. I'll let them claim victory as long as I can go back to a version of normal where I'm safe and even semi-happy.

"What do you need me to do?"

Anjelica prints out a picture of a small, wooden box with ornate sides, its top a sliding number puzzle. The little squares—one through eleven, plus an empty square to give them space to slide—are arranged in a four-by-three grid. "Take a good picture of this in your head. It shouldn't be hard. It's one of a kind."

I start to memorize the numbers—they're out of order—but she pulls it back then hands me a scrap of paper. "Memorize the address or not. It won't matter. There's no escaping all the surveillance cameras in this shop. But if you're able to acquire what I just showed you, you'll prove you've been telling the truth. About everything." That means the password.

I tighten my jaw to keep from losing it in front of them. "Not if, but when I do," I manage, my confidence dropping below my feet, "you and all your tentacles will be out of my life forever. *Si?*"

"*Si.*"

"One more thing," I say. "No box until Sofia is in the air, on her way to Rome."

Anjelica shakes her head. "When she's on her layover in Newark."

"Fine." I turn to go upstairs. "I'll be going out. There are things I need to do."

"Like what?"

"You'll be tracking me. You'll see. I'll be back, but not in time for dinner."

Never for dinner again. Or lunch. Or breakfast. I'll get my own drug-free food and water, thank you. But I keep quiet about that. From now on, I have no plans to talk to them more than absolutely necessary.

My first stop is the grocery store near the apartment. I grab a pair of scissors. Also, a new toothbrush and toothpaste. Then I borrow the cashier's phone—tell her that my battery died—to text Devin.

It's Tess. Meet me in Piazza Navona. Fontana di Nettuno

It the fountain of Neptune battling an octopus. All those tentacles.

He texts right back that he'll be there in half an hour, so I sit inside a gelato shop with a scoop of pistachio, then take the scissors to my bag.

I assumed the listening device was that bump inside the strap, but that's only doubled-up fabric. I move all my stuff to the grocery bag, turn the courier bag inside out, and grope every millimeter. Was there ever a bug? It's all perfectly flat. Except for the metal label. It says GUARDAMI. Translation, *watch me*. I'd bet a million dollars there's no such bag company.

Without a working strap, the bag is useless anyway. Then again, it might be useful to let them listen in at some point. I cut out the bug, drop it in with the groceries, and go to trash the courier bag. The woman behind the counter stops me. "*Non lo vuoi?*"

It brings me some joy to give it to her.

I sit there, dipping my spoon into my gelato, barely tasting it. I'll have no appetite until this is over, but I need to keep up my strength. I shovel in the rest so fast that my stomach doesn't have time to protest. But my gut churns at the realization that I'm about to scope out the scene of my next crime, a place with full surveillance. Then there's the matter of the password.

I can't just sit here and stress, so I'm out the door with another *grazie* from the woman behind the counter.

Devin is already standing in Piazza Navona, his back to the fountain, moving his line of sight from entrance to entrance, until he starts jogging toward me. "Are you okay?" he mouths.

I lean in. "Never better. Sort of."

"Where's your bag?"

I hold up the one from the grocery. Then I reach inside. "Our friend." Before I think it through, I toss it into the fountain. "I was going to save it for old time's sake, but it just hit me that they'll still monitor my calls and texts. If I need to mislead them, there's an app for that." I give a twirl. "I'm free!"

Devin dances me around.

And suddenly, I'm about to lose it. I crumple to the fountain's ledge, head between my knees. I don't need Devin to see me cry. Don't need anyone to. But I can't stop my back from heaving, my throat from sobbing. And I can't look up when someone—I assume Devin—sits next to me, his hand rubbing the small of my back. Otherwise, he lets me be.

Sooner than I'd expect, I manage to regroup, fish a napkin from my plastic bag, and blow my nose. "Sorry. I needed that."

"No doubt." He points to the fountain. "Meanwhile, your bug blends in nicely with the other coins."

"I'm sure it will be very happy there."

He takes my hand. "Does this mean it's over?"

I shake my head. "It's just beginning."

CHAPTER THIRTY-EIGHT

WE PASS BY THE ARTISTS ON OUR WAY OUT OF THE PIAZZA. If my painting is here—the woman in a red dress, holding a yellow umbrella under a blue sky, walking by the fountain—I have a credit card, and I plan to use it. The artist is still painting, but that picture is gone. Probably for the best. I can't be distracted right now.

I need to scope out the shop, which, according to the nav app, is two blocks away on Via dei Coronari, a street with small businesses selling everything from leather jackets to specialty food and antiques.

We walk along the cobblestones, dodging tourists and locals, while I give Devin the short version of today, especially the point when I lost every one of my sensibilities and told the Rossis that if Sofia left DC, I'd give them the map and the password.

"But you don't have the password."

"As long as she's on a plane, I can save my parents."

"Do you truly believe they'll make it that easy?"

I shake my head. "We both know. That's why I now need to find out what's in the box. If some key can wake me up from this nightmare…"

We go through the arched doorway of La Collina, *The Mountain.* The Mountain's children or grandchildren probably own the shop now. Regardless, the shop has three surveillance cameras, each tagged with a sign making their presence completely clear.

The shopkeeper is chatting with an older couple off to the side. He gives us a nod and keeps us in his sights like shopkeepers do with people our age, especially in a store where the prices of the jewelry and trinkets are more than your average person makes in a month or four.

The box is sitting in a case among several others near the corner to our far right, a tiny price tag by its side. I hold in a gasp. *25.000€ +*

Twenty-five *thousand* euros? Steal something worth twenty-five *thousand* euros? I refuse to be the subject of the next Italy true-crime documentary. And yet…

Devin leans over. "What's the plus sign?"

The shopkeeper comes over. *"Inglese?"*

Devin tells him, yes, he's from London. Then he asks about the box. I let him do the talking. If I come back tomorrow, he can assume I'm from London too.

"Do you have that kind of money?"

"You speak English. *Grazie.* No. Of course I don't," he says, "but I'm wondering if I might see it anyway. I adore puzzles."

"Through the glass you may see it. No touching unless you have the magic word."

"Magic word?" Devin says.

"*Una parola d'ordine.* Code word. Your plus sign, you called it. I cannot take this box from the case unless you tell me the word."

No wonder Anjelica seemed so smug.

"Linguine? Vino?" Devin smiles.

"Only one try per day," the man says.

Devin waves him off. "Gelato? Baffi." He points to the man's mustache.

I shake my head and tug Devin toward the exit.

Devin calls over his shoulder, "Rumpelstiltskin?"

The man laughs.

I don't. Not out the door. Not down the street. Not when I catch my toe on a cobblestone and practically throw an innocent stranger off his feet. I stop at the corner and lean against a building. "I am so screwed. I can't even touch the thing unless I have the password."

"Then we'll keep trying. Suppose we read him every word in the dictionary until—"

"You heard the man. Only one try per day. Besides, there's a high probability the password is a name or a phrase or a string of numbers."

"Did your cousin suggest that?"

I shake my head. "If you'd heard Vittoria, you'd know they're clueless. And desperate. And in a race against the Rossis."

"The spoils at the end of this must be worth so much more than a twenty-five-thousand-euro investment."

"Even more," I say, "if you have your resident thief steal it."

He gives me a quick squeeze. "Remember what you said before.

All you've got to do is free your parents from Sofia, then you're at liberty to live your life."

"But am I?" I say. "Are we? How far do their tentacles extend, and how many are there? Three? Three thousand? And if I don't keep up my end of the deal, they could kill us as an example to the next innocent girl who walks into their lives. I cannot have her blood on my hands. Yours, either, if they find out you're helping me. Leave. Leave now."

He hugs me again. "I am not leaving no matter how many times you tell me to."

"Then we need to go shopping," I say.

Devin steps back, his eyebrow arched. "I don't understand. You've never struck me as the type to believe that shopping is the answer to—Ah!" He taps at his phone. "Shop for a similar box. Affix a sliding-number toy on top and… Right. They're not naïve."

"No, but if, somehow, I can find the password, I'll need to go into thief mode. And that might take some things."

He swipes on directions to Rinascente, a trendy department store near the Trevi Fountain, then swipes them off. "Forget your plan. You cannot walk in there and steal that box. You'd land in jail. The other thefts? Petty. A slap on the wrist. But this?"

"This or death. What choice do I have?"

"A third option." He pulls up his beltloop. "Once your parents are safe, we explain it all to the police and get them to fetch it for you."

"Because the police are happy to deliver evidence just like that." I snap my fingers.

"Right then," he says. "Option four. We get our hands on twenty-five thousand euros to tempt the shopkeeper. Or... I take a sledge-hammer to the display and pull off a smash-and-grab. Or... You can always escape to Tahiti. I hear it's nice this time of year."

Despite everything, I'm still able to laugh.

Inside Rinascente, I buy the same courier bag I had. Minus the bug. "I got attached to it," I say. "Besides, when I walk in with it, the looks on their faces should be priceless."

By the time we come out, I've also bought a new pair of bright green Chucks, a bright green shirt, some makeup, and a pair of black leggings.

"If you're looking to assemble a disguise," Devin says as we're heading toward the Rossis, "I'm not sure you've succeeded."

"We'll see."

He prods me for more details.

"I can't," I say. "Not until I think this through."

He moves in front of me and takes me by the elbows. "I can help. I'm a decent thinker."

I look away because his pleading eyes are making it hard to keep everything inside. "You are, but you might also tell me all the ways I can fail. Not because you're negative, but because you're wonderfully practical. The last thing I need is to feel hopeless. When I tell you tomorrow, feel free to say that I'm totally delusional about my chance of success. And feel free to step back and let me do whatever alone."

He insists on walking me to my street. We stop at the corner, and I pick up dinner, breakfast, and three water bottles. "Nothing of theirs is going into my mouth."

He grabs the food. "Stay at our house. AdDad and Dance Mum would love it."

"Thanks, but no. If I rattle the Rossis enough, they could slip up again, and I might find something to get me out of this. Without jail. See you tomorrow?"

Devin grabs me in a hug and, this time, he doesn't let go. I don't either. If this were a movie, I'd pull back just enough to look at him, and our kiss would be epic. But this isn't a movie. This is real life, if real life were a nightmare.

I finally unclench the folds of his shirt I'd apparently grasped.

He loosens his grip as well, kisses the top of my head, and hands me the bag. "You will be at school tomorrow."

I nod.

"If not, I will have AdDad call the police."

"Good."

I sense him watching me all the way to the building, but I don't turn back. I want him to see me being braver than I am.

I breathe in a gulp of courage, take the three flights up, and burst into the apartment, my courier bag front and center, my arms swinging the shopping bags.

Neither of them comes out from the bedroom or the office. I creep up to my room, but no one's there either. *"Ciao?"* I repeat it louder. And again. I'm alone!

I race to the office in case they've left the canister on the table.

Of course not. And the safe door is shut. Even so, I give the handle a tug. It opens! Another slipup. I must have rattled them so much that they forgot to spin the lock after they shut the door.

I pull out the canister and the two books, but the framed picture with the letter isn't there. I've got this, though. I retrieve the copy from my shoe and open the canister. The real letter is already in position. I copy the decoded message onto a piece of paper.

Scatola contenitore calice libro lettere b f h l a i e c g d m

I know these words. Box, container, goblet, book, letter. I have no clue about the random letters unless...the password!?

I almost dance, but no. If that's the password, Anjelica would have given it to me days ago. "Steal this and you're free." If only. I almost wish she'd give me a sledgehammer, because that option is looking more tempting with each passing second.

I have only one hope. Vittoria seemed certain that my family has or had *il calice*. I still can't ask my dad, though, or the Rossis will call my bluff. Game over.

And if they catch me in here, game also over. I close the safe just like I found it. Back upstairs, I pull the monkey down, talking to him like I did before, then I place my bags on the shelf with the crucifix.

I start going through the Colonel's letter word by word, analyzing it for anything like a password. For all of ten seconds. The Rossis would have used every tentacle trying that.

And now I have nothing. I'm done. Spent. Exhausted. Mentally and physically.

"Oh, Nonno," I whisper, nearly praying. "If only you'd brought back *il calice*." I open the locket and look at him and Nonna for strength.

A door closes below. Two sets of footsteps head up the stairs.

The letter and decoded message go under my pillow. I lie back and play with the monkey.

Francesco is first through the doorway. "Seems you're good at making new friends."

I hold up the monkey and ask in near-perfect Italian if he has a name.

Francesco shakes his head.

I look at the monkey. "*Il tuo nome è* Triumph."

They're not amused by that. I pretend to be. If I look defeated, there's no guarantee Sofia will be on that plane in eighteen hours.

Anjelica sits on the bed, hovering over me like she still has some power.

I want to move away, but I force myself to lie still.

"So," she says. "You've seen your problem." She obviously means that I need the password and twenty-five thousand euros.

"I assume my credit card has a much lower limit."

"Oh, honey. You used up most of it tonight. A little shopping spree?"

"A girl has to do what a girl has to do. And I'm set for tomorrow. Is Sofia?"

Anjelica gets her on FaceTime. "Show her your bags."

Sofia scans the camera around the room and lands on her largest suitcase, open and half-packed. "I *so* hate to leave," she says, the sarcasm dripping. Then she turns the camera back on herself. "Are you sure your father was an only child?"

"Unless he's been hiding a sibling from me his whole life."

"And you're sure your *nonno* is dead?"

"Seriously?"

"Yeah. Sad." There is no empathy in her voice. "Equally sad are the things they call family heirlooms here. Cookie sheets. Wooden bowls. Alabaster eggs. The gold coins are nice. Silver dollars too. But not a goblet in sight. And believe me, I tore this house apart." She brings her face close to the camera. "I pity you. No password, no parents." She makes a slash motion across her throat.

I gasp. I shouldn't have.

Anjelica stands. "That's what I thought. When you become an orphan, remember it was you who set the timetable. If you hadn't pushed this, we'd still be playing our game. And once we'd gotten everything possible from your family, we would have disappeared from your life only to resurface later. Maybe here, maybe America. It was nice living there those years."

That's why they're so fluent. And that's why I need to get this done. If they slip back into the United States, they'd threaten me forever.

She pats me on the leg and brushes past Francesco to the stairs. "Tick-tock, tick-tock."

He gives me a warm smile. "Sleep well." He takes a step out and turns back. "You do realize the why of all this, don't you?"

I don't answer.

"I'll take that as a no." He pauses, but I still don't react. "We're only putting you through this to get what belongs to us. By all stories, your *nonno*—stupid, stupid, stupid—most likely pawned the goblet after the Colonel gave it to him. Or really, after the Colonel's wife did. Prematurely. Just to get a few lira for his trip.

At least that's what Arsenio and Florenza believe, what with their weeklong search in every little shop from Genova to Napoli."

Sounds like a last-ditch effort to get me to confide in him.

"Then there's the case of your *zia* Elena. She inherited the canister. Fair enough until she weaseled her way into possession of the book with the map when Agostina died. Believe me, we looked for that map in every one of Elena's drawers, pillows, pots, pans, and picture frames. Then, celebration! We had it! Or so we thought until your ultimatum today." His face softens. "You can tell me. Where did she keep it? Safe-deposit box?" He shakes his head. "No. She doesn't trust banks. None of them do."

"Maybe she's changed." I force a smile. "Or maybe she and her family never had it."

Francesco throws up his hands. "Tess, listen. I was asked to talk to you for one reason: to help you help yourself. Think hard. Maybe something I've said will help you find that one vital piece of information you have tucked in your memory. Honestly, we'd rather not hurt any of you. Murder brings out the authorities with a vengeance." He pauses for just a minute. "And now that you've turned out to be a dead end…"

"Have I?" But it doesn't come out with as much bravado as I'd like.

He taps his watch. "Time will tell." And he heads down the stairs.

My first thought is to shove the wardrobe to the doorway so they can't enter without warning. Three reasons stop me. First, if I block the steps, I have nowhere to flee. Second, if they're so intent on torturing or killing me, I have nothing but a ceramic cross, a flower vase, a pair of scissors, and a monkey figurine to defend myself. Third, they have to believe there's a chance I do have the password. Whatever happens from now through tomorrow, I need to keep reminding myself that they're not in this for the blood; they're in this for the treasure. And if, for some reason, I can get them what they want, I'll be...

My stomach sinks.

...Dead. No matter what Francesco just said, their self-preservation instincts will take over. Kill Tess. Kill her family. No loose ends.

I need that password.

CHAPTER THIRTY-NINE

I DO NOT WANT TO BE AT SCHOOL. WHEN SOFIA BOARDS THE plane, I need to skip out early anyway and, and...

There's a reason I wouldn't tell Devin my plan last night. Deep inside, I suspected it was crap and, by light of day, it is.

At least Sofia will be gone. My parents texted me in the middle of the night. They added two happy faces because she and I will have such fun together. Then two frowny faces, them with no girls there. If they knew the truth, their frowny faces would be screams, and my parents would be running off-grid, arms flailing.

Sofia said she'd take an Uber, but my parents insisted on driving her to the airport so she'd be safe at that time of the night/morning. Which is good. At least I'll know she's there. Though she could always turn around and disappear, which is why I refuse to tell them anything until she's FaceTimed me from inside the plane, right before phones off with the flight attendant warning her to hang up.

The school is dark—the parking lot, nearly empty. Even after a quick stop for a few extra supplies, I'm here an hour early.

I hoped not to see Francesco and Anjelica at all, but it's like they never sleep. Or maybe they're bats and sleep during the day. They didn't say a word about the now-drowned listening device. I'm guessing they're satisfied enough that I didn't trash my phone too. And they probably think they still have Signor Matteo in their pocket.

I sit at the back corner of the school building, trying to keep a kernel of optimism alive. Somehow, possibly, maybe, I might find the words to persuade the shopkeeper to show me the box. Out of the case. Or, in desperation, I might be able to convince the Rossis to give me more time, even if that means having Sofia stay with her tentacles in DC. Anything to keep us all alive until I can figure out a way to safety.

Except... I will never feel safe unless they're in jail. Or dead. And I will not turn into a murderer.

I press my palms against my temples. *Think, Tess, think. Goblets. Where would Nonno or Nonna have put a goblet?*

I've never seen one at home. Sofia didn't find one. The only goblets at my grandparents' house were fancy, crystal ones—a wedding gift. Nonna always hoped the whole set would break so she didn't feel obligated to use them when the gift-giver came over. Besides, *il calice* would be durable like the canister. Even the book, the map, and the letter are on stronger paper.

I open my locket. *Nonno, Nonna, speak to me.*

This is the only enduring thing Nonno ever brought from Rome. Why couldn't the Colonel have used a locket instead of—

Is it possible? What Francesco said last night. The Colonel's wife giving it to Nonno prematurely. Everyone being pissed.

I text Devin. Back corner of school ASAP.

He shows up in less than a minute. "Are you okay? I've been looking for—"

"Why didn't you text?"

He eases down next to me. "Didn't want you to not answer. I would have worried more."

"I'm worrying enough for the entire world. But tell me. Italian for *locket.*"

His phone app comes back with *medaglione.* "Like medallion," he says.

I shake my head, and his face falls like a kid who opens a birthday present to find a pair of boxers instead of a skateboard. "Try necklace."

"I know that one. *Collana.*"

I shake my head again. "Reverse it. Try *calice* again. Alternate meaning."

"Cup, glass, goblet, calyx. That's all."

"Calyx. What's that? Sounds scientific."

"Part of a flower, I believe?" He looks that up. "Right. It's another word for the sepal."

"What's that, Professor Botany?"

He hands me his phone. It's the part of a flower above the stem that acts as a protective layer for the bud and eventually encloses the petals.

I'd love someone to protect me with a layer until the Rossis—

I shove Devin's phone back at him. Whip off my locket. Show him the flower-not-a-flower. "*Calice?*" I whisper. "Calyx?"

I can't get it open fast enough. I want to rip Nonno and Nonna from their places, but I tug her picture out. The surface behind is as smooth as can be. "Please, Nonno." I ease out his picture. Engraved behind are initials. C.C.T.

Devin is leaning so closely I can barely see the locket anymore. "The Colonel's initials? His wife's?"

I shake my head. "His last name would have been Alessandro like ours."

"Then you think...?" He doesn't finish his question.

I don't think. I know. This is the password. C.C.T. *Chi cerca, trova.* Whoever searches, finds. It's what my parents said as I left. It's the saying Sofia also finished. Or sort of did. "*Non trova.*" I did hear her right.

Suddenly, last night's plan might work. Might work. It'll either set me free or land me in jail.

I turn to Devin, hoping he sees the plea in my eyes. "Please be my friend and give me time to think this through. Then later, when I talk to you and Bright and Nicolas, please play along."

He strokes my hair and goes in for a kiss, but I can't. I need to keep as clear a head as possible. I turn my head, letting his lips brush my cheek, and I walk away.

CHAPTER FORTY

TODAY'S SUBJECT IS MEDIA: FILM, TV, MAGAZINE, RADIO, newspaper. First thing, Signorina Emma puts on, arguably, the most famous Italian movie, *La Dolce Vita*. She gives us the plot to help us understand because there will be no subtitles. Even if there were, it wouldn't matter.

I see nothing, I hear nothing, I understand nothing. Instead, I run through every possible scenario, trying to find the ultimate one. I know exactly what I need to do.

When the movie finishes, I find Signor Matteo and tell him that before noon, Devin and I need to leave for the day. Nicolas and Bright shortly after. "I'm making everything right for both of us," I say. He asks if I need anything else. "Just please answer your phone if I call. I might need a translator urgently."

He gestures for mine, keys in a number. "New number." He bought a burner just in case they're monitoring his.

I wave mine. *"Capisco."*

"I know you do," he says. "*In bocca al lupo.*"

"Thanks." Carly taught me that one. Literally, into the wolf's mouth, which is their way to say good luck. But it feels like that's where I'm headed.

It's not for another hour that I'm able to get alone time with Devin, Bright, and Nicolas. "I need help on a project," I say.

"Ooh!" Bright says. "You decided? Individual or group?"

"Individual." Then I lean in. "It's not exactly school-related, but Signor Matteo knows about it and will excuse you from class."

"Sounds important," Nicolas says.

He has no clue. "It'll sound more like a practical joke."

"I'm in! What? Why?"

"I'll tell you the what, and if you do it, I'll tell you the why later."

Bright leans way in. "But Tess, please, tell—"

"I'm in," Devin says, cutting her off.

"I'm still in," Nicolas says. "Just promise you won't leave us hanging forever. I cannot live the rest of my life chasing theories."

"Fine," Bright says. "What do we do?"

"Something you were born for, Bright. Be a really good actor." I open her oversized purse and slip in a bag.

"Don't I get one?" Nicolas asks.

"It's for both of you," I say. "You have connected supporting roles. When Devin texts that it's time..."

I give them the rest of their instructions. Devin hands them the address of the gelato shop.

"Why are you taking Devin with you?" Bright says. "Where are you going?"

"Why? Because he's the best one for the part. Where? If I tell you, you might overthink your role. And I need you to be amazing."

Bright still tries to weasel out more details, but that's a losing battle. She stops when I pull her aside and give her my permission to make her play for Devin.

Nicolas looks hurt, but he'll get over it, especially when he learns everything.

I give them each a hug. Signor Matteo will find you when it's time. I'm taking Devin with me now." I don't need him yet, but his presence gives me hope I can pull this off.

We walk to a nearby park, and I explain why I'm so sure *parola d'ordine* is inside the locket. But all the while, he stares into space like I'm invisible. I finally nudge him.

"Terribly sorry. I'm trying to find flaws in your logic. Other than the fact that C.C.T. isn't a word per se, I can't. If that's not the password, I'll be in utter shock."

"So will Bright if I call this off. And Nicolas, if I can't give him a real story."

"I'd make one up for you, but you're the one with the imagination."

"I'm hoping this imagination has put together a solid plan." We find a bench, and I tell him every last detail, sounding more and more like a master criminal. I take a breath.

He arches his eyebrow. "You're rather enjoying this, aren't you?"

"This being what?"

"Sleuthing, finding clues. Being Sherlock Holmes. Or maybe his sister, Enola."

I shake my head. "I'm just doing what I need to." But he's not wrong. There's a thrill in figuring out the next move. Maybe it is in the genes.

"What do you think?" I ask when I finish.

"It should work. Or..."

"Don't bother saying it. Though I hear jail is nice this time of year."

CHAPTER FORTY-ONE

DEVIN SITS WITH ME ON A BENCH UNDER A PAIR OF STONE PINES while I monitor Sofia's plane. He's suspiciously silent. Like this has finally gotten to his nerves as well. And that's making me rethink everything.

I can't.

Instead, I pull out a pen and our syllabus.

Devin flashes a crooked smile. "Schoolwork on such a day?"

"Timeline." At the top, I jot down the exact time I left the Rossis to steal the canister. I write down the trains I took, the time I arrived at Viale Europa, all the details. Then, by each day of the syllabus, I add every step of every task. "I might need it," I finally say. "You'll keep it for me in case I get arrested or killed?"

"Stop saying that." But he takes it from me anyway, stands, and paces a wide circle twice around us before he pulls up his beltloop, and sits again.

"What's with that beltloop thing? It's not like your pants are ever sagging."

"Bad habit. My other tell, I suppose. Wearing my emotions on my trousers."

That's worth a smile. "Please tell me it's a good story. Something really fun. I could use some fun right now."

"Sorry to disappoint," he says. "It's truly mundane unless, of course, you've been kind enough to forget the story of the frogs."

"The frogs? I don't remember anything about frogs, year six, toothbrushes, pudgy you."

"Right," he says. "Then I'll skip right to my cross-country training and how it started melting away the weight faster than Mum could buy me new trousers. So, I was forever tugging them up by the beltloops. And that is the most fun story I can tell you right now. Sorry."

We sit in silence again. And again, I refresh an airline app that differentiates between planes leaving the gate and leaving the ground. If Anjelica and Francesco are monitoring me, they must be laughing over my obsessiveness.

Twenty minutes later, my phone lights up. FaceTime. Sofia rolls her eyes. "I'm on the plane. See?"

"Disconnect your earbuds and tap the person next to you."

She does.

The woman has a baby on her lap. She wouldn't be Sofia's accomplice. At least I hope not, for the baby's sake.

"Sorry to bother," I say, "but my cousin next to you? I'm supposed to make sure she's on the plane home and not flying off to Aruba like she did last year. Where are you headed?"

"Newark."

"Thank you. You see, our grandmother is in the hospital, probably won't pull through, and my cousin has this phobia about sick people. And sorry. Too much information."

The flight attendant comes around and reminds Sofia to turn off her phone.

"Wait," I say, hoping to get the flight attendant's attention. "How soon before the plane takes off?"

"We're pushing back now, so she needs to hang up."

Sofia waggles her head, mimicking the flight attendant. "I need to hang up." And the phone goes dark.

"Time to alert your parents?"

I jump.

Devin's about to apologize, but I wave him off. "Not until they're in the air for ten minutes, close to the Delaware border."

"Delaware?"

I give him a quick geography lesson, hoping to waste all the minutes. But no. And no to something else. "I'm not immediately calling my parents either. Not until I get the box. It's my insurance policy against anyone waiting to take Sofia's place. But when I do call…holy crap. I need to find a way to tell them the whole story so they won't freak out."

"They'll freak out no matter what you say."

"There's freaking out and going full-on ballistic." I stand. "It's time."

We wind through the roads, getting closer and closer to La Collina. Halfway there, I duck down a street, barely wide enough for motorcycles and pedestrians. I open my bag and, over the same blue shirt I wore with my first burglary and the break-in with Devin, I slip on the new green one.

"Looks like you borrowed that from a sumo wrestler," he says.

"Exaggerate much? It's only a couple sizes too big." But I tuck it into the front of my jeans. "Better?"

He doesn't answer, too kind to remind me it's not a real disguise. He checks his phone instead. "I'll text them."

As he rounds the corner, I ease my back down the stone of a building and change from my flip-flops to the new green Chucks. I uncap the black eyeliner and before I can bring it to my face, Bright grabs it from my hand. "My job, remember?"

"You don't have to do this, you know." I look to her and Nicolas, then Devin. "You either. You can leave once you're done. See me tomorrow."

"It's just a practical joke," Nicolas says. "Right?"

Bright sighs. "Of course not, Nicolas. We all know there's something else going on. Now, eyes closed, Tess." It feels like she's slathering on three thousand layers of makeup, but when she has me open my eyes and holds a small mirror in front of my face, I don't look like a raccoon. And I don't look like me either. She moves the lipstick toward my mouth, and I start to take it away from her—"I can do that."—but she puts a death grip on it. "My job."

Now I really don't look like me. I stand, my legs buckling like a just-born horse.

"You don't look so good," Nicolas says.

Bright slaps him on the arm. "The makeup is awesome."

"That's not what I mean."

"I'm fine," I say. "I'm better than fine. I'm ready. And there's still time for you to back out, but if you do, I need to know. Now."

"Whatever this is," Bright says, "I'm in. But promise to tell us later. Really promise."

"You'll know by tomorrow. I swear."

I turn and I don't look back.

CHAPTER FORTY-TWO

La Collina is four blocks away. Four blocks to run through my contingency plan in case they do bail and I'm on my own.

I'll be okay. I've stolen before. Three times. Just not in public. Not with surveillance cameras. And not something worth 25,000 euros. I try to strip the cost from my mind. My plans have all worked, and this one will, too, especially because I'm rock-solid sure about the password. C.C.T. Unless they're looking for the words and not the initials.

Devin's right. With all the movies and shows I've watched, with all the secure sites I've visited, I've never seen a password only three letters long. But the Colonel set this up soon after World War II, long before technology, when it was all real spy stuff, when passwords were sometimes full dialogues. That's the issue. If I say to the shopkeeper, *"Chi cerca, trova,"* and he comes back with a second sentence, he might expect me to respond with a third.

I press my temples. I need to walk in self-assured.

First move, I turn the corner and pass the gelato shop. Next, I imagine I'm about to go into a cheap accessories store at any mall in the world. My heartbeat doesn't buy that. But I straighten my back and inhale every speck of confidence I've ever known. Here goes.

I pull open the door. Even though I remember they'd be here, the TELECAMERE DI SORVEGLIANZA IN USO signs momentarily smack my confidence away. Then there's another issue—I'm the only customer. Three or four other people would be ideal, but...

The box is in the case to my right. I go left to browse just like any normal person, keeping half a step back from the counters so I won't slip and leave fingerprints.

A man, different than the one last night, comes from the back. Surveillance cameras in use. *"Buongiorno."*

I give a wave. The plan is to speak in a higher voice than normal and say as little as possible. No talking means less chance to notice my American accent. When Devin and I were waiting for Sofia's plane to take off, I practiced the words I'd need, recording my voice and comparing it to the voice in the app. Devin said it was perfect, which means it will do.

The shopkeeper is probably about sixty years old with a goatee. He's no taller than I am. Unless he has a bouncer in the back or a gun behind the counter, I'm physically safe. He asks if I'm looking for something.

I nod. *"Una scatola."* I hold my hands to reflect the size and shape of the box.

He asks how much I'm willing to spend.

I smile and shrug.

The shopkeeper points out several boxes in that case.

I shake my head and stroll around the case that spans the width of the shop, pausing twice, then curving right until I step faster as in: *Aha! There it is!*

If my heart beat any harder, it would give out. Then I'd be dead. And I wouldn't need to worry about anything. But a bigger part of me desperately wants to triumph. Fully.

The shopkeeper explains that this is a very special item, placed here by an important man who wants it bought only by a particular person. He flashes the price tag.

I hope my nod looks like the money doesn't mean anything. *"Posso vederlo per favore?"*

He can't show me without the password.

"Un momento, per favore." I need to decide now. C.C.T. or *che cerce trova.* I have one chance. One chance only. The Rossis will never give me a second one tomorrow.

My heart beats faster. C.C.T.? *Che cerce trova?*

Suddenly, it's clear. Everyone's been desperately searching for *il calice,* so it must be what's engraved in there.

I say it in Italian. "Chee. Chee. Tee."

His eyes open. His mustache twitches. *"Ripeti, per favore?"*

I repeat it. "Chee. Chee. Tee."

He pulls out his phone. Who is he calling? The Rossis? Zia Elena? I feel the blood drain from my face. But he puts it on speaker and has me repeat the password again.

The voice at the other end gives a chuckle. *"Mostraglielo."* Show it to her.

I keep my internal celebration to a minimum. There's still the part where I steal the box.

The shopkeeper takes the phone off speaker and listens for a couple seconds before he tucks the phone into his suit coat and pulls out a set of keys. He unlocks the case, eases out the box, and places it on a velvet pad on the counter.

His eyes seem full of questions, but all I can do is say, *"Grazie."*

Before I'm able to touch it, he covers the box with his hand. *"La sua carta di credito per favore. O contanti."*

Please, no. He needs a credit card or cash. I have only fourteen euros. And worse, the credit card has my name. I fight the impulse to grab the box and run.

"If anything goes wonky," Devin said, "promise me you won't panic. You may have to improvise but promise me you'll stick to the plan."

I promised, which means I need to say something I didn't practice. The words echo in my head as a native Italian would speak them, but imagining the sound doesn't guarantee it'll come out that way. Improvise.

I open the flap of my bag, unzip my little purse and start pulling out my wallet, but the telltale navy cover of my U.S. passport comes up with it. I close the flap.

Why does he need it? *"Carta di credito? Perché?"* My coughing starts. On purpose. To, hopefully, hide my accent. I only want to look. *"Voglio solo vederlo."* I cough some more.

"Stai bene?"

I hold up a hand, signal that I'm fine, and the coughing eases up. His hand doesn't, though. No credit card. No box.

Maybe he won't look. Maybe the card will just sit on the counter under that paw of his.

This time when I reach into my bag, I unlock my phone, send a pretyped text to the group, then I do pull out my credit card.

I give another cough to keep up the act, flash him the front side of the card, then place it upside-down on the counter.

He turns it over. *Fantastico.* "Alessandro! Tess Alessandro!" He says how happy he is to meet me. Shakes my hand. Then he lifts his off the box.

If only a busload of tourists would show up and cause a huge distraction because now, I need to grab both the box and my credit card. And not get caught.

The plan. Stick to the plan.

The eleven numbers on the top of the box are in random order but not the same as yesterday. Someone's been playing with it. I slide the numbers and line up the one, two, three, and four on the top row. The shopkeeper seems fascinated.

Someone, please, come in. Have him look away for three seconds. Just three.

But the shopkeeper stays glued as I maneuver the five to the left of the second row.

If I were tending shop, I would have slid all the numbers in order a long time ago. He has to know what's in here. Maybe he's watching to see my reaction. Or to make sure I don't grab and go.

"*Sei.*"

I look up and smile. Yes, it's time for the number six. I slide it up, to the left, slide the nine down, the rest of the row over—

"Ahh! *Aiutami! Aiutami!*" A high-pitched, bloodcurdling scream and a call for help comes from outside. *"Sangue! Sta sanguinando!"* Someone's bleeding.

I leave the box and start toward the window. The shopkeeper's right behind me.

Before he can look up, I move back, slide the box into my bag, walk out the door, and sidestep a girl, now joined by a woman, both bent over a kid, blood dripping from his nose.

CHAPTER FORTY-THREE

IT'S NEARLY IMPOSSIBLE, BUT I KEEP MYSELF FROM RUNNING. Brisk walk. Brisk walk. Past the gelato shop. *Don't look back, Tess. Don't look back.*

I have to. Just one glimpse and—

"Ahh!" I'm sprawled, facedown, on the cobblestones. My knee is probably bloodied, and so is my chin. I grope for the box.

It's not smashed under me. Somehow, it's propped against the side of my waist. In that split second, between the moment when the toe of my Chucks caught on a cobblestone and I wound up falling face-first on the ground, my instincts must've kicked in—the same ones from the swimming pool/volleyball incident—and I shoved the bag to my side.

I start to ease up just as two people run out from the gelato shop. They ask if I'm okay. No, I'm not. I need to get out of here or I'm dead. Either the Rossis will kill me or my cellmate will. A woman stoops beside me, a light hand on my shoulder. I want to tell her I'm fine and to leave me alone and, especially, to forget my face, but I didn't practice those words with Devin, and my Italian will sound way too American.

But maybe those three years of high school French won't. "*Je ne parle pas italien. Mais je suis bien. Merci. Grazie.*"

After I tell them I don't speak Italian, but I'm fine, I pick myself up, push past them, and hustle down the narrow street, my bag pressed against my chin and my knee aching like hell.

I ignore this glitch in the plan, take the next right, then—

The credit card! I didn't take the credit card. Now, the police will have my name and my fingerprints. But I can't go back. I can't panic.

I go to our meeting spot. Devin takes one look at my face, and I wave him off.

"Yes, I had a nice trip." But that's all I say. I take off the green Chucks, the green shirt, and my jeans. I'm now a girl in a blue shirt, leggings, and black flip-flops. I take a quick look at my knee. The double pants situation protected the skin from breaking, but my knee is an angry red and it's already starting to tighten up.

Devin hands me makeup remover wipes. I press one to my chin. It stings, but there's no blood. And while I go full-on removal, he gets out my little purse—I threw away that bug too—and stuffs my shirt, pants, and shoes into my bag. He drops a new Italia National Football Team hat in my lap, his contribution, and walks off with my courier bag, the box intact and inside.

I tuck my hair in the cap, the shortened piece—the one Anjelica cut—not fully cooperating, and I move on.

I should have learned from my accident, but I can't help myself. Again. Instead of taking an alternate route away from the shop, I double back, fully understanding why criminals feel the need to return to the scene of the crime.

Even from the opposite side of the street, the small puddle of red from Nicolas's "bloody" nose stands out like a stoplight. Bright's scream echoes in my memory. The shopkeeper stands in the door, looking up the street, down the street. Then comes the approaching sound of sirens.

I continue walking as if I need to be somewhere. And I do. Anywhere but here. Professionals are trained to see through makeup and clothing changes, at least on the shows and movies I've seen. And the girl with a scraped chin and a limp will be memorable.

I get to Parco Adriano, a park adjoining Castel Sant'Angelo across the Tiber River. I strategically chose it in case the Rossis come after me. It's just a three- or four-minute run to a police station. If I can still run.

The station would not be my first choice of safe havens. They'll soon have my name, fingerprints, and the surveillance video from La Collina. So now especially, it's inevitable. I'll be talking to them at some point. Just not yet.

I focus forward to the huge, round building, the emperor Hadrian's mausoleum. Any other day, I'd take it all in, but Hadrian will have to wait. Devin is standing between a pair of tall, conical trees.

It's only when I reach him that I cry or laugh or both. I can't distinguish. After two minutes of celebrating, I sit. Abruptly.

"What's wrong?" he says. "Are you badly injured?"

"Worse." I blow out a breath. "I had to leave my credit card in the shop. Name, fingerprints, everything."

"Oh, bugger," he says. "Let's not panic. You promised you wouldn't."

"I'm not, but the plan needs to change."

He raises his eyebrow.

"I now need to follow this through to the end."

"To what end?" he says.

"The end-end." I blow out a breath. "I need to be the one who puts together all the Colonel's objects. I need to get my hands, my actual hands, on whatever the Rossis are willing to kill for." I may not need to, but I desperately want to.

Devin just looks at me. "Have you gone mad? You said you just needed to get the password. Then the box. And now…" He shakes his head. "Fine. How do you plan to do that without Anjelica and Francesco on your bum?"

"Don't forget the police." I give half a laugh. "It's just a matter of time before they track me down. I can't exactly flee a foreign country with a forged passport unless you know a forger who can fix mine."

He shakes his head. "But the credit card. You'll claim it was stolen. That will explain away everything."

"Why would they believe me? There's video evidence, not just from today but from last night too. Oh, God. They'll show you were with me."

"I wasn't with you today."

"Doesn't matter," I say. "I promise I will take all the blame for making you my unwitting accomplice. And I will do this because my best chance, my only hope to stay out of jail, is to tell the police the whole story, from beginning to end. And have something tangible to show for it."

"You do realize the box is tangible."   When I don't bother to answer, he jabs at my phone. "And you also realize it's just a matter of time before the Rossis come after you."

"Right. Back to the plan." I have Devin take a video of me from my phone, walking with the box, enough trees in the background so that they know I'm away from La Collina.

I text it to Anjelica and my phone rings immediately. FaceTime.

"Finally," she says.

"What? No thank you? No bravo? No appreciation whatsoever? You should at least wave that rally towel I took from my *zia*."

"Where are you?" she says. "Bring it here. And what happened to your chin?"

"What happened to my chin? I'm badass. That's what happened. As for your other questions: A. You know where I am. B. Give me a minute to breathe, will you? C. The box is no longer with me. It's with someone I trust. And don't bother to guess who. You'll be wrong. I'll bring it to you when Sofia is in the air from Newark to Rome."

"We're coming to get you."

"Do what you want, but I've left explicit instructions that the box not be given to anyone but me. Or the police. Otherwise, you do know that wood burns."

Her eyes open wider. "You're a monster." Then she relaxes. "No. You wouldn't."

"Try me."

"Fine." She snarls. "Now what?"

"I checked a few minutes ago. Sofia's next flight is scheduled to leave in just under two hours. Once the flight attendant makes her get off the phone, and once I confirm that the plane is well on its way, I will call you. Meanwhile, sit tight." I almost hang up, but it suddenly hits me. "Where's Francesco?"

She gives a laugh. "Almost there."

"Great." I ignore the pain and start jogging. "I am two minutes from the police station, so you might want to call him off. But before you go, remember what you said the morning of the canister? You called me weak and soft. You might want to add conniving and calculating to that. Just saying." I end the call. And stop. And rub my knee.

Devin comes up by my side. "All that sass. Do you, purposely, want to lose your head?"

"It's keeping me sane, but now I need to rethink part of the plan."

"Again?" Devin moves around, holds me by my elbows, and looks me in the eye. "Fine, and I will help with any plan unless it puts my Italian family in jeopardy. You cannot hide there."

"My plan doesn't need to involve you. If you want to leave, I'll manage." I say it like I mean it. "There's still a lot to do. And none of it's illegal. Well, not anymore." I give him a brief hug then step back and turn. "Feel free to walk the other way."

"Are you kidding?" he says. "Not until we open the box."

"After that?"

"If you can act that cheeky to people threatening to blow up your very existence, I might be able to bear this for a while."

Devin and I move to within a dozen yards of the police station while my phone continues to blow up. Anjelica. Francesco. Sofia. They all send intimidating emojis. Then Sofia sends a stabbing gif. If they want to rattle me, it won't happen. Not anymore.

Then comes a text from Bright and Nicolas: *When r we meeting?* It's our code that they're on school grounds.

"They're safe." I show Devin.

He gives a grin. "You do know I get their texts too." He FaceTimes them. "You were brilliant. I watched from around the corner. That scream, Bright! Outrageously brilliant. Nosebleed, Nicolas, highly successful."

Nicolas laughs. "When the woman hovering over me said the blood looked thin as food coloring, I thought I was going to have a real nosebleed."

"Sorry," I say. "Guess I added too much water and not enough syrup to the tomato paste."

"No worries," Bright says. "I saved the day."

Nicolas laughs. "She said I was on blood thinners. And she cried that I might die."

"Then I handed him a wad of tissues, and he tilted his head back and told everyone he was fine, and the crowd cleared. And Tess? Where were you?"

"Right there. Inside the shop. But I left before the whole thing was over."

"It's over?" Bright says. "You can tell us everything?"

I shake my head. "The story will be better, I promise. Really, really amazing if you wait until tomorrow."

My words will come true no matter what.

CHAPTER FORTY-FOUR

WE STAND OUTSIDE AN *ALIMENTARI*, A SMALL GROCERY STORE, just a block from the police station, figuring out our next moves. But our plans, our threats, nothing at all will matter until we open the box.

I put tiles one through five in order at the shop. I slide the six to its spot. Then seven, eight, and nine. But ten and eleven will not cooperate. I try it. He tries it. I try again. The other numbers are all messed up now. Finally, we get smart and watch a video.

Slide, slide, slide, slide. Done.

"Ready?" I open it before he can answer.

My stomach drops. Inside is something marked *confezione colorante*. Tucked to the side is a slip of paper. Devin plugs the words into his app to make sure we translate it accurately.

If you are reading this, you did not explode the dye pack. Congratulations! Lift it out slowly. Think carefully. Carry on.

"Carry on and do what?" he says.

I ease out the dye pack. Underneath is another sliding puzzle. This one, though, has eleven letters of the alphabet.

"Let's do this." Devin puts the A in its place, the B, the C.

"Stop." I point to the two words. *Pensa attentamente.* Think carefully. "Could be another dye pack underneath. We played it predictably with the numbers, but..."

"What do you propose?"

I stare at the letters. A, B, C, D—"Wait. Why's there an M? That's the thirteenth letter of the alphabet. It should go from A to K."

"Right," he says. "No K. No J. Hmm." He shakes his head. "I can't think of any Italian words with a J or K. Can you?"

"Which means J and K wouldn't have been in the Colonel's letter..."

"Therefore, not in the decoded message."

Eleven letters: *B F H L A I E C G D M*

With the tutorial again, we get them in order much faster this time.

I give the letter-puzzle lid a light tug. It pops up. This compartment has another dye pack. Below it, a thick, brass key. And written in dye-pack red, as if to disappear if the pack exploded, *Fila 11.*

"*Fila* means row?"

He nods. "As in eleventh row." I wait for him to say *eleventh row of what,* but he doesn't. I assume we're thinking the same thing. We'll know when we get there. Ostia Antica.

I've had Devin take multiple pictures every step along the way in case of whatever. He holds up the dye packs. "Toss them?"

I shake my head. "What if they turn out to be important?"

"What if they explode all over us, marking us as criminals?"

He looks to one side. The other. "Sit tight." He trots off without another word.

"Where are you going?"

He doesn't turn back.

Serves me right for not cluing him in earlier. I sit tight, very tight, on the curb just outside the *alimentari*, but I can't just stare into space, each muscle in my body freezing up. Doing nothing is better than doing something stupid. I'm so close to the finish line, it'd be easy to get sloppy. The Rossis did.

If only they'd slipped up enough for me to record their threats or get proof that they forced me to steal. The only proof out there is video footage of me stealing a 25,000-euro box. And possibly more of me going in and out of the Villa Borghese Museum and the university library, which doesn't prove anything except that I was there when things went missing. The only bit of proof I really have, Devin has, is Signor Matteo's napkin.

Poor Signor Matteo. Even if he's sorry for whatever got him involved, he brought it on himself. Me, I was just born into the wrong extended family. If I need to drag him to the police, I will. This is survival. I can't be soft if I want to get my life back to...

Not normal. After this, things will change forever. For me. Within me. I'm not the same girl who needed to pack three black-jean, blue-shirt outfits. I'm not the same girl who tiptoed onto that plane, quivering with every step. I'm not that girl who felt like a fraud, a phony, an impostor with each new experience. I'm not that girl anymore.

Even still, I'm scared.

CHAPTER FORTY-FIVE

MY KNEE IS THROBBING. I PULL A FIVE-EURO NOTE FROM MY wallet, ease the dye packs into the courier bag, and hope that for these couple minutes they don't rub up against something and explode all over the box.

Inside the store, I buy a package of frozen vegetables. Back outside, dye packs safe, I sit and balance the vegetables on my knee. And I check the airline app again.

Sofia's plane is still on time. But Devin's been gone for twenty-four minutes. To me, *sit tight* without an explanation means five, ten at most. What if he got hit by a car and is lying unconscious in the emergency room? Or in a ditch by the side of the road? What if—

The hair on my neck bristles. If the Rossis think I was bluffing and he's the one with the box, they could have tracked him down, tied him up, and are now torturing him as I sit here with the birds chirping and the sun shining and the breeze gently blowing.

I text him. Just a question mark.

No answer. Ten minutes later, there hasn't even been the three-dot promise of an answer.

I stand, the less-than-frozen vegetables tucked under my arm, the dye packs gently balanced in the palm of my hand. Pace down the street, away from the police station. Back toward the *alimentari*. Away. Back. Away. Back.

Devin!

I punch him in the shoulder. "Where have you been? What did you do? Are you okay?"

"I was fine until you beat me up."

I rub his arm. "Sorry."

"No," he says, "I'm sorry. It just took longer than I thought."

I blow out a breath. "Well, never ever ever leave again without giving me a timeline."

He looks at his phone. "Fifty minutes. See what you mean. But aren't you the least bit curious where I was and what I did and what I discovered?"

"Fine. Where were you? What did you do? What did you discover?"

"Last one first," he says. "While I was waiting, I pulled up this." He shows me a website about *difesa legittima*, legitimate defense. It's an Italian law in which a person can't be punished for acts committed under threat of violence. The law may be for self-defense, like for killing a home intruder, but we decide it should apply to anything I've done. Maybe.

"At least it's something," I say, "because we both know this will end with the police. But… Where were you? What did you do?" I poke at the plastic bag he's holding.

He pulls out a box of zipper bags. "For your dye packs."

"That took almost an hour? I could have knit a grass carrier in that time. And didn't you notice? *Alimentari?* Right here?"

Then he holds out a cell phone. "This will be very useful, don't you think?"

"Who's is it?"

"Your new mobile. I might not have twenty-five thousand euros for a box, but I do have forty euros and change for a burner phone. It doesn't have many minutes, you can't load all the apps, but it should do for now."

"I forgive you."

We laugh. My timer chimes. Sofia's plane is scheduled to depart in five minutes. I FaceTime her on my old phone, but it immediately says Unavailable.

I call again. Unavailable. A third time, and she finally answers. "What, already?"

"You know the deal," I say. "I talk to your seatmate. Then you flag down a flight attendant after they tell you to turn off devices."

"What's the point?" Sofia moves her phone around so I can see she's on an international-sized plane. "You do know that I wasn't the only one in the United States. I wasn't the only one in the DC area or even in your neighborhood. It was so cute. Your parents thought I was out with my little high school pals each night."

I want to yell at her, yell at someone, but my throat clenches.

"Here's the deal," she says. "Until we get the box, we are not finished with you or your family. Is that clear?"

I find my own voice. "So. If I don't give you the box, your people are going to kill everyone I know in the U.S."

"Why stop there? You have family just kilometers from wherever you are. They've been working against us for years now. I'd be happy to shed a little blood in Rome too."

The woman next to her leans away.

Sofia turns to her. "Sorry. Just practicing for an acting role."

The woman visibly relaxes.

I don't. "How did a high school girl like you get to be a killer so young?"

"Oh, *cara*. High school? Please. That was eight years ago. I'm the one who taught my older sister. You've met her."

"Signora Roma? She's your—"

Sofia laughs. "That batty old mother of ours? I'm talking about Anjelica." She ends the call.

I stare at the dark screen, shivers coming in waves. I turn to Devin. "They... We... I..."

He puts pressure on my hand so that I lower the phone. "I saw."

"You did?"

"You didn't notice? I had my head against..."

"They'll never leave me alone. My life will never be my life anymore."

"She could be bluffing."

I shake my head. "It took more than three people to pull this off—six if you count Signora Roma, Il Creepo, and Signor Matteo.

Then add whoever's been following me and whoever videoed Carly's accident and whoever made my passport and whoever, supposedly, bugged my parents' phones at work. And I have to believe it would take more than Signor Matteo to arrange for me—me, one little, insignificant person—to get accepted to this exclusive, nearly-no-one-gets-in program then get placed with some of the most dangerous people on—"

I stand. Move away from Devin. "You? How did you get in? Why did you become friends with me?"

"I make good marks in school. I'm charming, right?"

I can't bring myself to move.

"Tess. I'm sorry if I'm making you freak out, but you should know me by now. Me, Devin Kessinger-Scott."

I should, but I'm not sure I know anything anymore.

He moves to take my hand, then doesn't. "Look at me, Tess," he says. "You know me."

I shake my head. "I only know the person you want me to see. Let's start with the Ferrari. You have one, I know."

He shakes his head. "But my family does. And a Maserati. We're rich, but you never asked about that."

"And yet you're so careful. No drinking. No swearing. No doing anything you could get in trouble for. Except you're fine with aiding and abetting me, a criminal. What's that about?"

"It's complicated." He tugs up his beltloop. "On one hand, I promised my family I wouldn't get into any sticky situations or compromising positions. Something ugly that could play out in the British media."

I just look at him.

"On the other hand, why did I get into this sticky situation? My parents would be proud. I told you how they got detained at that rally. As for getting into Exchange Roma, it was easy. My father. He's actually a high-ranking diplomat."

"A diplomat? What does that mean?"

"It means he's the type of British official who works in the interest of the U.K. He's based in London but also has responsibilities elsewhere. If you want, I can have him ring up the prime minister, who will vouch for him. Meanwhile…"

He shows me pictures of their family on three different sites, including a *Guardian* feature article on *The Most Unassuming, High-Profile Family in London.*

"As for me picking you," he says while I'm reading, "think back. It was you who started it. Drawing my eyebrow." He raises it. "Any normal person would have stopped to question you."

"You're right, you're right." I hand back his phone and look at him. "Sorry. I'm slightly paranoid right now."

"As am I," he says. "Not just for your sake, but for my family's. Anjelica and Francesco have you at my Italian house quite often. Who's to say they won't target Family Roma as well?"

"You should just leave. We'll stage a big, ugly fight right here. I'll call Bright and tell her all about it so the Rossis know that I will never speak to you again. That you're cruel and—"

He pulls me close, my cheek settling on his chest. "Not happening."

I want to nestle in until this business is over, but it won't go away on its own.

I allow myself a minute, then turn just enough to check the

airline app. The plane has left the gate. The weather conditions are fine. In minutes Sofia will be airborne, this time on a much longer flight. Even if she parachutes off the plane, it won't change what I'm about to do.

I call Anjelica. "What's with your sister, not confirming like I asked?"

"You've discovered our little secret," she says. "She can be a bigger bitch than I've ever been. Bad genes, I suspect."

I wave off the rest of the small talk. "You do know that my aunt and cousins—"

"Which?" Anjelica says. "You do know that we're your cousins too. Me, Sofia, and that too-good brother of ours and his wife, whose office you visited at Villa Borghese. And let's not forget Signora Roma, your *zia* Rosa."

"If you're trying to shock me, Anjelica, sorry. I figured out that connection forever ago. Though the part about your brother and his too-goodness is new."

"Well, listen to you."

"Yeah, listen to me. Listen hard, because here's the deal. If you agree, I can have Elena's side bring the map to a designated spot. I will text you the exact time and place. In exchange, you will bring the letter inside the canister."

"And the box? How can I trust that you won't give it to them?"

"You still have my passport. If you also bring that, you'll get the box. *Una mano lava l'altra.*" I pause. "However, if you don't follow that exactly, they'll get the box. Indirectly, that is. I have two envelopes. One contains the whereabouts of the box. The other, not."

292

"Instead," she says, "what if—"

"Nonnegotiable." I end the call.

Then I call Vittoria from the burner. "I have news."

"News?" she says. "*Prego.* Tell me is *il calice.* Tell me, Chicky. You know where it is."

I smile. "*Si. Il calice,* I know where it is."

She squeals and starts rattling off something to whoever's with her. In Italian, and I actually understand most of it. She's telling Zia Elena that they almost have it.

Yeah, not so much.

"Where is it?" Vittoria says. "Where we can see it? You tell me, we get it, and we can share like was supposed to be."

"Except we still need one piece. If you bring the map, the real map, the one on Zia Elena's nightstand—and I will know the difference—our other cousins will give you the canister back, with the letter."

She's relaying all this to Zia Elena then apparently mutes the phone for a moment. "Why would we? The letter. We decoded months ago."

She's bluffing. "Then you know the ten letters at the end?"

"*Si.* All ten."

I laugh. "Except there are eleven letters. Apparently, you do need what they have. If you follow my instructions, there's a bigger payoff for you."

"What is that?"

"You'll be getting a text any second now." I nod to Devin, who sends it.

"The box! How you got it?"

"Does it matter?"

"No," Vittoria says. "But how I can be sure you will give it to us and not to *la famiglia* Martorelli?"

"To who?"

"Giovanni and Claudia Martorelli. You call them Francesco and Anjelica Rossi."

Good to know their real names. I tell her about the two envelopes and assure her that the box is in a safe location. "As for why I would give it to you? You're the family I know. We visited you, you visited us. *Si?*"

"We are true family. Remember that."

After the call ends, I use my original phone to send separate texts to Vittoria and Anjelica. It's set. At approximately 16:30, you will receive the exact time and place for the swap. If you're not within 30 minutes of the Colosseum then, start heading there.

They'll expect the text to come from this number, so I add. The next text will come from an Italian phone number. Follow the instructions exactly.

That gives Devin and me ninety minutes, which should be enough time if we move fast.

We get to the meeting spot, the Colosseum skate park, within five minutes and comb back some dirt underneath a bank of bushes. I wrap my original phone in a plastic baggie, set it down, and brush a thin layer over it. It's not visible, but still trackable. And if it's gone when we return, I can live with that. Without it, I have my freedom.

For now.

CHAPTER FORTY-SIX

IN MY MIND, WE'D BE USING A COMBINATION OF BUS, TRAIN, AND foot power to get to Ostia Antica, but Devin's right. If the bus and train are running late or if we miss a connection, we won't make it with enough time before closing to do what we need.

The good thing about being near a major tourist attraction—it takes barely a minute to grab a taxi.

It's hot, and the driver isn't using his air-conditioning, but it's better that way. I didn't realize how claustrophobic I've felt until now as we're racing down the streets, the cap off, my head half out of the window, my hair whipping every which way. Until Devin grabs hold of it with one hand and rubs his eye with the other.

I don't feel like apologizing. I do too much of that in life. "Am I doing the right thing?" I say instead.

"I can't think of another way to do this. Except, perhaps, to call my father. I never underestimate him. He is a wicked negotiator."

"Can he negotiate a truce between criminals? Does he deal with criminals?"

"He may have. Terrorists are criminals."

"And he's negotiated with terrorists?"

He gives a chuckle. "Truly, I haven't a clue."

"Here's what I do know. Or have learned." I doubt the driver speaks much English, but in case he does, I keep my voice low. "You can't reason with unreasonable people. And when I see Sofia hold a knife to my parents' throats or threaten to blow up our house or drip poison into their already-drugged mouths and, in real time, crash my friend's car with her in it, I consider that at least slightly unreasonable."

Devin gives a sad nod.

"But as soon as we're done, yes. He could be valuable."

"How so?"

"Is he fluent in Italian? Or know an interpreter? Have influence with the Italian police?"

"No. Probably. Possibly."

We're about a minute from Ostia Antica. Devin texts the picture of the nightstand map to my burner so we both have it. I enlarge the picture, really looking at the careful, handwritten coordinates.

"One of a kind," Devin whispers.

The taxi lets us out, he buys our tickets, and we go in.

Before I focus on anything, I smell it.

Perfume.

CHAPTER FORTY-SEVEN

"You look like you've seen a ghost," Devin says.

"It's her. Signora Roma." I tuck my hair into the Italia National Football Team cap and pull it low on my brow. "My phone is at the Colosseum. How could the Rossis know I'd be here?"

"Think about it," Devin says. "They must've suspected that, eventually, all roads lead to Ostia Antica."

True. If they're hoping to find whatever's here today, just over an hour before closing, they'd need someone in place. Signora Roma. Also, Il Creepo, who might be her husband, which would make him Uncle Creepo. He's sitting on a low wall up ahead.

I stop and look for a safer route past him, but the best way may be to blend in.

The ruins here are busy but not crowded. We wait until a family of four starts forward, then we fall into their shadows. They pause to read something in a book, but we continue on, walking right by Il Creepo as if we were your average tourists.

I'd prefer to see Signora Roma, not just smell her, so she doesn't blindside me with her bony hand on my shoulder when I least expect it. "Her scent will give her away, right, Devin?"

He agrees, but not like he entirely believes it. Neither do I.

Even though her scent has faded, it's nearly impossible to keep from glancing left, right, left, right, and not in a touristy way. I try to stop looking like the hunted and, instead, focus on the sights spread before us like enormous brick sandcastles that have been half-leveled here and mostly leveled there.

Among the apartments and other buildings, according to a quick video we watched in the taxi, are private baths, public restrooms, something like a fast-food restaurant, and an amphitheater. We're passing that now. According to both maps, we're nearing the Curia, their version of city hall.

The exact intersection of G and 7 puts us to the side of seven steps leading up to the Curia's grounds. A brick retaining wall, as high as the top step, runs to either side. Just above, on a patch of front lawn, is a tall, mostly intact column. We agree. This column, this landmark, could be our starting spot for the six paces west and two paces north.

"How big are paces?" Devin asks.

It sounds rhetorical, or I'm translating it that way because there is no right answer. "Which way is north?" I say instead.

According to the compass app, two paces north lands us on top of the retaining wall. Six large paces west, and we're back on the lower level at a pair of uneven, rectangular stones at the wall's side. "An unremarkable spot. No one would bother with it."

"Unless," Devin says, "they, too, are graced with a map, book, letter, canister, locket, and box. Or they're those people." Two couples, who look like they're taking a much-needed break, are sitting on our stones. The one man who's moaning about his aching feet—in American English—makes it sound like they'll be there a while.

In case we were wrong about the paces, we try several times more from different starting spots, but those two stones make the most sense. And the people are still there.

"I've got this." I walk right up to them. "Excuse me, but can you take our picture?"

"You're American!" one of the women says.

"Close," I say. "Canadian." Before she can ask for our life story, I hand her my burner. "And I hate to ask this favor, but me and my brother, our parents met right here during a tour. Would you mind if we moved you all for a minute?"

It works like a charm. She takes a few pictures, I sit to review them, and they leave.

"I'd ask how you arrived at that ploy," Devin says, "but the more important point is that I'm not your brother. And I'd kiss you right here in an unbrotherly fashion, but those people are still watching."

"And we shouldn't blow our cover." I kiss him on the cheek anyway. But we have only forty-three minutes until closing time, so I pivot away before he can respond.

Both stones are pockmarked with all sorts of shapes, but otherwise, they're solid—no place to insert a key. "Not surprising," Devin says. "The key was lying right next to *Fila Eleven,* and there are no rows here."

"What about the eleven on the map grid?"

He shakes his head. "The numbers are at the top, so I'd think it would say column eleven, but we can keep it in mind." Then he sits to inspect the stones at eye level. "Tess!"

On one of the stones, in the space between them, someone deliberately carved *650M SE*.

"Six hundred fifty meters *sud-est*, southeast." Devin pulls up a map. "It's a cemetery."

"How appropriate. Our final resting place. Unless we screwed up, and we're off on a wild-goose chase." But it makes sense, and the clock is ticking. The cemetery, too, closes soon.

On our way out of Ostia Antica, I catch a whiff of Signora Roma near the entrance, but once we're onto the street, it's pure, outskirts-of-Rome air. The nav app shows a nine-minute walk to the cemetery, but I push through the pain, and we reach the entrance in six.

The late sun is filtering through the trees, and though it may not be misty here, I get that damp, creepy feeling from all the gray grave markers and the telltale cemetery silence that feels like someone or something could seize you at any moment.

I shake that off. We only have thirty-one minutes till closing, and I can't do this another day. Even without tracking devices, the Rossis would hunt me down at Devin's. Or they'd hold AdDad and family captive until they turned me over.

The rows here aren't numbered, so we count them as we pass. Four, five, six, sev—

A man jumps into our path.

I scream. I think Devin does too.

The man laughs like this is a regular thing for him. His name is Giorgio, according to the patch on his coveralls, and by the rake in one hand and the bucket in the other, he's a groundskeeper. He asks if we need help. We say we're fine and keep counting. Eight, nine, ten...

"Eleven!" We make a right turn down the unpaved path taking us past grave marker after grave marker. We reach the end.

Devin shakes his head. "I was sure we'd know it when we saw it."

I nod. Except for slight variations, the markers are essentially the same and have no obvious use for a key. We pause at the last one to regroup.

Nino Ruggeri

14 Aprile 1934 - 20 Settembre 1970

"Look." I point to that inscription then to the next marker and the one after that. "These people died in the 1960s or 70s."

"I'm sorry," Devin says, "but I'm not seeing your point."

"*Il Colonnello* wrote that letter soon after World War Two. They could have added rows since then."

We have two choices. Either go down every one of them until we find something marked *Alessandro*—that image gives me a shiver—or we find the groundskeeper.

My first reaction: no groundskeeper. He could be a tentacle outfitted with gravedigging equipment. But if the Rossis knew we'd wind up here, Rosa and Il Creepo would be here instead.

Near the entrance, Giorgio shows us a map that differentiates the new area from the older one.

Old Row Eleven turns out to be Row Twenty-Eight. And when we turn down this one, about halfway, there's an unmarked mausoleum, the only structure that could be worth all this terror I've been through. And it has a lock.

CHAPTER FORTY-EIGHT

THE KEY FITS. THE KEY TURNS. THE DOOR RELEASES, BUT JUST A sliver. "If you'd like the honors…" I say.

"The honor of being first inside the creepy mausoleum?" Devin draws even with me. "Right, then. I am thrilled to act as—"

Before he can get out the next word, I push on the door.

"—Ironman. Or…you've just proven, in a genderless manner, that you are."

It's pitch-black inside, but the area is so small, our phone flashlights light it up. White marble benches line each of the four white marble walls, all so immaculate like someone cleans the entire place daily. Front and center is a white marble tomb with a marble statue of a man in military garb lying in repose. "The Colonel," I whisper. "Is this the treasure? Finding his burial site?"

"If he's playing one enormous prank."

There has to be more, and I shudder at the thought of what I need to do next. I inch closer to the tomb, working up the nerve to lift the lid. My fingers flex to the beat of my heart in anticipation of seeing a fully decomposed body, snakes and spiders, moths and maggots weaving their way among the bones. "I will never be ready for what we're about to see."

"Nor will I," Devin says. "You opened this mausoleum. The least I can do is help with this. One, two, three!" No way this opens. At least no obvious way.

"Might there be a release outside?" He takes the key and goes out while I stay in here.

I crouch next to the tomb to inspect the floor, wall-to-wall marble tiles. Maybe one of them lifts and unlocks the lid. I knock on one, the next, the next, and on down the line. These all feel solid. I turn the corner and do the same on the front side of the tomb. Same. Other side. Same. Behind it. Same, same—

Slam!

I scream. Jump up.

It's just Devin. "So sorry. I didn't remember the door slamming the first time."

He hands back the key, I catch my breath, and we finish knocking on the remaining tiles. I shake my head. "The walls are solid marble. The benches, solid marble. The floor and ceiling, solid marble."

"It's like we're entombed ourselves," Devin says.

"Great." I go to the other side of the Colonel and inspect his shoes, laces, pants, belt, jacket, face, hat. Everything is sculpted from the same piece of marble. Except his medals, metal medals, each with a different symbol: star, cross, coin, sunburst. Each symbol with a different number: four, seven, six, two. The coin with the number six protrudes more than the others.

I push on it. Nothing. I try to lift it straight up then flip it right, left, front, back.

"Allow me?" Devin slides the coin to the side where it rests neatly on top of the sunburst. Underneath is a disk. He presses it.

A latch releases the lid, and—

Puh!

We jump back. A pocket of air spits some substance. Poison? Cloud of death? But it's more like dust. And I'm feeling okay. Creeped out, but okay.

"That may have been like breaking a vacuum seal for the first time in years," he says.

I go with that, and we open the lid a little more. Nothing else spits at us. A little higher. Higher. We shine our phone light in. "Stairs?"

"Stairs," Devin says. "Thank goodness. But that calls up the question, where do they lead?"

"I, for one, refuse to think anymore. Let's just go."

The lid slides back as easily as if the hinges had been greased every day. We step up to the top and start our climb down, our phone lights not reaching the bottom, not until we're twelve steps lower. Even here, though a little dusty, it's cleaner than I'd ever expect. The Colonel must have arranged to keep this whole place preserved.

Twenty-two steps later, we reach a landing. The wall to the right has a door with a brass lock that's similar to a bicycle combination chain lock. Four little wheels with numbers zero through nine. They rotate.

"It's the numbers on the medals," Devin says. "Four, seven, six, two."

"Well done, you." My brain, though, is screaming to get the hell out of here before the Rossis somehow catch up to me. But I stand solid as he rolls the numbers.

The lock clicks. And he opens the heavy wooden door to what looks like a long tunnel.

I hold up my phone light. "Was this fully charged?"

"Just half," Devin says. "It's a pity too. I nearly brought my oil lantern but thought better of it."

Funny, but I can't laugh right now. I just move faster, grateful that the floor is paved and the concrete walls aren't crumbling, though I wouldn't want to inspect them. It smells surprisingly dry too.

We reach the end, a tiled wall. Eight of the tiles in front of us, stacked one on top of the other and twice as long as the surrounding ones, each have a string of ten letters. At either side of each tile is a slightly depressed space nearly the same length. "Another sliding game."

"Right," Devin says, "but what are the rules?"

I shake my head. "Maybe we test it out. Try sliding the top one over."

He pushes the tile fully to the right.

Ping! Ping! Ping! Pebbles falls from the ceiling. Then comes a full shower of them. We jump to the side, but not before we get hammered with a hailstorm of dirt and rocks. The walls and floor may be finished, but the ceiling is a mass of debris. I shake as much as possible from my hair.

"Looks like the construction crew missed a spot," Devin says. "Do we try another tile and hope it doesn't cause an avalanche?"

"Just move it slowly."

He does. Double the mass of debris falls on us, up nearly to my ankles.

I brush myself off. "I refuse to get buried alive underneath a tomb in a mausoleum."

"Technically, a cenotaph, a tomb with nothing buried there."

"Is there a reason we're getting technical?"

"Sorry," he says.

"I don't mean to snap. We're just so close to the end and…"

"I know. Maybe it's time we call the authorities and let them—"

"No." I stand back and look at the tiles again. There's one small black dot above the column of movable tiles and another dot directly below. I try to wipe them off, but they're permanent.

"You have that dangerous look," Devin says.

His words barely register. The letters, the dots. They mean something.

```
A  B  C  D  E  F  G  H  I  J
G  H  I  J  K  L  M  N  O  P
I  J  K  L  M  N  O  P  Q  R
A  B  C  D  E  F  G  H  I  J
D  E  F  G  H  I  J  K  L  M
P  Q  R  S  T  U  V  W  X  Y
B  C  D  E  F  G  H  I  J  K
E  F  G  H  I  J  L  M  N  O
```

"It's another code," I finally say. "It has to be."

"And not the one that opened the second layer of the box," Devin says. "Only eight rows here." He pulls out both versions of the letter from his pocket. "Shall we try the Italian one?"

I nod. There'd be nothing English about this. It has to be—

I step forward, holding my arm out so he won't follow. "Stand back. Get ready to run."

He doesn't stand back. Instead, he lowers my arm to move an inch ahead.

"You are either the kindest, most protective person in the world or the world's biggest idiot."

"Thank you," he says. "Though, whatever you're about to do, do it already because I'm not the world's bravest."

I center the C of the top tile under that black dot, grab Devin's arm, and dash back. But nothing falls.

"Either you're right," he says, "or we've already dislodged the debris from that row."

I tiptoe forward. "Hopefully, from the next row too." I slide the second tile so that the H is underneath the C.

"So far so good," he says. "I assume the real test comes next. What is the real test? If I may ask."

I don't want him stepping forward to be my hero. Yet he won't leave my side as I reach for the third tile. "Ready?" I slide the I underneath the H then stumble back as fast as I can.

Ping! Ping!

We run. But nothing more falls.

"Residual stones, perhaps?"

I want to believe he's right, desperately need to. The next one will tell.

We take a small step forward, kicking the debris out of our way. Nothing. Another. Nothing. One step at a time, my confidence builds. I am right. I just have to prove it.

I slide the fourth tile, line up a second C with the marks, and make no move to run.

Devin tugs me back anyway.

"It's okay. We're good."

"We're good?" He stares up as if daring the ceiling to pound down on us. "For now. We still have four more."

I open my locket, Nonno and Nonna smiling out at me. "C-C-T. *Chi cerce.* Whoever searches…"

"…finds."

In succession, I slide the E, the R, the C. Each move comes without debris but with a small click we didn't hear before.

"Because we were running," Devin says, "to avoid the cave-in."

"And because I was sure I might kill you."

"Then you would've been dead too."

"No. You would have fallen in so gentlemanly a way as to protect my head and leave an air pocket for me to breathe. Then I'd have to live the rest of my life with all the guilt that—"

"You're stalling," he says.

"I am stalling. What if there's nothing back here? Or what if it leads to another series of puzzles? I was so sure Ostia Antica was the end. And now? We'll have the Rossis where we want them. Zia Elena's side too. But what if this isn't the end? What if it's repeat, repeat, re—"

"Slide it. Just slide it, already."

I let my fingers linger on the last tile, the final E.

Slide!

CHAPTER FORTY-NINE

It's not just one click, but a series of them. Eight altogether. A jagged gap appears where the permanent tiles meet the empty sliding spaces. The gap continues down to the floor and forms a door.

I take a half step in, Devin's breath on my neck. "Wait," I say. "I have this vision of tripping a trigger that closes the door and traps us forever. Stay out here? Save me if it happens?"

I move forward.

It's a small chamber, empty except for another marble crypt in the middle. This one is larger with no Colonel in repose—just one word chiseled into the side: TROVA. Finds.

Goosebumps. But what did I find?

This brass lock on this crypt is in plain view as if to say, "You've come this far. No more games." Or maybe that's wishful thinking again.

I slide the key in. *Please turn.* "Thank you."

"Thank you for what?" Devin calls. "What are you doing? Tell me everything. It sucks to be the Royal Guard."

"There's another crypt, which probably won't seal me in, but you never know. Stay there until I say it's safe."

This lid opens easier than the one upstairs. In place of a body or bones or rocks or stairs are a dozen bundles of fabric. Bands of tape hold the grayish felt in place. I stand and stare.

The one on the far left is nearly the width of the crypt. It lifts easily, but it's half my height, two-thirds of my wingspan, and is too cumbersome for me, fully and safely, to pull out by myself.

"Everything okay?" Devin calls.

"Should be. Come on in."

He peeks through the door as if adding weight to this room would trigger absolute devastation. But he quickly straightens. "What's all this?"

It's what I'd hoped for from the first time I saw the posters in the Borghese Museum's office, and yet, I didn't dare to dream. "Paintings. Thefts from museums or family collections. Spoils of war."

I'd like nothing more than to lift them all out, peel back the felt and place them around this room like a small, private museum. But I refuse to be responsible for destroying what might be a treasure. And yet, we need to confirm what I suspect before we make our next move.

We lay one of the bundles on the ground as if it were a newborn baby. The tape is starchy and no longer sticky, but the felt has been wrapped for so long, it remains fully in place.

I peel back one flap, then another. Underneath is fluffy, off-white material.

"Batting," Devin says. "Someone took great care with this."

It's only now that we can see that the corners of an ornate, gold picture frame have been protected by heavy corrugated cardboard. Beyond that, brushstrokes. I want to see more. I want to have more. Just this one painting, an amazing souvenir to cherish forever. Or to sell on the black market and use the money to buy—

I'm not a thief. I'm better than that. Better than them all. Except Nonno. He left and did right by his family. "Right?"

"Whatever you say."

"I say, we did it!" I hold up my hand for a high five.

Devin goes to slap it back, but instead, he grabs onto my hand and pulls me to his chest. I look up at him. He, down at me. Maybe it's the adrenaline rush, maybe it's extreme relief, but this kiss, this one, lingers and lingers and feels so right.

We come up for air and I take a slight step back. "We should, hmm, make some calls."

"Right." Except we have no reception down here.

We rewrap the painting, return it to its slot, close the lid of the crypt, and close the door behind us. We decide not to scramble the letters. It might cause a cave-in.

Back upstairs, we slide the crypt lid back into place, the Colonel's medal, too, then lock the mausoleum door from the outside.

I resist the urge to stand there and guard the place. We'd be like a beacon pointing to its importance. Besides, the cemetery closes in six minutes. We move toward the entrance instead.

I text Anjelica. North side, Colosseum Skatepark in 20

minutes. 17:15. Do not show up more than 5 minutes early or you will forfeit your rights to the box.

I'm about to send the same one to Vittoria, but I change my mind. East side, Colosseum Skatepark in 20 minutes. 17:15. Do not show up more than 5 minutes early or you will forfeit your rights to the box.

It's a decision I make on my own with only myself to blame if it turns sour. Zia Elena's side may not be fully honorable, but they are family, and they didn't threaten to kill anyone.

Devin is busy with his calls anyway. First, to AdDad. "I promise I'm fine. I'll send you a selfie if you want. Just meet us here. And yes, call them if you will."

Them, who? His parents in London? The police? All fine.

I've already dialed the main Rome police station. I do have the legitimate defense law on my side. Even if that's questionable, I'd rather answer for everything I did than live with the Rossis out there, waiting to get even.

Devin looked them up by their real names. They're wanted for forgery, embezzlement, conspiracy, and a whole list of offenses. Capturing them can only tip the scales in my favor.

A man answers.

"*Mi chiamo Tess Alessandro,*" I say. "*Americano. So parlare un po' di italiano. Ma parli inglese?*"

"Yes," says the voice. "I speak English."

"*Grazie.* I have information about a criminal family. The Martorellis. They have been threatening my life and the life of my family. Do you know who I'm talking about?"

"One moment." He transfers me to the on-duty commander, Commander Mancusi.

I repeat what I just said.

"Are you now in danger?" she asks.

"I'm safe now, but they're expecting to meet me in fifteen minutes." I give her the location.

"The Martorellis? Which?"

"Giovanni and Claudia. They've been going by Anjelica and Francesco Rossi." I give her the address of the apartment.

"How do we know it is really them?"

"I can text you a picture." It's the family photo in the kitchen, the one I took with Devin's phone. "But I'm an exchange student from America. I've been living with them for the past two weeks. Please. Can you send someone fast?" I look up and pinch the bridge of my nose to stop the tears.

"We will dispatch a team. Do not meet them there."

"I won't." I give her my phone number and location, and she insists on sending an officer here to meet us. It sounds like AdDad has already taken care of that, but right now, please, send me a whole police squad.

Before she ends the conversation, she has me enter her direct number into my phone. I text the photo. Then I slump down on the cemetery side of the entrance gate. And I sob.

CHAPTER FIFTY

GIORGIO COMES AROUND TO TELL US IT'S CLOSING TIME. He points to me. "*Può essere difficile perdere una persona cara.*" It's hard to lose a loved one.

I'm about to correct him, but in general terms, he's right. It is hard. I thank him instead.

Then he stands aside. Two police officers have shown up. One comes over to make sure I'm not hurt.

"*Sto bene,*" I say. "These are tears of relief. *Lacrime di,* um, not scared, *non spaventato.*"

"I understand relief," the other says. "My partner not speak much English."

From what I can tell, he's asking Giorgio to let us stay for a while. I have a feeling it will take more than a while to sort this out.

Another car comes screeching up. AdDad. He wraps each of us in a hug. "I broke every traffic law. But don't tell them."

"He knows," Devin says. "He speaks English."

The officer waves him off. "No catch. No problem. No do again." He asks for our story.

Suddenly, my knee is throbbing.

Giorgio fetches chairs for the five of us while I start with Sofia threatening my parents with a knife and being forced to take the canister. "From my *zia*," I add, hoping it sounds less criminal. "It had some yarn in it, but that's all." And I don't want to admit to anything else I did, not yet, so I start telling them about Carly and the other threats.

My phone rings. I put Commander Mancusi on speaker. "I want you to know we arrested Giovanni and Claudia Martorelli. They were where you said they would be."

I thank her profusely. "Can I ask? Did they have a letter with them? A canister?"

"Letter?"

"Correspondence. Silver container."

"Ah. *Minuto*." She's apparently muted the phone. "No. No letter. No container. But they both had weapons. You are very lucky."

"I know. *Grazie, grazie, grazie.*"

"We will talk later? I will come to you. Or you will come to the station?"

I look up to AdDad, who nods. "You will not be alone."

I can't help it. The tears start again. I compose myself fast, ready to go on with the story, but the officer asks what brought us to the cemetery.

"We need to show you."

Devin and I take them through the process of opening the door and the crypt. When they see the stairs, one of the officers whistles.

I nod. "We were surprised too."

We head down and through the corridor, this time brightly illuminated by the officers' flashlights, our steps punctuated by "*Oh, mio Dio!*" and "*Cavolo!*" and "*Mamma mia!*"

Before I open the second crypt, I turn to them. "We'll need an art expert."

"An art expert?"

"*Esperto d'arte,*" AdDad says. He turns to us. "Why?"

"I think these paintings have been missing for decades."

I open the crypt and unwrap that one corner again.

"No more," the officer says. "We get the experts."

Back upstairs, they alert Commander Mancusi, who promises to get museum representatives here shortly. "Our officers will stand guard until then."

One of them stays there. The other walks with us to the entrance gate and hands us off to a second pair of officers. They already know our names and enough of the story to ask for my key to the Rossis'/Martorellis' apartment. It's their job to escort us out of there.

I don't want to go, but I have no choice. We head to AdDad's car.

"It's not fair," I say, trying not to sound like a brat. "After what I went through, I deserve to see how it comes out. I mean, I didn't get to watch them haul away Anjelica and Francesco—or whatever their names are."

"I am sure you will see in the news." AdDad stops at a light and turns to look at me. "Are your parents okay? I would be, you say, freaking."

My parents. I need to tell them everything, but… "Where do I begin?" I ask AdDad.

"You call them on FaceTime," he says. "They will see you are not hurt. You tell them you are fine, and you smile. But you also cry. You smile too hard, and we think you are hiding something."

It makes sense, but I don't want them to be alone. Also, someone—not me—needs to convince them to see a doctor. I need Aunt Debbie, but I don't know her number.

Before we go to the Rossis to pick up my things, AdDad swings by the Colosseum Skatepark. My phone is just where we left it. I don't call, though. I text.

It's Tess. First, truly, I'm fine. I just took this picture with Devin and his exchange dad.

I hit Send then start typing the rest. Can you do me a favor? Can you

My phone rings. Aunt Debbie.

"Tess? What do you mean you're truly fine? That's what people say when they're not."

"Really. I'm in one piece. No real cuts or bruises, no internal organ damage."

"You're still scaring me. I'm switching to FaceTime." She does.

"See?" I say. "I mean I scraped my chin when I stupidly tripped earlier today. Otherwise…" I show her that I'm safe and in a car with Devin and AdDad. "I need to ask. When did you last see my mom and dad? Are they fine? Are they safe?"

"I talked to your mom this morning. She wanted my recipe for strudel."

AdDad turns around. "Just tell her, Tess."

"Don't freak out," I say. "I know you will, but don't." I take a breath. "The Rossis, my exchange family, they're not who they pretended to be. Neither is Sofia. You met her, right?"

"Nice girl. Didn't strike me as the homesick type, though."

"She's not. She's the one who put Beanie Cubbie in your office as a warning to me. I made her leave." Then I give her the very shortest version of how the Rossis threatened to kill my parents. And I assure her that the Italian authorities will be there to pick Sofia up when she lands. "But I need to know. How are my mom and dad? The truth."

"The truth? They've been better. They're trying to shake some bug they caught last week or so, but they can't seem to."

I knew it, but it still catches me off guard. I breathe in four, hold two—

"Tess? Now, what's wrong."

I nod on the exhale. "I'm fine. But here's what you need to do. Please, leave now and get my parents to the hospital. They've been drugged, something addictive that may have them go through withdrawal."

She's already walking from her office to her car. "I'll get your mom first. Then we'll pick up your dad. Be ready to answer when they call. If they don't see you right away, they'll be on the next plane. You know that."

"I do. And make sure they understand I truly am fine. I'm handling things here."

"Tess, you've always been amazing, but now..." Aunt Debbie shakes her head. "No words, but I love you."

"Now," says AdDad. "We get you home and fed."

It hits me. My eyes well with tears. "I don't have a home. I don't have money. I don't have my passport. I don't know where to go."

"You always have a home with us." AdDad reaches back, grabs my hand, and holds it the rest of the way to the Rossis' apartment.

An officer is stationed at the entrance to the street, a space waiting for AdDad's car. He walks us down the cobblestones to the building, telling us how they needed to break open the door. The Martorellis installed an unpickable lock, and my key didn't work.

I give a laugh. "Figures. They lied about pretty much everything."

"You never used the key?" AdDad says.

"They told me they'd always be here for me."

Another officer is stationed upstairs. The door frame is noticeably broken. "They move out?" he says. "Before today?"

"No. They were here this morning." I go in.

The place is cleaned out. No furniture, no pictures, no safe. In the kitchen, no dishes or pots or pans. Just one lone blue towel. Zia Elena's. "Can I have this?"

The officer nods. "Everything still here, I think, is yours." He points to the spiral stairs.

I take them up, one by one, hopefully for the last time. I put extra weight on the sixth and ninth steps, making them squeak as loudly as possible, but it doesn't seem as loud as the night I tried to sneak down when—surprise!—they were speaking English.

My room is pretty much how I left it this morning. My suitcases are under the bed, my clothes and shoes are in the wardrobe, my toiletry caddy is on the desk. The monkey is there. So is the vase.

The crucifix camera is missing. In its place, the yarn from the canister. Only two other things are different. They've left my money, credit card, and driver's license in the middle of the bed. Next to my passport, my real passport.

The officer points to it. "You should carry this with you."

"They made me carry this one." I fish out the fake and hold it out to him. "Please take it."

It's too crowded in the room with all of us in there, so Devin, AdDad, and the officer wait for me at the bottom of the stairs, which is good. I don't need everyone staring while I pack. And while I take a long look at the other new object in the room.

Leaning against the foot of the bed is the painting from Piazza Navona—the woman in her red dress, holding a yellow umbrella under a blue sky, walking by the fountain. On the back is a sticky note with two words: *Bonne fille*. In French, *good girl*. Maybe a hint to where they were headed next or something to throw the police off their tails. Either way, it feels like they left me a reward. After all, *una mano lava l'altra*. They expected to escape with the paintings, so they gave me one in return.

As much as I'd love to erase this whole time from my memory, I never will. And now, finally, I might have the chance to experience the Rome I imagined that day.

CHAPTER FIFTY-ONE

By the time we get to AdDad's house, Dance Mum has already arranged for an attorney to be here. Signor Diamante greets us at the door. He's a friend of the family and has Devin's dad's approval as well.

At first glance, with his jet-black hair and sharp features, I'm totally intimidated. But then he smiles and gently pats my shoulder, and he's won me over. If he can do that in three seconds, he's probably amazing at his job.

We sit in the living room, and I tell him every detail. He listens and nods and asks a few questions. Then I ask him one. "Will I be arrested?"

"Oh, Tess," he says. "No, no, no." And he assures me that I will not become another girl in another bone-chilling documentary. And he will be with me any time I talk to the police.

He stays there for dinner, and afterward I excuse myself to

AdDad's office, which doubles as my guest room for the night. It may be small, but it's larger than the tower room, and it won't come with death threats. I go in there to FaceTime Carly, to apologize. And my heartbeat rivals its pace during some of the scariest parts from earlier in the day.

"Tess!" She sounds like her old self again.

Before she can start talking and talking, I blurt out four words. "I am so sorry."

"I know, but seriously? A blown tire can happen to anyone."

Then I tell her everything. And I apologize again. And again.

"Stop it or I'm hanging up." She moves her finger closer and closer to the screen.

"Fine. Talk."

She laughs. "So, you know how, sometimes, bad things happen for a good reason? You made me call Dr. Abrams, but I still wasn't convinced. Then due to circumstances beyond your control, I landed in the hospital. Do *not* apologize. Pain aside, I had the best time there. No one can stop Dr. Carly CureKids now. I'm just glad you're okay, but what's with your chin?"

Before I can laugh, AdDad knocks on the door. "Two detectives are here to talk to you."

I end the call with Carly and get my parents on FaceTime. They're home from the hospital and insist they're feeling well enough to be in on every conversation.

Signor Diamante, my new BFF sitting next to me, takes the lead, though. "These detectives," he says, "are here to talk to you about your *zia* Rosa and her friend."

They were unable to find Rosa and Cornelio, aka Il Creepo—who's not my uncle—at Ostia Antica but assure me that they are actively searching for them. For my own sanity, I decide that while the Rossis are real threats to me, Rosa and Cornelio are not.

The officer asks me to describe each time I saw the two of them. I do, then they want me to describe everything the Rossis forced me to do.

Signor Diamante guides the conversation.

I sketch the canister for them. Then Devin and I bring out every scrap of evidence we have. The pictures on his phone from Zia Elena's apartment, then pictures of the letter, bookstore and library books, and the box itself. Next, all my shoe papers, my timeline, the yarn, and the photo the Rossis hung in my window. I show them everything but Signor Matteo's napkin. I promised I'd protect him, and I will unless it's absolutely necessary to protect myself.

"Now, this box," one of the detectives says. "Do you have it still?"

Signor Diamante nods. "Bring it here."

I hand it to the detective.

"We questioned the owner of La Collina," she says.

I want to see him and apologize, but I nod so she'll go on.

The box, she explains, was originally given to the Mountain for safekeeping until it was claimed by the person with *la parola d'ordine*. The twenty-five-thousand-euro price tag was a way of discouraging people and also his way of making the other items look like bargains. "You had the password," the detective says. "Then she is yours. The credit card was a precaution."

We wrap up after midnight. Mostly. Just as the detectives stand to leave, Commander Mancusi stops by. She wants to meet us. And to tell us they have Sofia in custody. "But there is something else I want to say. And watch your faces." She tries to hold back a smile.

"The art experts. They believe the pieces of artwork you found are what you suspected. They are valuable originals by Italian and Dutch masters."

I look at Devin. He looks at me. And every bit of energy that shocked me into action for all these days has turned into a massive blush of triumph. I pump my fist. "Yes! Yes, yes, yes!"

Commander Mancusi laughs. The experts, she explains, believe the paintings were first sent to a home in the Italian countryside when Italy joined the war. Then they were seized by forces apparently headed by the Colonel. "They suspect he hid more works of art elsewhere." She looks me in the eye. "Tess, would you like to help us find them?"

"Me?" I shake my head. "I think I'm retired."

She laughs and gives me a pat on the knee. "We leave now. You will be here until when?"

"I'm not sure." I hold up my phone. "Mom? Dad?"

They look at one another. I can see the worry in their faces. And if they insist that I come home, I will.

But I can't hold my breath and wait for an answer. "I'm sure you want to see me right away," I say. "And I want to see you. But I also need to be here, finish school, be in Rome the way it should have been all along. Does that make sense?"

They look at one another again. "It does," my mom says, "but we'll give you our answer tomorrow."

We leave it at that.

And I laugh inside. Just a week ago, I was crying to go home. And now, I'd cry to stay.

CHAPTER FIFTY-TWO

SOMETHING IS DIFFERENT. I SENSE IT THE MINUTE I WAKE UP, even before I open my eyes. But it's not that I'm in a different room. The pervasive feeling of dread is gone.

Mostly. There is one loose end.

No one has mentioned Zia Elena, Arsenio, Florenza, and Vittoria. Including me. But I need to say something today.

I roll over and look at my phone. 10:47. I'm missing school. More importantly, I've missed the drama. I wouldn't blame Devin if he already told Bright and Nicolas everything. But they've texted both Devin and me at least twenty times, and he hasn't responded either. The last one from Bright: RU dead or something?

I can at least ease that worry. Very very long story. Tell u everything later. Up most of the night. Rt now me + pillow

I dress quickly and go downstairs, where AdDad has apparently baked everything he knows how. He's taken the day off work. "You might call it stress baking, but today it's happiness baking. Happy you are here."

"I'm sure I'll be going soon."

"No, no. You stay." Even if he doesn't need another body in the house, he's good at faking it. "Flavia wants you to stay. She will tell you when she comes back after morning class."

I grab a biscotti. Almond and anise. Food hasn't tasted this good since the dinner at the top of the Spanish Steps. I was so trusting then. And I need to be trustworthy now. I tell AdDad about talking to the police again.

Devin comes out at that moment. "What did you forget?"

"My Italian family. I didn't mention them at all."

"Because..." Devin says.

I take a beat to get my words going. "Remember when I told them to meet me at the east side of the skate park?" I know he doesn't because I didn't show him.

He shakes his head.

"Well, I did. I needed the police to catch the Rossis no matter what. And I was worried that two different families could cause so much confusion, the Rossis might escape."

"That makes sense," Devin says, "but aren't you worried about the other family?"

"Yes, no. Maybe." I never saw Zia Elena's side commit a crime. Not here. Not when we visited them. Not when they visited us. Unless snooping is a crime. And there's the fact that I actually committed a crime against them. Twice.

I call Signor Diamante, who suggests I leave the matter alone for now.

I'm good with that.

Then I text my parents to tell them I'm up. They FaceTime me right away, 5:00 a.m. for them. I confirm I'm still fine for the seventh time since last night, except I have more questions.

My dad nods. "Go ahead. Shoot!" he says. "Wait. Didn't mean that." His laugh isn't all the way back, but I let it go. "Whatcha got for me?"

"You've never told me about the Rossis, the Martorellis, whoever. Why?"

He blows out a breath. "Rosa's branch broke off before I was born, so it's almost like they never existed. Still, yes, you should know everything, good and bad. So, for starters…

"When I was a boy, as kids do, I'd whine for an extra cookie or one more ride on the roller coaster. And Nonno would shake his finger at me. 'Don't be like the Colonel.' I thought it was a saying everyone knew. But when no one in third grade did, I asked Nonno what it meant. It was like a dark cloud covered his face. He sat me down and told me that when the Colonel didn't get his way, he'd do bad stuff to people. That's all he'd say."

"Rosa must have learned well. Maybe Zia Elena too."

My dad nods. "But not Nonno. I believe I told you this story. He'd just turned fifteen when he cheated his own friend out of money. Only two lira, but still. That's when he realized he was becoming his father and got the hell out of there."

"It sounds a little familiar, but why didn't I know the rest?"

My dad shakes his head. "I suppose we're so busy with what's happening today and what's supposed to happen tomorrow that we forget about yesterday."

"We should stop doing that," I say.

"Agreed. Piecing things together these past hours..." He shakes his head, almost in tears. "I am so sorry, Tess. But I think I know how you got mixed up in this whole business."

"How?"

He wipes the corner of his eye. "In one of our conversations, Arsenio mentioned that you were guaranteed to get accepted to Exchange Roma. That he knew people who knew people, and that's the way things worked around there. Then he laughed it off as a joke."

"It's okay, Dad. You didn't know what that meant."

"But I ignored my Spidey sense. I was so excited for you."

"You were." I hate seeing him feeling so guilty. "It's not your fault. Though, if you did know we were illegal heirs to an artwork fortune..." I laugh.

So does he. Then he gets serious again. "I guess the paintings have jogged my memory because I'm recalling other bits that Nonno told me over the years. This one is especially relevant."

I turn up the volume so I won't miss a word.

"Toward the end of the war, the Colonel was arrested for stealing, but he never paid the price for it. Somehow, he put full blame on a scapegoat who was later executed for disloyalty. The Colonel turned honest after that, not because he was sorry, but because he was scared."

"You knew the Colonel stole paintings?"

My dad shakes his head. "I assumed it was money. He did live a very comfortable life."

"You know," I say, "if I'd taken just one painting, *we* could live a very comfortable life."

My mom grabs the phone. "Tess!"

"Just kidding. But if I start to come home with a hubcap collection, stop me, okay?"

They laugh, but my mom keeps hold of the phone. "In all seriousness, now, don't get any ideas, Tess. No treasure hunting. Not if you want to stay and finish the program, that is."

"You mean I can stay? I'll promise anything."

"Don't get all dramatic on us," she says. "But yes. Devin's family really wants you to. You must have made an amazing impression. We always think you make a good impression, but we're your parents."

"And I've proven you right. You're welcome." I give a laugh. "And as my reward, answer this. Did you know that Arsenio, Florenza, and Vittoria searched the houses when they were in town for the funeral?"

"We suspected so," she says. "I walked in on them looking around and not like normal guests."

"Did they ask about *il calice*?"

"Even if they had," my dad says, "it would've gone right over my head. And if they'd mentioned a locket, I would have played dumb. They may not be like Rosa's side, but they would have tried to wheedle it away from me. It was always yours."

Devin has been sitting here, hanging on every word. Also, drawing his own family tree.

"Any deep, dark secrets?" I ask when the call ends.

"One never knows," he says, purposefully raising his eyebrow. "You of all people should understand that."

I over-grin. "You think? And just when I thought Arsenio wanted me here for me."

"Right. Arsenio. He guaranteed your father that you'd get into Exchange Roma. How does that figure into your living with the evil family? Do you know?"

"Here's my best guess," I say. "Arsenio gets me to apply to Exchange Roma and leaks that info to the Rossis. He knows they'll do whatever it takes to gather all the pieces. Maybe he and Florenza were on that trip or maybe they were here, watching, waiting to swoop in and, well, you can guess the rest."

Devin nods. "Contact them. See if you're right."

"I tried. My parents did too. As of last night, they're gone. Poof! Vanished! Thin air!" I give a shrug. "Oh, well. If they're on the run, so be it."

"So be it? Who are you and what have to done to my tie-up-all-loose-strings pal Tess?"

"Don't worry," I say. "She'll be back. Just give her some time to bounce from jittery kitten to untamed tiger and anything in between. You'll discover the real me soon enough. I'll discover the real me, whoever I am now. Who knows? You might end up hating me."

"You don't completely believe that, do you?"

"Not anymore." I start to lean my head on his shoulder but pop up. "True confession?"

"About what?"

"About Zia Elena's side of the family. I feel safer knowing they're out there."

Devin moves away like I'm some contaminated stranger.

"Think about it," I say. "The police didn't catch Signora Roma and Il Creepo. And if the Rossi/Martorelli network is as big as they made it sound, less chance they'll focus on me if they're worried about Zia Elena. Besides...Zia Elena, Vittoria...never mind."

"Never mind, what? You're looking to the side again."

"Oh dear," I say. "And just when I thought I had that perfected."

"You never completely did." He raises his eyebrow.

"Another truth is, I really like Zia Elena. And even with her threats, I sort of like Vittoria. So, part of me wants them to be safe." I shrug. "Maybe I've inherited a little evil."

"You? No. Maybe you want to be a little evil. There's power in that. In a twisted way. But a suggestion from someone who may've tried. Don't pretend to be something you can't."

"And yet," I say, "I pretended to be a thief. And I did it pretty well."

He grabs my hand. Pulls me outside. Away from the windows.

This time, the kiss is epic.

CHAPTER FIFTY-THREE

We're excused from school for the day—Dance Mum called in and said there was a family emergency that involved us both—but I need to go back.

"Otherwise, Bright and Nicolas won't leave us alone," I tell Devin.

We get there toward the end of lunch when everyone is either in the cafeteria or outside at the picnic tables. First thing, we knock on Signor Matteo's door.

He rushes up and hugs us both. After too many profuse apologies for his involvement, he asks if we're okay.

I assure him we are, but his brow stays furrowed.

"And you are too," I tell him. "The Rossis will always believe that you were true to them."

His face relaxes. "*Grazie. Grazie. Grazie. Un milione di volte grazie.*" And he hugs us once again before he walks us to our classroom. No one else is there yet, but it'll only be a minute or two. "You will be staying for the full term, no?"

"I am."

"Again, I am so grateful that you removed the danger from my life and the life of my family; I will give you anything you want. I am the reason your world became cruel."

"No," I say. "They are the reason. You were a victim like me."

"*Non importa. Qualsiasi cosa, davvero qualsiasi cosa.*"

I tell him, no, I don't need anything, that he was here for me when I needed him, but he won't let up until I promise. I'll let him know if I need anything. Anything.

The class starts trickling in. A few people ask where we were, but Devin and I have been so busy getting answers, we forgot to come up with a story. Now we need one. Bright and Nicolas are rushing up.

"When you weren't here," she says, "we thought you were either dead or arrested."

Nicolas nods. "Or you'd taken the ferry to Albania and eloped."

"Exactly." Bright slings her arm around my shoulder. "Tell me you stole a wedding ring from that shop. That's why you used us."

I hold out my left hand. "No ring."

"Then why? You promised you'd tell us everything."

"You were right, Bright. It wasn't a joke," I say. "I desperately needed something in the shop, but I didn't have the money for it. I needed you to be a distraction."

"You stole it? You're a thief?"

"That's part of the story, but it's totally out of context."

Bright's eyes grow wide. "You're even more interesting than I thought."

"You think I'm interesting?"

"That's why I targeted you."

I just look at her.

"What? You were sitting by yourself that first day, writing or drawing or whatever, but you especially looked so sure of yourself. You're the only one who didn't look nervous."

I'd admit exactly how nervous I was, but I love that she's seeing a different side of me. I'm pretty much that girl now.

"Then I especially stuck around because you caught Devin's attention right away."

"Aha! That's the real reason." I laugh. "And you stayed close to me so I wouldn't totally move in on him."

"Maybe. A little. But now you can move in all you want." She winks at Nicolas, whose grin can't get any bigger. "But honest truth, I decided to hang around you because I wanted your interesting-ness to rub off on me. And now, maybe it did. You promised! Tell us everything! All the gory details!"

I'm saved by Signorina Emma, who comes in, clapping her hands. *"Per quelli di voi interessati a realizzare un progetto artistico..."*

For those of you interested in art for your project? She knows?

But she taps at the computer and the big screen flashes on. It's a news story.

I don't catch all the words, but I don't need to. They're talking about the capture of the Martorellis, and they're showing stock photos of the paintings from the crypt. They end the story with one sentence—basically, that the police have not yet disclosed how this all came about, but that some unnamed sources are responsible for this amazing find.

I turn to Devin, whose face is as red as mine feels.

"Seriously," Bright says, not even trying to speak in Italian. "You? You captured an international crime ring?"

I try not to react.

"Doesn't get more interesting than that."

I smile. "I guess it doesn't."

CHAPTER FIFTY-FOUR

IT'S THREE WEEKS LATER. MY PARENTS FLEW OUT FOR A LONG weekend just to see me for themselves. I took them to the crypt and to Villa Borghese and a few of the other places I went with the Rossis those first few days. Including Naples, where my dad bought that watch.

They're back home now. Here, all the publicity has died down. Mostly. Maybe I shouldn't have posted that haiku the next day.

Those twelve impostors,
fixed to walls, can now bow to
the originals

I claimed it was only inspired by the story, but with Bright as your friend, word tends to get around. It's fine. Better than fine. I'm touring with her and her family here in Italy during that week when

I was supposed to be staying with Zia Elena's side. And Bright's parents, who are not rich or famous—they make high-end window coverings; who knew?—have been gathering tips from a rich and famous client who has experience dealing with the press.

Even still, reporters occasionally call or knock at the door. They want Devin and me on all the Italian, U.S., and BBC network shows—news and true crime. Well, me mostly.

I'm not ready.

That conquering-hero stand I took, the one that gave the Rossis the nonnegotiable ultimatum? I can now point to three thousand different ways it could have ended in disaster. Which is why a lot of my swagger has gone into retreat. If I ever have to summon it again, though, I know it exists.

There's another thing I know. I'm like a giant pot of minestrone. I'm not exactly sure what's inside, but in whole, I love it. It's real. It's true. It's the new Tess, who's really not so different from the old Tess. Except I'm now refusing to obsess over that question: How did I get here?

I'm here because I can handle it.

On the surface, that may sound like I'm ready for all those interviews, but I could use a little time and space. I hear the reporters will give me many more opportunities.

After Italy, with Bright and me joining Nicolas at Devin's house—his parents have invited us for an "extended holiday"—they'll stay on my tail. But his parents, too, have experience with the press.

I have no clue how the media found my number, but when I

asked my parents about changing it, they told me that everything might die down by the time I get home. Meanwhile, they loaded up my burner cell, which allows me to turn off my official phone when I want privacy.

I check it pretty often, though. Like now. It's a text from yet another number I don't recognize. I read them all anyway. Then delete, delete, delete.

This one, though, I read again. And again.

Hey, Chicky! You won. This time.

Vittoria.

I shiver. But I need to reply.

Where are

Backspace, backspace, backspace.

I hit a speed dial number instead.

"Tess? Is everything okay?"

"It's great, Commander Mancusi. But I need to know. Were you serious about me helping you track down more missing art?"

"Absolutely."

I laugh. My mom is going to kill me.

ACKNOWLEDGMENTS

I teethed on Nancy Drew, the Hardy Boys, and Encyclopedia Brown; dove further into reading with Agatha Christie; spread my wings with Donald Westlake, Mary Higgins Clark, Harry Kemelman, Dashiell Hammett, and whatever my parents had at home. So, it might naturally follow that I would fall hard into writing mysteries and thrillers. Except...

Except, I was so in awe of these books—the premises, the construction, the twists and turns, and, especially how they made me feel—I never dared to dream that I'd try writing one. And then...

And then in conversation, my agent Jennie Dunham mentioned something-something (you should) something-something (thriller) something. Yeah. No. But my self-doubt morphed into a spark of interest then into an opportunity. Thanks, Jennie, for your confidence in me and connecting me with (thank you!) Brendan Deneen, who skillfully shepherded this concept through its early stages. Thanks, too, to Jack Heller and his team at Assemble. Not only did you greenlight this for me, but you—along with Caitlin de Lisser-Ellen—provided invaluable feedback and guidance.

Then, what an amazing and rewarding whirlwind to have Sourcebooks come on board when the story was known as *Exchange* and the book was far from fully realized. Huge thanks to Eliza Swift for taking that chance, and to Wendy McClure, who most wonderfully joined this team. A shout-out to Ploy Siripant for the perfect cover; to Cassie Gutman, Kelsey Fenske, and Jenny Lopez for production assistance; Sydnee Thompson for copyediting; and Danielle McNaughton for internal design.

Grazie, grazie, grazie to my Italian-to-English translator, Manuela Liace, who swept in with no notice and barely enough time to edit my misworded, translation-app Italian, especially the phrase which would have thrown the whole context of a certain passage into the gutter. You were a lifesaver, Manuela! Any errors in her translation are my responsibility.

Same error message applies to my (unnamed) Brit-speak editor who helped me further develop Devin's voice. Before you, I'd've never known the difference between pants and trousers.

Then there's my undying appreciation to Dick Feldman for tiptoeing around me—giving me space to create—during those twelve-plus-hour writing-and-revising days. And to Paige Feldman and Cassie Feldman for being my brainstormers, my idea bouncers, and my cheerleaders; for reading everything from first concepts to full stories and being unafraid to tell me, *Seriously, that doesn't work.* To you, to my family and my friends: You always give me the best reason to find my way home.

ABOUT THE AUTHOR

Award-winning author Jody Feldman (The Gollywhopper Games middle-grade series) may have liked to become a treasure hunter, codebreaker, movie director, or architect, but realized she could explore all that and more as an author. When she's not totally obsessing over the next plot twist, you might find her watching football, solving puzzles, traveling to new places (including Rome!), or at home in St. Louis, Missouri, baking the best secret-recipe oatmeal cookies you'll ever eat. *No Way Home* is her YA debut. Learn more at www.jodyfeldman.com.